KILLER THEATER

"I heard what happened at the theater," Moire began. "Do you think the show will go on?"

"I don't know if that's been decided or even discussed yet." It seemed like everyone in town was interested in knowing if the show would continue. Then it hit me: Was there anyone in particular who might want the show to close before it opened? Somebody who might gain by seeing TOTS shut down?

One of the line cooks called Moire's name, and she told him she'd be right over. She eased the cash drawer closed. "If I were Ava Turner, you wouldn't get me to go back there."

"Why not?"

"Are you kidding?" The diner owner's right eyebrow formed a question. "If somebody was trying to kill me and missed and got the wrong person or something," she said in a hushed tone, "I'd be afraid they'd try again." She gave me a meaningful look. "And what if they succeeded?"

Moire twirled and headed for the kitchen.

The woman had a point. What if the killer did try again? I decided it might be worth trying to talk to Ava Turner once more. Her life could still be in jeopardy. . . .

Books by J.R. Ripley

DIE, DIE BIRDIE

TOWHEE GET YOUR GUN

THE WOODPECKER ALWAYS PECKS TWICE

TO KILL A HUMMINGBIRD

CHICKADEE CHICKADEE BANG BANG

HOW THE FINCH STOLE CHRISTMAS

FOWL OF THE HOUSE OF USHER

A BIRDER'S GUIDE TO MURDER

CARDINAL SIN

Published by Kensington Publishing Corporation

Towhee Get Your Gun

J.R. Ripley

KENSINGTON BOOKS
www.kensingtonbooks.com

KENSINGTON BOOKS are published by

Kensington Publishing Corp.
119 West 40th Street
New York, NY 10018

All Kensington titles, imprints, and distributed lines are available at special quantity discounts for bulk purchases for sales promotion, premiums, fund-raising, educational, or institutional use.

Special book excerpts or customized printings can also be created to fit specific needs. For details, write or phone the office of the Kensington Sales Manager: Attn.: Sales Department. Kensington Publishing Corp., 119 West 40th Street, New York, NY 10018. Phone: 1-800-221-2647.

Kensington and the K logo Reg. U.S. Pat. & TM Off.

First Lyrical e-book edition: January 2017

First printing: April 2019
ISBN-13: 978-1-4967-1970-6
ISBN-10: 1-4967-1970-0

ISBN-13: 978-1-4967-1971-3 (ebook)
ISBN-10: 1-4967-1971-9 (ebook)

10 9 8 7 6 5 4 3 2 1

Printed in the United States of America

Thank you to John Scognamiglio and the whole Kensington crew for the incredible job you do; to Priya Doraswamy at Lotus Lane Literary; and my family, friends, and fans. Together, you make what I do possible and worth the doing.

1

"That's the third time this week," I complained, brushing back a lock of limp brown hair that refused to stay put.

"Maybe you should go over and say something," Kim replied, and it sounded very much like a dare. She wore the same khaki culottes and green T-shirt that I did, so why did hers look fresh and sharp while my clothes looked dumpy and dowdy?

I frowned, looking at the ratty blue and white camper van parked outside my front door. "Maybe I will." I wasn't exaggerating. This was the third time in under a week that someone working on the place next door had parked their beat-up old Winnebago at the curb directly in front of Birds & Bees. Definitely a man.

He'd also been trampling through my flower beds. Mom and I had purchased six trays of petunias from a local greenhouse. We painstakingly planted them one Sunday morning between the sidewalk and the white picket fence in an effort to give the front some color. I noticed, walking out to the mailbox, that the entire corner of the bed nearest his vehicle was a mushy pulp of purple and green. The worker had been using my flowerbed as a shortcut.

To paraphrase a song in Rodgers and Hammerstein's musical *Carousel,* June flowers were busting out all over. And this guy was busting up my flowers.

I wasn't sure who he was. There'd been a lot of workers in and out of the empty storefront of late. I'd only seen snatches of the back of his head. Definitely a man.

Not only was the thing an eyesore, it blocked the view out my main window. It also blocked potential customers' view into the store. Definitely not good for business. And I could use all the business I could get.

"Well," Kim chided, "what are you waiting for?"

"I'm thinking." I tapped my toe in sync with a downy woodpecker rhythmically stabbing away at a tray of peanut butter suet suspended in a cage feeder that dangled from the porch on a green chain. The downy woodpecker is a smaller member of the woodpecker family with fluffy black and white plumage. The one feeding now was a female. I could tell because the bird lacked the distinctive red patch on the back of its head that the males bear. Though short-billed, the bantam-sized woodpecker had no trouble extracting the peanut butter treat from behind the metal grill.

Kim and I grew up together. She was my best friend and a working partner, albeit part-time, in Birds & Bees, the shop we'd opened a couple of months back. Our store catered to bird-feeding and bird-watching enthusiasts and also carried a few supplies for bee-keepers. We were not a sex-ed shop for preteens, and I was getting tired of the joke.

In addition to the store's stock, we had started a small garden out front with plants to support bird and bee populations, like holly, milkweed, and assorted wildflowers, depending on the time of year. With summer just around the corner, options were nearly endless. The little town of Ruby Lake is located in an area of western North Carolina that boasts a robust growing climate.

Mom and I had also planted a row of pulmonaria tucked up against the front porch. The flowering plant also known as lungwort did well in the shade and was especially popular with both bees and hummingbirds.

The camper van blocking the view of Ruby Lake, the town's eponymously named medium-sized natural lake, was a rusting blue hulk with near-bald tires and a sagging white shell. Its windows looked like they'd last been washed during the Nixon administration.

Kim was right. It was time to stop whining and do something. The ruined flower beds had been the last straw. "I'll be right back."

I pushed out the French doors and walked determinedly toward the camper van. I couldn't help grimacing at the tattered bright red NC STATE WOLFPACK bumper sticker on the back as the door of the camper flew open.

The Wolfpack were practically the mortal enemies of my own school's team, the University of North Carolina Tar Heels. Not that such things mattered to me. I was hardly the rah-rah type. And, after all, I had many friends who'd attended NCSU. Not to mention a certain unmentionable ex-boyfriend. It was a terrific school. Just so long as its alumni didn't park their wrecks in front of my place-of-business-slash-home.

"Hi," said the young man in blue jeans and a white tee, stepping from inside. I placed him at my age, give or take a couple years. I'm thirty-four and plan to be for many years to come.

The stranger ran his fingers through a shock of wavy brown hair, then stuck his hand out with a smile. "Paul Anderson."

"Hello," I said, reluctantly shaking his hand. "I'm Amy Simms." I nodded my chin toward the shop. "This is my store." And my home, I could have added.

"Oh." He beamed. "You're the pet shop lady." He stuffed his hands into his denim jacket.

I smothered a frown. "I don't sell pets. I sell birding supplies, birdseed, nesting boxes—"

He cut me off. "Got it." He slammed the door of his camper shut, then kicked it again with his boot when it refused to stay shut. "Thing never latches right." He started to turn away. "If you don't mind, I'm sort of busy right now."

I noticed bits of purple and green plant material on the bottoms of his boots. My petunias. "Listen, Mr. Anderson—"

Anderson stopped and raised his hand. "Paul, remember?"

How could I forget? "Listen"—I cleared my throat—"Paul, about your Winnebago—"

The young man's brow shot up. "This isn't a Winnebago."

Was this guy going to chop off every sentence I started? "Well"—I bit my lip—"your camper van—"

The guy chopped me off again. "Camper van? I'll have you know this is a 1987 Holiday Rambler, Amy." He slapped it lovingly on the side, and I expected the shell to separate from the truck. "With a Ford Econoline three-fifty chassis and a four-sixty engine under the hood."

I didn't know what all those numbers meant, but I knew enough about men to know that such things impressed them. Me, not so much. "Fine. But your Holiday Bumbler—"

"Rambler."

"Rambler"—I paused to let some steam off—"is blocking my store."

Paul looked confused. "It's on the street."

"Yes. I know, but still—"

"This baby's a real collectible."

"Looks to me like your baby's collecting mostly mud and rust," I said, stepping off the curb and assessing the monstrosity more closely. It was also collecting stares from locals and tourists alike. A car tooted and I jumped back quickly to the sidewalk.

Paul cocked his head. "Have you got a problem with me?" he said with surprise. "With my Rambler?"

"That's what I've been trying to tell you. I would appreciate it if you would park it somewhere else."

He shook his head. "This is convenient, you know?"

"Convenient for what?" It certainly wasn't convenient for me. I pointed to the empty storefront next store that abutted mine. "Why not park it there? That's where you're working, right?"

"Yeah," he said slowly. He grabbed my extended arm and swiveled my hand toward the curb. "Fire hydrant, see?"

I pulled my arm free. I saw.

"So I can't park there." Paul Anderson shrugged. "Gotta park here."

I sighed. "But it's blocking my store."

Paul Anderson's brow wriggled. "I'm not exactly parked on your sidewalk. I'm on the road." He shook his head. "Perfectly legal."

I pointed at his tan harness boots. "You see that?"

"You like my boots?"

"No." I shook my head. "That's my flowers your boots are wearing. You're trampling my flowers."

"Oh." He rubbed the top of his boot against his calf. "Sorry about that. Maybe you should think about plastic."

"Plastic?" I could feel the pressure building up behind my eyes. Why were we suddenly talking about plastic?

"Yeah, flowers, you know? I've seen them in the store. You plant those puppies and you'll never have to worry about people trampling your flowers again. I'm thinking of adding some to my flower boxes." There were several empty metal flower boxes outside the storefront and along the front edge of the out-door sales area.

"Plastic flowers don't do our endangered bee population a fat lot of good."

"Huh. I never thought about that," he replied, looking thoughtfully at his own empty flower boxes.

"I'd rather you simply stay on the sidewalk."

He scraped the soles of his boots on the cement, leaving a smeared trail of petunia guts in their wake. "I'll try." He held up his hand. "Scout's honor."

I looked at his hand and frowned. "That's not scout's honor. That's a peace sign."

He twisted his lips and looked at his fingers. "Really?"

I rolled my eyes. "Really. You need three fingers, not two and—" I stopped. "Oh, never mind. What are they working on over there, anyway?" I asked, changing the subject. I didn't feel like giving this grown man Boy Scouts lessons. "I've been meaning to go over and introduce myself to the new owner but haven't had the chance."

Paul beamed. "Well, you just did."

"Did what?" I asked, already fearing the answer.

"Meet the new owner." His hazel eyes sparkled as the sun came out from behind the clouds that had been obscuring the morning.

"You bought the old garden center?" The place next to mine had been a garden shop with a large outdoor area that extended all the way to my house and interior space on the other side. With Brewer's Garden Center out of business, I'd thought adding a few flowering plants for sale at my place might help me pull in some of their old customers.

Paul Anderson beamed. "Yep. You might say I'm reopening the garden center. Even keeping the old name." He scratched his cheek. "Sort of."

"You?" Paul Anderson did not look like the gardening type. I followed him to the door of the closed storefront.

"Only this time it'll be a beer garden."

"Beer? You're turning this place into a bar?" He stepped inside the dark and dusty space, and I had no choice but to follow. The inside smelled of fresh sawdust.

"Yep. Into a beer garden and brew pub." He stretched out his hands. "Brewer's Biergarten." He tapped the neon sign spread out on the new bar top. "Funny coincidence, don't you think? Brewer's Garden Center." His brow went up suggestively. "I'm a brewer. Brewer's Biergarten?"

I stifled a groan. "Funny is one way of looking at it." There it was in bright red, foot-tall letters: BREWER'S BIERGARTEN. I couldn't wait to see it all lit up at night. Not.

"Wanna see the equipment? It's in back. I've already got the wort kettle set up and the—"

I cut him off. After all, it was my turn. "No, thanks. And what's a wort kettle?" I instantly regretted opening my mouth and snapped it shut. I had not meant to get this guy started when what I wanted to do was to get this guy stopped.

It wasn't that I was against beer or even brew pubs. Lord knew I enjoyed my fair share. But right next to Birds & Bees, my business and my home—that I could do without. I could also do without Paul Anderson. Especially when he was parked on my front steps.

Paul waved and plowed through a pair of swinging shutter half-doors. "Wort is the liquid you extract from the malted barley. From there, you add yeast and, presto, beer!" He smiled sheepishly. "Well, at least that's it in a nutshell."

From a nut job, I thought. I stared suspiciously at all the shiny equipment, vats, pipes, and doohickeys of unimaginable purposes. It all looked practically medieval against the exposed red brick background. "Look." I cleared my throat and backed out toward the street. "About your Scrambler."

"Rambler," Paul corrected. "It's my home, not a plate of scrambled eggs." He laughed.

"Your home?" I tapped my foot at the door. "And just how long are you planning on making that—that thing your home?"

Paul Anderson shrugged. He thrust his hands in his back pockets. "That's hard to tell." His eyes took a swing around the store. "Until I get settled. You can see for yourself there's a lot to do here."

"I'll say." The place looked more a wreck than my own store had when I'd taken over the old Queen Anne Victorian-era house mere months before. "Couldn't you park your *home* around back?" I knew the garden center had a large parking area behind the store. Plenty of space for cars. They'd even kept large slatted wooden bins of soil and pine straw back there for their customers. Surely there was room for his vehicle.

Paul shook his head. "No room. Lots of construction materials, equipment, you know?"

"You know, there are laws against living on the street." Okay, I was bluffing. Sort of. Come to think of it, weren't there laws against opening places that sold alcohol? Permits required? Did this guy have any of those? The man seemed a bit oblivious. I made a mental note to check with the building department.

Paul smiled. "Nobody's complained so far. Besides, it'll only be for a few months."

As much as I was tempted to file a complaint, I knew I wouldn't either. In the end, I was a live-and-let-live kind of person.

Then the *few months* line sunk in. "Over my dead body."

Okay, so I'm a hypocrite. Aren't we all one time or another? I could imagine the noise, the late nights, the fights. The drunks stumbling over to Birds & Bees looking for a place to spend the night. The house had been an inn for years, after all. No, this was not going to end well.

"You got something against beer? Or gardens?" Paul Anderson inquired. "Or maybe people having fun?"

"Fun?" I crossed my arms. "What's that supposed to mean?"

"It means people having a good time, enjoying each other's company. Capital F-U-N."

"I know what fun means. What I don't know is what your game is."

"No game, Amy. I'm merely an entrepreneur out to build my business." He nodded toward Birds & Bees. "Just like you."

Okay, so he had me there. I was disliking this guy more and more by the minute. "What made you decide to start your bar here? In Ruby Lake?"

"Biergarten."

I rolled my eyes. "Biergarten."

I stepped aside as Gertrude Hammer, Gertie, town

curmudgeon, ambled past, pushing a grocery cart that had no doubt been stolen from Lakeside Market. I say no doubt because the green plastic LAKESIDE MARKET placard was still welded to the back of the cart.

"I heard it was a nice little town," Paul replied. His close-set hazel eyes scanned me from head to toe. "Full of friendly people." Paul popped open the passenger-side door of his truck and pulled out a battered toolbox, which he dropped carelessly to the sidewalk, where it landed with an ear-splitting rattle. "At least that's what my buddy said."

"Ha!" We both heard Gertie snort from ten feet away. Gertie spun around, letting the grocery cart roll free. "Not Simms!" She had on a baggy gray sweat suit and a pair of shoes that looked like they might have been made from triceratops hide.

Gertie had sold me the house and, while I'd felt ripped off and foolish at the time, for some reason she'd been desperate to buy it back from me. I hadn't figured out why yet. The cart bounced down the curb and into the street.

The tour van in its path screeched to a halt. I leapt into the road and retrieved it. "Here you go," I said with a flourish, whipping the cart into old Gertie's hands. Gertrude's about a million years old, give or take an epoch.

"Thanks," Gertie spat. Her eyes fixed on me. "Watch out for this one. She's a death magnet."

With that, the old woman gave her cart a shove and continued up the street.

"Death magnet?" I huffed and stamped my foot.

Paul laughed. "Man, Craig told me Ruby Lake

had potential, but he never told me what a bunch of characters you all were!"

"Craig?" I felt a terrible tension creeping up my neck, the blood draining from my face.

"Yeah." Paul's teeth flashed white against his swarthy complexion. "Craig Bigelow. He's the friend who turned me on to this place. We're partners. I can't wait till he gets here."

My heart went cold. I clenched my fists.

"You okay?"

Craig Bigelow—rhymes with gigolo, of course— was the man who'd taken my heart and broken it into six pieces. One for each year we'd been together. He wasn't the only reason I'd left Raleigh and returned to Ruby Lake, but he was a big one.

"I don't know him at all." I turned on my heel and retreated.

2

"Well?" asked Kim, sliding shut the cash register and handing a woman a receipt. The woman's companion hefted a twenty-pound bag of unshelled black oil sunflower seeds, our bread and butter so to speak, over his left shoulder. The sunflower seeds were our biggest seller. They're cheap and plentiful, and attract a wide variety of birds to backyard feeders.

"Well what?" I asked, holding the door open as our customers departed.

"Is he going to move his camper?"

"We agreed to table the discussion for now," I answered. I picked up the broom and dustpan and circled around the front counter, my arms working quickly.

Kim planted her feet in my path. "Spill it."

I glanced up at her, giving her ankle boots a quick swipe with the tip of the broom.

"Hey!" She stepped back. "These are Rockports!"

"Serves you right." I tried to squeeze by her. "You're in my way."

"Fine." Kim moved to one side, plopping her butt down on the counter. "But I know you. You clean when you're upset."

I leaned the broom against the corner near the window. "Fine. You want me to spill? I'm spilling. His name is Paul Anderson and he's opening a brew pub." I paused as if he were going to interrupt me, then continued. "A *biergarten*," I self-corrected. "And I'm afraid I let him or the situation or my own frustration," I admitted, "get the best of me."

"A beer garden?" Kim took a swig from the water bottle she kept near the register. "Cool."

"Yes, I guess so."

"Beats having an empty shop next door, doesn't it?"

Kim was right. "Yes. That it does." An empty shop doesn't drive business. "Anyway, like I said, the owner's name is Paul Anderson. The guy with the . . ." I stumbled. "Rambler, I think he said. So he's going to be living in it for a while. Until he gets settled, he says."

"Is he single?"

I looked down my nose at her. "I don't know."

"He is good looking. Don't you think?"

"I suppose." In a rattle-my-cage sort of way. "But what do you care? You're seeing someone, remember?"

"Yeah, yeah." Kim waved her hand at me. "I remember. In fact, Randy and I are planning to flip a house together."

"You are? Since when?" Kim followed me to the far rear of the store, where a small kitchenette served both staff and customers. I poured us each a glass of sweet tea from the jug in the under-the-counter fridge.

"Since Randy heard about this great deal on a place over on Maple Lane. The old man that lived there had to move into a retirement home. Rolling Acres."

I nodded and licked my lips. I knew the place. Rolling Acres was a senior living facility out on the other end of the lake. As I recalled, there was one main building and a number of separate bungalows.

Kim grabbed an open bag of peanut butter sandwich cookies. She offered them to me. I shook my head no but grabbed three before she could pull the bag back.

"In fact," Kim said, biting down on a cookie, "I think you know the guy that owned the house."

"Really?" I said, chewing. "Who?"

"That old guy who feeds the birds."

My brow quirked up. "You're going to have to do better than that. Do you know how many old guys we get in here who feed birds?" Senior citizens were a large percentage of the business. They had the time, the money, and the interest in backyard bird watching and feeding.

Kim laughed. "Sorry." She snapped her fingers. "It was that Mister—Mister . . ." She brightened. "Wincer? Whiskers?"

"Withers?" I offered, setting down my glass.

"Yeah, that's it. Randy said he's getting a great deal on the place."

"I didn't know Floyd had sold his house." I sat in

one of the rockers and leaned back, folding my hands in my lap. "Come to think of it, I haven't seen Floyd in the store lately."

Floyd Withers was a retired banker whose wife had passed away fairly recently. He had become a regular birdseed customer. He didn't know diddly about birds, or bird feeders, for that matter, but his wife had been a bird lover and continuing to take care of the birds seemed to be his way of remembering her.

"I guess that's why." Kim sat beside me.

"What do you know about flipping houses?" I asked Kim. Kim's a long-legged blonde whose devilish blue eyes normally convinced men to do anything that would have required her to get her hands dirty.

"Nothing," she readily admitted. "Randy knows all that stuff. I'm going to be his helper."

Randy Vincent was a local property manager. He owned a string of cabins at Ruby Lake and around town. He'd been separated for over a year from his wife, Lynda, who shared the business. Kim and Randy had been dating for months with Lynda's blessing. According to Kim, the divorce would be final in a couple of months.

"Good luck with that," I said. *And good luck to Randy*, I thought. With Kim as a helper, he was going to need all the luck he could get. Kim was a great woman and a hard worker in her own way, but she knew as much about rehabbing a house as I knew about brewing beer.

Squat.

I stopped rocking and stared out the back window. "I haven't told you the worst thing about Paul Anderson yet."

"What?"

"He's friends with Craig," I said, struggling to remain detached.

"No." Kim leaned sideways and gripped my wrist.

"Yes." I locked on to her brilliant blue eyes. The kind of eyes I could only wish I had. "And it gets worse."

Kim laughed as she shook her head. "No offense, but what could be worse than the guy next door knowing Craig?"

I started rocking again, quickly, squeezing the handle of my mug so hard I thought it was going to shatter between my fingers. "Being partners with him."

"No!" Kim gasped, her hands clamping down on the rocker's armrests.

The chime at the door sounded, and we both rose.

"Hi, Amy. Hey, Kim." It was only Cousin Riley, one of my aunt Betty's kids from her first husband, Fred Foxcombe. Aunt Betty is Mom's twin sister. They are fraternal twins and very similar physically, even though this is not always the case with fraternal twins. However, Mom and Aunt Betty's personalities were anything but similar. My aunt Betty can be spontaneous and change course in the blink of an eye. Mom's always been on much more of an even keel. Aunt Betty lives across town with her third husband, Sterling. Mom, tired of living alone since Dad passed, lives on the third floor of Birds & Bees in an apartment with me.

"Hello, Riley." I wiped my hands on my apron

while sending Kim eye signals that she should keep mum on the whole ex-boyfriend-coming-to-town thing. No point in spreading the news around Ruby Lake any sooner than it was bound to spread anyway.

"What brings you here?" At first look, I'd have guessed a tornado. His flannel shirt was wrinkled and untucked, and his hair couldn't make up its mind which way to go. He appeared not to have shaved in a week.

"Weren't you working at the theater today?" Kim asked.

Riley nodded. "I just came from there." He wiped his hand with a soiled hanky and stuffed it back in the front pocket of his jeans. "Did you hear what happened?"

Riley's the sort of jack-of-all-trades you find in any small town. Earning his living doing a little of this and a little of that. And a lot of loafing. So it was no surprise that he enjoyed working in the local community theater. He also considered himself something of an actor. Not too many folks in town agreed with that personal assessment.

"I heard the curtain broke," Kim answered.

I shot Kim a look.

She shrugged. "Anita telephoned while you were out."

That explained a lot. Anita Brown is the town's dispatcher. She's also quite adept at spreading any news around town.

"Hey, it wasn't my fault!" Riley said, pulling out his old hanky and rubbing it over his face. "That place is old. I ain't responsible for the curtain rods."

"Did anybody get hurt?" I asked.

Riley nodded. "Afraid so. Robert LaChance and Coralie Sampson."

Kim and I gasped in unison. "Not seriously, I hope," I said, grabbing Riley's forearm.

"LaChance broke his arm and Coralie's got a busted foot."

I winced. I'm a bit of an empathetic pain sufferer. Just hearing about other peoples' injuries caused me discomfort.

Riley nodded. "At least Miss Turner didn't get hurt." Like his twin sister, Rhonda, Cousin Riley had thick brown hair, hazel eyes, and a generous nose. Those eyes now shimmered with relief.

"Ava Turner?" I asked, eyes growing wide.

"The movie star?" Kim said.

Riley's head bobbed some more. "Mind if I get some of that tea?" He nodded toward Kim's half-empty glass.

"Help yourself," I said, following Riley to the kitchenette. Any sarcasm I might have injected was lost on my cousin. "So, you say Miss Turner was there?"

I waited as Riley filled his glass, drained it, then filled it once more. "That's right." He wiped his mouth with the back of his sleeve. Better than that dirty handkerchief, I supposed. "Not two feet away when that big, old iron rod hit the ground. *Splat!*" He shoved his open palm downward. "Lucky she didn't get clobbered herself."

"That's terrible," Kim said.

"I'll say." I rinsed out the now-empty pitcher in the sink. I'd brew some more tea upstairs later.

"Were Robert and Coralie in the cast or the crew?"

"Both were in the show," Riley answered. "I'm not sure what Lou is going to do now. I offered to fill in for Robert, but he and the director said my carpentry was too important and that they couldn't afford to lose me."

Sure. "Who's Lou?"

Kim filled in for Riley, who had his hand in the cookie bag. "Lou Ferris is the overall theater manager and generally acts as stage manager, too, over at the Ruby Lake Theater On The Square. He's been there for years. I'm surprised you didn't know that."

I shrugged. "Doesn't ring a bell."

"Lou says the show's in a real pickle," Riley commented. "We're supposed to open in a week. You know how the town counts on the income from those shows. But without a couple of actors to fill in, he says the theater might have to shut down."

"Shut down?" gasped Kim.

Riley washed his hands in the sink, then ran his fingers down the sides of his pants, leaving wet streaks that did nothing to improve his appearance. "You know the old place has been losing money for years. And the building needs a good amount of work."

"They can't do that," I said. "Local theater is important to a town like Ruby Lake. Plus, the tourists patronize the theater every summer."

And summer was just around the corner. I toweled up the mess around the sink that Riley had created. "We need TOTS!" I exclaimed, throwing the towel down at the edge of the counter.

Riley looked at me. "So you'll do it?"

My eyes squeezed together. "Do what?"

"Take over Coralie's part," Riley said quickly, as if I should have known. "I already told everybody you would."

I should have known.

"Yes!" squealed Kim. "She'll do it!"

"No!" I shouted back. "I won't."

3

"What did you say the name of this show is?"

It was the next morning and we were on our way to the Theater On The Square, most often referred to by locals as TOTS, down on the west side of Ruby Lake's main square. Kim was driving. I was fuming. Riley and Rhonda, his sister, were taking up space in the back seat. Mom was watching the store.

How had I let myself get talked into performing in a community theater production? Kim and I had argued for an hour. She'd finally talked me into doing the show, albeit grudgingly, partly because I was getting a headache from going round in circles on the subject, and partly because she'd told me that I'd be doing the town a favor by helping to save the show.

Not that I thought my taking over a minor role in the musical was a big enough favor that the town would, as a consequence, want to show their appreciation by nixing the whole eminent domain process that Birds & Bees was potentially facing.

"Annie Get Your Gun," Kim replied in answer to my question. She turned her head toward me. "Or in this case, Amy Get Your Gun."

"Very funny. Please keep your eyes on the road."

"Yes, Mom." We drove past city hall, the local history museum, and the theater's front entrance. There it was in all its glory, the marquee: ANNIE GET YOUR GUN—STARRING RUBY LAKE'S OWN AVA TURNER.

Kim angled into the theater's side lot, where about ten other cars were already parked.

"Isn't Ava Turner a little old," I said, slamming the car door shut behind me, "to be playing Annie Oakley?"

Kim glanced nervously over her shoulder. "Shush." She waved her hand at me. "Keep your voice down."

"Why? There's nobody out here but us."

Kim grabbed her purse from the backseat and locked the car. "Ava Turner played the role of Annie on Broadway," she said. *"In New York."*

"I know where Broadway is." I was a huge Broadway fan, after all. Broadway music was the theme song to my life.

Rhonda started around the building toward the front, facing the square. "Miss Turner was asked to play the role."

"By the director himself," her brother added with a touch of reverence.

Rhonda went on. "Besides, Miss Turner's done a lot to support the theater and this town."

"She's a great lady," Riley put in.

"She's very private," added Rhonda. "You know, this is the first time she has agreed to participate in one of our local productions." My cousin gave me a look meant to imply that I should be both duly impressed and grateful for the honor Miss Turner had bestowed upon our town.

While I mulled over their words, we entered the elegant old theater lobby, which was done up in shades of red and gold. Photos of the myriad stars—local, regional, and national—cluttered the gold leaf wallpaper.

Photographs of Ava Turner, arguably Ruby Lake's most famous citizen, occupied the place of honor, a shrine of sorts, between the doors leading to the seats. I studied several of the photos. The actress had never varied from her auburn hair, most often flowing, long, bouncy locks with that classic pin-curl look, but occasionally cut shorter for a dramatic role. Her eyes were a beautiful shade of green beneath perfectly shaped eyebrows.

"Who is directing this show, anyway?" I wondered aloud.

"August Mantooth," Cousin Rhonda said with reverence.

"August Mantooth?" I stopped in my tracks. "Cute. Stage name?"

Riley looked at me funny. "Geez, Amy, it's the man's real name. I hope you're going to behave yourself."

I flushed. Cousin Riley was admonishing me to behave myself? I bit the inside of my cheek and vowed to be on my best behavior.

"Mr. Mantooth came all the way from New Jersey to direct." This from Cousin Rhonda, Riley's fraternal twin, just like Mom and Aunt Betty. Twins tend to run in families, and they have a long history of running in mine. If I ever had kids, I figured there just might be twins in my future.

Rhonda and Riley, to this day, behave like two proverbial peas in a pod. They also have a younger brother, Rudy, four years my junior, who is nothing like them. Of course, he was from Aunt Betty's Husband Number Two, so it was to be expected. The twins are nearly four years older than me, making them thirty-eight. Having never married, Rhonda was yet a Foxcombe.

Rhonda, who, for as long as I'd known her, had worn her thick brown hair in a fifties bouffant, tugged at the large string of pearls around her neck. "I'll be in back, if you need me." She wriggled her fingers and ducked through a dark doorway to our left.

Rhonda was working hair and makeup on the production. Her brother, Riley, left with her. But before leaving, he laid a hand on my shoulder and said, "Just follow the steps down to the stage. Everybody should be there by now. Except Miss Turner. I'll go pick her up myself later."

"You chauffeur Ava Turner to the theater every day?" asked Kim.

"Of course," replied Riley. "You don't expect her to drive herself, do you? She's a star." With that, he departed.

There was no need to observe Cousin Riley's directions. All we had to do was follow the sound of arguing coming from a dark corner of the stage. There was also an incessant hammering coming from backstage that rattled the boards beneath my feet.

"What have I gotten myself into?" I muttered. I turned to Kim. "What have *you* gotten me into?"

Kim grinned sheepishly. "I hear showbiz folk can be a bit high-strung." She patted my shoulder. "Don't worry. It'll be fun."

"Great." Paul Anderson's admonishment the day before that I didn't know what fun was reverberated in my head. "Why don't I see if I can get you a part in the show?"

Kim ignored the suggestion. "Call me when you need a ride back to the shop." Riley and Rhonda lived downtown and could walk to and from the theater if they wanted to.

Kim turned to go, and I latched on to her arm. "Where do you think you're going?"

"Back to Birds and Bees." She gently pried her arm free. "You don't want your mother to be stuck there alone all day, do you? Besides, Randy's coming by later and he's going to show me plans for the flip."

"Fine." I frowned. "But don't think I'm going to forget you, Kim."

Kim grinned. "Hope not!"

I watched Kim disappear up the ramp, then turned and followed the sound of raised voices, all the while attempting to drown out the sound of whoever, probably Riley, was pounding so hard I could feel two of my fillings coming loose.

The stage was deserted. A lone spotlight from the booth in back provided little illumination to the black stage. I crossed in front of the orchestra pit, toward the sound of the voices. I stopped dead in my tracks as I heard a man's brusque speech.

"I'm telling you, it was no accident!" the man snarled. "Somebody tried to kill me."

"Now, Robert, why would anybody—"

Robert? I thought I recognized that voice. Robert LaChance, the car dealer. Not a person I'd be putting on my Christmas list this year or any other for that matter. He'd treated his ex-wife, and my dear friend, Tiffany, very poorly. To make matters worse, I was sure that he was somehow involved in the plot to get the street widened and my store rezoned. I just couldn't prove it.

"I don't know why," Robert cut him off. "But they are."

I slowly pulled back the deep purple curtain with my index finger and peered through the tiny gap. Robert LaChance, arm in a cast and sling, had his face pressed up against a second man, whom I didn't recognize. Robert wore a sharp pinstriped suit. Tiffany called it his sleazy used-car-salesman costume.

The second man was an obese fellow pushing fifty with a cherubic face and a blond crewcut. His fleshy nose looked like it had been smeared across his face with a butter knife. By contrast, he dressed more casually, in khakis and a white short-sleeve polo. "I know there may have been a few accidents . . ." He wheezed, tugging at his collar. I noticed a line of sweat along his forehead.

"Accidents?" Robert laughed sourly. "First," he said, holding out his fingers, "somebody tries to run Riley off the road. Next, we get a string of thefts—"

"I wouldn't call them thefts exactly," cut in the second man.

"Lou," said Robert with little patience, "several of the cast and crew have reported missing personal items."

Lou. I realized this must be the theater manager, Lou Ferris.

Lou hitched up his pants. "Tiny, little things," he said, pinching his fingers together.

Robert snarled. "What about the fire?"

"Fire?" I snapped my mouth shut. I hadn't meant to say that out loud. Both men turned my way. Figuring the jig was up, I pushed my way through the heavy curtain. "Hi, I'm Amy Simms." I extended my hand.

"Lou Ferris," the big man replied. His grip was doughy and warm, like a proofed loaf ready for the oven. "Welcome."

"Thanks. I see you're into birds, too."

"Excuse me?" Lou said.

I looked pointedly at the tiny tattoo on the inside of his wrist. "The bird. A swallow, isn't it?"

"Ooh." Lou smiled. "Yeah. Sometimes I forget it's there." He rubbed his wrist.

"It's beautiful." Not that I'd get one tattooed to my wrist, but it really was a lovely lavender and teal sketch of a swallow.

"Thanks, I got this—"

Robert interrupted the manager. "Yeah, yeah. Can we cut this little bird lovers convention short?"

I turned to the car dealer. "Hello, Robert."

Robert's jaw worked back and forth. "Miss Simms. I hear you will be replacing Coralie."

"That's right."

"Let's hope you don't suffer the same fate," the car dealer said ominously.

"Excuse me?"

Lou interjected. "Miss Sampson suffered a foot injury." Lou gave Robert an ugly look. "That's why you're here."

"Yes, Riley told me there had been an accident."

"Hah!" Robert snorted. "Somebody tried to kill Coralie. Broke her foot, and she's lucky it wasn't her head." Robert pushed his cast toward me. "Me, too."

"It was an accident," Lou said, visibly struggling to retain his composure.

Robert practically spat as he said, "Somebody rigged the damn curtain rod and tried to crush us!"

Lou waved his hand. "Really, I think *crushed* is too strong a word."

"That curtain rod is two-inch-thick iron. Don't tell me crushed is too strong a word!" Robert scratched at his nose with this cast. "It was sabotage."

I pulled at my lip. "Sabotage? Who'd do a thing like that?"

"Nobody," Lou replied quickly.

"You're blind, Lou." Robert shook his good arm at the other man.

Watching and listening to the two men, I knew something strange was going on here, but I had no idea what. Whatever it was, I wanted no part of it. I was beginning to think that showbiz was not the biz for me and said so. "I'm not sure I'm really right for the part, Mr. Ferris. And I am rather busy with my own business, Birds and Bees?"

"Nonsense," the theater manager said, clasping my hands in his. "You'll do fine."

A heavy vibration shook the ground, and a large man with a lavish white beard and a mustache that stretched out to infinity in two directions bounded, penguin-like, down the black steps toward us. "I'd say she'll do perfectly!" he said with a singsong lilt.

I turned toward the gentleman. I guessed he was in his late fifties or early sixties. But they had clearly been hard years. Dark gray eyes glowed unwaveringly at me, and his long black coat swirled around him like it was alive. I wondered how he did that. Black cuffed trousers hung loose over his dress shoes. He carried a white silk scarf wrapped several times around his neck.

"Your eyes are as green as the hills of Eire, mademoiselle," he said, putting a point to his mustache.

"August," said Lou. "This is Amy Simms. She's replacing Coralie."

"Ahh." He grabbed my hand and kissed it in an extravagant gesture. "August Mantooth at your service." He bowed. "You will be playing the role of Winnie."

"Who?" My brow wrinkled up and I rubbed my nose. Mantooth smelled heavily of spicy cologne.

"Dolly Tate's sister." This from Robert, his voice hard.

"What? Not a chance!"

We all turned. There, at the corner of the stage, a woman in skintight beige pants, a pink blouse, and pink heels was staring down on us with an angry red face.

And I knew her. Sort of. She was me. Sort of. Because her name was Amy, too. She was the ex-wife of Derek Harlan, an attorney who'd helped me out recently. She'd also warned me to stay away from him. She'd said something about how she'd kill me if I didn't.

Something told me she wasn't quite over the man.

"That woman"—she thrust her arm out and pointed—"is not going to play my sister!"

"Now, now, Amy," August Mantooth began, waddling back up the short flight of stairs toward the woman. "Let's not have any theatrics." He guffawed at his small joke and shot me a quick wink. "I'm sure whatever the trouble is, we can sort it out."

The two disappeared.

I turned to Lou Ferris and Robert. Why didn't Robert disappear as well? What was he doing here anyway? If his arm was broken and he was no longer in the show, why didn't he go back where he belonged? To LaChance Motors.

"You were saying something about a fire?" I said.

Lou gave Robert a warning look. "It was nothing. This is an old structure. We have certain"—his tongue played over his lips a moment—"electrical issues."

Robert snorted and looked at his watch. "I've got things to do." He gave me a look, which made me worried that those things had something to do with me.

Lou pulled me toward the stage. "Come, let me introduce you."

He led me out on stage and yelled for someone to

turn up the stage lights. In a minute, the stage was washed with bright white lights.

August dropped Amy Harlan's hand and scooted over to the end of the stage. "Will somebody please make that hammering stop?"

"Sorry!" came a muffled cry from behind the stage. A moment later, a face I recognized popped out from behind a prop wall. "You want me to stop?"

"Please," August Mantooth replied. "Can't you continue whatever it is you are doing later?"

"But Lou said we needed to get the rest of this scenery done by tomorrow."

"Aaron?" I interrupted. "What are you doing here? I mean, I know what you're doing here." Working, obviously. I moved closer. "But I'm surprised to see you." Aaron Maddley is a farmer by trade, but also a skilled craftsman. He had built a number of bluebird houses for me to sell at Birds & Bees, each one beautifully handcrafted and assembled. Unfortunately, I'd also practically accused him and/or his sister of murder.

"Hello, Amy," he answered curtly, his fingers tightening around the claw hammer hanging at his side.

"Lou isn't directing this show," August said, tossing his scarf over his left shoulder. "I am. So, if you don't mind?" He waved Aaron away with a flick of the fingers.

"Catch you later?" I called, rising up on my tiptoes, but Aaron gave no answer.

Lou whistled for the crew and cast to gather around. I recognized several of the faces, like Mayor MacDonald; Ben Harlan, Amy Harlan's former father-in-law; Dick Feller, who worked over at the Ruby Lake Motor Inn; Amy Harlan, of course; and a couple of the crew. Lots of the faces were new to me. I hadn't been back in Ruby Lake long, so that was no surprise.

"Everybody, this is Amy Simms," explained Lou. "August, I will leave you to make the introductions." The theater manager started for the stairs at the left side of the stage. "I'll be in my office if you need me."

August made the introductions and handed me a well-worn script. "Our next rehearsal is at seven this evening. Please be prompt."

I promised I would.

August clapped his hands to silence everyone. "I'll keep this brief, ladies and gentlemen. As you all are aware, there have been some accidents."

He paused as members of the cast and crew started whispering with one another. "Enough! I called you all together this morning to introduce you to your newest cast member and to tell you that yes, indeed, the show will go on."

The director paused once again, looking decidedly annoyed, as a smattering of applause erupted.

"Quiet, everybody!" A nattily dressed man in a brown suit with the largest hands I'd ever seen stamped the floor. His suit was straight out of the Wild West.

"Who's that?" I whispered to Dick Feller beside me.

"T-Bone Crawford," Dick replied out of the corner of his mouth, so softly his lips barely moved. The man could have been a ventriloquist. "He's portraying Davenport."

I nodded briefly. The character of Charlie Davenport, the manager of Buffalo Bill Cody's Wild West show was one of the major players in the cast. T-Bone Crawford was not a tall man, but he was stocky, with coal-black hair and thick lips.

Dick's hand went to the side of his mouth. "He's an ex-con."

"What did he do?" I couldn't help but ask.

T-Bone Crawford turned his hard green eyes on me and glared.

Dick stepped away and I clammed up.

"I'm beginning to have second thoughts about this show," Amy Harlan pouted, pulling at her hair and raking her steely gaze over me.

"I'm beginning to think this whole damn show is cursed," Mac MacDonald grumbled in reply.

"Enough." August Mantooth cleared his throat and glared at the mayor. "There is no such thing as a curse, despite what certain persons might intimate." His eyes passed slowly over us all. "Merely cursed critics."

This brought several chuckles.

"Excuse me, Miss Turner. May I speak with you privately?"

We all looked to the dimly lit back of the theater house. Ava Turner, in a sleek red dress with flouncy sleeves, was striding down toward the stage. A tall, slender woman in a denim jacket and jeans followed along, matching the former movie star's long stride with her own quick little steps.

"Not now," said Ava, stopping and looking down her nose at the woman. "I'm rather busy."

"But Miss Turner—"

"Later, darling." She gave the other woman a patronizing tap on the shoulder. I noticed a large diamond ring on her right index finger and an equally large emerald on her middle finger.

Riley hurried down the steps and took Ava Turner's hand. "Miss Turner, what are you doing here?" Riley looked nonplussed. "I wasn't supposed to pick you up till later."

"Yes, I didn't want to disturb you for our little meeting," added August, moving closer.

"Thank you, darling," Ava said, allowing Riley to help her up the steps. "My neighbor offered to provide a lift."

The woman on the floor cocked her head up toward the stage. "Miss Turner," she began, a white cotton blouse peeking out of her jacket, "if you want to talk later—"

"Not now, Patsy!" barked August.

"But—"

The director towered over her. "Please go check on the wardrobe for Ms. Simms." His eyes raked over me. "You may be required to make some alterations."

I fidgeted uneasily, unsure if that was a compliment or an insult.

"Yes, Mr. Mantooth." The woman's shoulders sagged and she skulked off.

"You'll have to pardon Ms. Klein," August said, turning to me. "She's quite useful, filling in wherever needed, but sometimes her zealousness gets to the point that she makes a pest of herself."

Ava Turner pushed herself between me and the director and stuck out her hand. "Ava Turner," she said, her voice soft as silk. "Call me Ava." Her head twisted to August. "Do you need me for anything? I wanted to have a word with Ms. Rhonda about my makeup."

"No, my dear. Rehearsal's at seven," replied the director, bowing slightly. He tilted his head back and clapped. "You're all free to go or get on with whatever you were doing!"

"Wait." Ben Harlan stepped forward. Ben's a lawyer, or maybe a semi-retired one, but he always dresses like he's got a date in court. Today was no exception with his crisp brown suit, yellow shirt, and navy tie. "I understand that Amy's taking Coralie's role, but who's going to play Frank Butler, what with Robert out with a broken arm?"

"Not to worry. Our new sharpshooter couldn't make it this morning, but he's promised to be here this evening," August replied. "I've already sent a script over to him."

"Okay if I get back to work?" I heard Aaron yell from beyond.

"By all means!" shouted August Mantooth.

With that, Ms. Turner turned and headed backstage. She'd never even asked me my name.

"So we're done here?" I asked, rolling the script up in my hands. Time to call Kim and get back to my real work.

August pressed his hand into my shoulder. "Try to read the script before this evening, Miss Simms. We are terribly behind schedule, and we do open in less than a week, you know."

The sound of hammering started up once more, and I couldn't wait to leave. I heard someone power up a vacuum cleaner in another room. The theater was a sudden cacophony of voices, sawing, pounding, and miscellaneous mayhem. I didn't understand how anyone could think under such circumstances, let alone act.

I promised August I would try to read through the script. Maybe I could get Mom or Kim to run my lines with me.

As I turned to leave, we all heard the scream.

4

I raced to the sound of the scream, the director close on my heels.

"Miss Turner, are you all right?" I knelt beside the movie star, who laid sprawled out on the floor in a most unladylike fashion. "What happened?"

A stagehand pulled out his cell phone and snapped a picture.

"Knock it off!" I commanded.

He sheepishly thrust his phone in his back pocket and hovered.

Ava was rubbing her head. "I don't know," she said weakly. "I was on my way to my dressing room when something hit me." She propped herself up with her right hand pressed against the ground.

August Mantooth leaned over and picked up a piece of lumber the size of a small baseball bat. "This?" He rotated the wood around in his hand.

I drew in a breath. A sharp two-inch nail protruded from one end of the board.

"What's going on?" Aaron Maddley appeared suddenly, hammer in hand. He glanced at me and Miss Turner, then the director. "What are you doing with that thing?"

"Have you seen that before?" I asked, holding Ava Turner's hand and looking up at Aaron.

He shrugged. "A scrap of wood, so what?"

"So somebody just hit Miss Turner with it," August said, his teeth worrying his lower lip.

"What?" Aaron looked from the wood to me.

"She could have been killed," I added. If that nail had connected with her skull, of that there was no doubt.

"I don't know," Aaron said slowly, stepping over me. "Looks to me like it might have fallen off this shelf."

I frowned. There was a dusty pile of wood scraps laying haphazardly on an open shelf bracketed to the wall. In fact, there were several shelves littered with odds and ends that appeared to have been pack-ratted away until needed. If ever.

But how could a piece of wood falling off a shelf, even with the help of an invisible imp, hit the actress hard enough in the head to knock her down?

Mac MacDonald scurried over and lifted Miss Turner to her feet. "Miss Turner, are you all right? Shall I fetch a doctor? Let me take you to a doctor."

She leaned against the mayor and batted her eyelashes. "I am feeling a bit woozy."

T-Bone Crawford, the ex-con, appeared. He held a tall, clear glass of water, which he extended to the actress. She ignored him.

"She's woozy, see?" Mayor MacDonald gingerly explored her scalp with his fingers.

The skeptic in me wondered if he was thinking about asking for her endorsement in his reelection campaign.

"Maybe we should call an ambulance," Aaron said.

"I'll take her to the medical center," offered Cousin Riley, watching anxiously beside Rhonda, who was clutching a hairbrush. "It will be quicker."

"Good idea," Mac said. "I'm going, too."

We all agreed that was the best plan of action, and Riley and the mayor led the actress away.

I rose and dusted myself off. I noticed Aaron hadn't offered me his hand but rather had drifted away. Probably to go bang on something.

Dick Feller was whispering in low tones with Lou Ferris near the curtain pulleys. Dick was playing Foster Wilson, a hotel owner, in the musical. Dick's real-life role is Ruby Lake Motor Inn's front desk manager. Talk about typecasting.

August stood holding the deadly-looking scrap of lumber. He gave it a second look and reached his finger out toward the nail.

"I wouldn't touch that if I were you."

He raised his brow quizzically. "I do not plan to cut myself."

I shook my head. "That's not it," I replied. "The police are going to want to see that. It's evidence."

His brows pinched together. "Evidence of what? You heard Mr. Maddley."

"Attempted murder, of course." I reached for the board. "I believe Mr. Maddley is very much mistaken."

"Murder?" August gasped. He pulled his hand away. "Oh, no. That cannot be!"

I shrugged and reached once more. "But it is."

The director shook his head so hard his whole body quivered. "No, no, no." He dropped the board and grabbed my wrists. "Do you know what that would mean? Police. Investigations." He inhaled sharply. "They might close down my show!" His eyes widened.

"Somebody just tried to kill your star. Don't you think that's more important? Besides, without Miss Turner, you don't have a show."

August frowned. "I'll tell you what. Let's keep this between us for now. You say murder, Mr. Maddley says accident. So who's to say for certain?"

"I'm pretty sure—" The director didn't give me a chance to finish my answer.

"If anything further untoward occurs, I will personally report it to the authorities." He held out his hand. "Agreed?"

I hesitated. "Immediately?"

He nodded solemnly. "Immediately."

Against my better judgment, we shook on it.

Not that it mattered.

Once on the street, I fished my phone from my purse and dialed Kim's number. The sooner she came and got me, the better I'd feel.

No answer. Straight to voice mail. I glared at the phone. "Great." Birds & Bees was approximately three miles away. While the walk might have done me good, I was in no mood for a crosstown hike. At least I'd chosen one-inch closed-toe heels instead of something more outrageous.

T-Bone Crawford, aka Charlie Davenport, came hurrying out the front door beside the ticket booth.

There was a matte-black motorcycle helmet in his left hand.

"Mr. Crawford, right?" I stepped forward. He paused, looking past me, and nodded.

"That's right. Thibodaux. Folks call me T-Bone."

I'd been wondering about that. What sort of mother names her child T-Bone? I held out my hand. "I'm the other Amy. Amy Simms."

Crawford winced as I felt my small hand being engulfed by his. "Sorry," I joked. "I guess I don't know my own strength."

T-Bone Crawford fluttered his free hand. "It's nothing," he replied, emotionlessly. He picked at his opposite hand. "I must've picked up a splinter someplace."

The ex-con turned abruptly and crossed the street. He threw his right leg over the seat of a big black and chrome Harley. Casting a quick last look at me, he started the bike's engine and roared off.

It seemed I was anything but Miss Popularity today. First Aaron Maddley treated me with an icy demeanor, and now T-Bone Crawford had taken off without so much as a wave good-bye. I was beginning to wonder if it was me. Was it something I'd said, smelled like, or done?

As I started along the sidewalk, silently cursing the entire male species, Robert LaChance came hauling out of the TOTS parking lot in a flashy silver German convertible, rear wheels spinning. The car dealer slammed on the brakes when he saw me.

"Hey!" He bent over, and a moment later, the booming sounds of Taylor Swift faded. "Watch where you're going, Simms!"

"You could have killed me," I reprimanded him, looking down at the front bumper a mere foot from my thighs.

"Yeah, but I didn't."

I ignored the callous remark and started walking.

Robert honked and I spun around. "What?" I said. "You want to back up and try again?"

He grinned. "Are you planning on walking all the way to your shop?"

My jaw dropped. "I seem to have left my wings at home."

"So you want a ride or what?" He gestured toward the empty passenger seat.

Robert LaChance was offering me a ride? What was the man up to?

"You want to make up your mind?" Robert's fingertips played along the dash like a sandpiper running along the shoreline. "I haven't got all day."

I hurried to the passenger side and climbed in, sinking into the warm, luxurious Italian leather. "Nice car," I remarked.

"Sell it to you for forty-five grand," Robert said, shifting into gear and sliding out onto the road.

"Too rich for my blood," I said.

He raised an eyebrow as he said, "Sell that place of yours and you'll be able to afford a car like this and then some."

I shifted my weight as he took the corner onto Lake Shore Drive much too quickly. He was a one-armed maniac behind the wheel. "What is it about my house that makes everybody want it so badly?"

"I don't know what you mean."

"What I mean," I replied, fighting to keep flying

hair from whipping my eyes, "is that you, the mayor, and Gertie Hammer are cooking up something." I faced him head-on. "I want to know what."

"Like I said, I have no idea what you're talking about."

"Oh, really," I said, as he pulled up outside my house, "then how come I got a letter from the town's planning commission informing me that they propose to widen this intersection?" I pointed to the corner of my property. "And demolish my house through eminent domain?"

"Really?" Robert LaChance sounded anything but surprised. An actor he was not. It was probably best for everybody's sake that he was no longer able to play the part of Frank Butler in *Annie Get Your Gun*. Probably the only good acting he did was when he tried to convince a prospective buyer how reliable one of his crummy used cars was.

"What do you know about T-Bone Crawford?" I asked, changing the subject. Maybe this he would answer.

"Crawford?" Robert shrugged. "Not much. He's a decent auto mechanic. Why?"

"Just curious." I reached for the door handle. "Wait? Does T-Bone work for you?"

Robert rubbed his fingers along his cast. "So what if he does?"

I took that for a yes. "So you know he's an ex-con?"

"Is there a point to all these questions?" Robert taunted, without really answering once again.

I climbed out and slammed the car door.

Robert leaned toward me, his elbow on the car's

passenger-side window ledge. "Maybe you should think about selling the place, Simms. You know, I've got an empty space in a commercial property not a mile up the road that would be perfect for your little bird store. I'll make you a good deal."

"Thanks." I yanked at my purse strap. "But I have no intention of moving."

"Well, now." Robert smiled evilly. "You might not have a say in the matter."

I bit back every curse I could think of as Robert and his fancy foreign convertible sped away. Tiffany was lucky to be rid of the man.

5

"What's in the box?" I asked.

My mother and Kim were sitting cross-legged on the floor in front of the sales counter. Both Mom's and Kim's eyes were fixated on whatever was inside the cardboard box between them.

Whatever it was, it was making small scratching and thrashing sounds.

Mom signaled for me to keep my voice down. "I found it on the porch," she said softly.

Kim looked up, then back down. "It's a bird."

I leaned over and peered inside. "A towhee, to be precise," I said. "An eastern towhee." I helped my mother to her feet.

"Thank you, Amy." Mom suffers from muscular dystrophy. It had been getting worse for a while, but these days seemed to be in a holding pattern, thank goodness.

"What's that?"

The three of us looked up. Esther Pilaster, or Esther the Pester, as I sometimes thought of her, trundled toward us from the back of the store. She was balancing a mug of coffee in one hand and a plate of cookies in the other. One of my throws was draped over her shoulders.

Esther is a renter I inherited with the house. She'd leased an apartment on the second floor from Gertie Hammer before the house was mine, and I'd been forced to continue the lease. I couldn't wait until that lease came to an end and the woman found a new place to live. She treated my store like an extension of her living room, no matter how many times I asked her politely not to.

Case in point, now. Drinking the beverages and eating the cookies that I put out expressly for the customers.

"I thought you said this place was no pets?" Esther Pilaster barked.

"It is." I eyed Esther carefully. I had my suspicions that the woman was keeping a cat. I'm allergic to cats. Seriously. I also suspected her of smoking in the apartment, though I had expressly forbidden it.

"Then what's your mother doing with a pet bird?"

Esther's a small, narrow-shouldered, elflike septuagenarian with a hawkish nose, sagging eyelids, and silvery hair normally pulled back tightly into a four-inch ponytail held in place with an elastic black velvet hair tie. She had gray-blue eyes, wispy white eyebrows, and uneven teeth. And no filter between her thoughts and her voice box.

"It is not a pet." I lifted the box to the counter and ran my hand along the little bird's tail. I turned to

Kim. "You say you found it outside?" One of its wings seemed wrong somehow.

Kim rose and dusted herself off. "Your mom found it. I found Barbara on the floor with Sammy when I got back."

"Sammy?"

"That's his name," said Mom.

My brows rose. "You named the bird Sammy?"

Mom pushed up her slender shoulders. "Why not?" She stroked the crown of the little bird's head. "Besides, he reminds me a little of Sammy Davis Jr."

I didn't want to know how or why a towhee could remind my mom of Sammy Davis Jr., an entertainer and Rat Packer who had died when I was a little kid, so I went another way. "Because we can't keep him is why not," I said, studying the towhee more closely. "He looks like he's been injured."

"He doesn't look like a Sammy," Esther remarked, dropping a cookie crumb in the box.

I quickly pulled out the cookie. "Birds don't eat cookies," I said. And no, he didn't look like a Sammy. He didn't look like a Frank Sinatra or a Dean Martin either.

"How do you know? You didn't give him a chance," was Esther's reply.

"They aren't good for them." I rolled my eyes. "See how his wing doesn't fold back all the way?" I ran my fingernail lightly along its feathers.

"Yeah." Kim leaned over me. "He definitely can't fly. If it's a he." She twisted her head to look me in the eye. "Is it a he?"

"Yes, I think so." The little towhee was about seven inches long, from its head to its long, rounded tail.

The bird was smaller than a robin, larger than a sparrow—to which the towhee is related. Towhees are distinctive looking with warm, reddish-brown sides contrasting with their white chests and bellies.

"If I remember correctly"—I strolled to the bookshelves and extracted a copy of the Audubon field guide for Eastern Region birds—"the males are more of a black in color—along the tail, wings, head, neck . . ." I scanned the tome's index, then turned to the eastern towhee page. "See?"

Mom and Kim nodded. Kim was holding the box. We looked from the book to the bird and back again.

"The females, like this one"—I tapped the opposite page—"are dark brown where the males are black." I carefully replaced the book. It was store merchandise, after all. "I wonder who left him."

"I think it was the children," Mom said.

"Children?"

My mother nodded while she tugged at her fingers. "I saw two children, a boy and a girl, on the porch. I went out to see if I could help them, but they ran off before I arrived." She glanced out the front window. "That was when I found the box at the door."

"I saw them, too," put in Esther. "From my window." Esther's window looks out over the front of the store. "Troublemakers, if you ask me."

"What are you going to do with him?" asked Kim as we returned the cardboard box to the counter.

"Take him to the vet, I suppose."

"I could take care of him," Esther said unexpectedly.

I cocked my head. What was the Pester up to? "No,

thank you, Esther. I'm sure this little guy will need some professional medical care."

"Harrumph," coughed Esther, spilling coffee on my throw. At least it washed away the clinging cookie crumbs. "I was only offering."

Right, I thought. She probably wanted to feed the bird to the cat she was hiding up in her apartment. After fattening it up on cookies.

"There's a vet three blocks away," offered my mother. "You remember Dr. Buchman? We used to take Snowy to him."

I smiled. I remembered our little bichon, Snowy— named after the dog in the Tintin books. "Doc Buchman's still practicing?" The man had seemed so old when I was a teenager.

Mom explained that Dr. Buchman was working part-time. "His daughter, Jane, has joined the practice. She does most of the work now."

I draped my arm over my mom's shoulders. "Thanks for helping out. Why don't you go rest for a while?"

Mom said she would. Much to my relief, she took Esther's arm and asked her to help her up the stairs. My mother is extremely perspicacious and always looking out for me. We looked out for each other. Mom would probably have my soiled throw washed, folded, and fluffed by afternoon.

I grabbed a clean towel from the kitchen and laid it gently along the bottom of the box. The little towhee gave three high-pitched whistles and hopped atop the towel.

"Hold down the fort," I said to Kim as she held the

door while I maneuvered the box out to the van. "And thanks for coming to pick me back up at TOTS."

Kim blushed. "Oops. I was supposed to do that, wasn't I? Sorry."

"Don't be. I caught a ride with Robert LaChance."

"Ugh. Now I'm really sorry."

I laughed. "We had an interesting conversation."

"About what?"

"About Birds and Bees."

"You still think he and the mayor are trying to drive you out of business?"

"I'd bet my life on it," I answered, shutting the van's cargo doors.

Come to think of it, I realized as I drove off, that was, at least figuratively, exactly what I was doing.

Buchman's Veterinary Medicine was located at the corner of a mostly residential street. If I remembered correctly, Dr. Buchman lived in the house next door.

A young girl in blue scrubs looked up from the desk, where she'd been staring at a computer screen. "Can I help you?"

I glanced around the waiting room. It seemed so much smaller than I remembered and poorly lit. A casually dressed middle-aged man sat on a bench. The collie at the other end of the orange leash he was holding eyed me eagerly.

I set the box down on the desk between the girl and myself. "I found this bird. Well, I didn't find it exactly." The towhee fluttered its wings, then settled into a corner of the box, staring up at me with striking red eyes. "I'm sure he's injured."

"Aww." She stuck her finger in the box. "Poor thing. We'll get you fixed up." She looked back to me. "New patient?"

I nodded and she handed me a form and a pen. I filled out the new patient card and was led to Examination Room 2.

Moments later, a second woman in blue scrubs and a white lab coat entered, carrying an electronic tablet. She looked in the box, then at me. "Amy Simms?" Her honey-blond hair was tied in a ponytail and tucked under the collar of the white coat. She had a lovely face and didn't appear to be wearing any makeup.

I nodded. "You must be Dr. Buchman's daughter."

She smiled. "Jane. Pop's down in Charlotte seeing his cardiologist."

"We must have been in school about the same time."

"I think I was a couple of years behind you. I remember Mr. and Mrs. Simms from high school." Both Mom and Dad had been high school teachers.

"I heard you were back in town." The vet reached into the box and held the bird gently in her cupped hands. "A towhee?"

I smiled. "Very good."

Jane nodded. "I don't think the wing is broken, but I'll shoot an x-ray."

I said okay. I wasn't sure how much this whole trip to the vet was going to cost me, but, whatever the charges, I wasn't going to let that stop me.

I sat while she left with the towhee. There was a slight medicinal smell to the small room. I thumbed through a tired-looking dog magazine. Several minutes later, Jane returned and placed Sammy back in his cardboard box. Jane's assistant handed her an x-ray. She examined it for a moment, then faced me.

I braced my knees as I awaited the verdict.

"If anything," the vet said, "it's only a hairline fracture of the left ulna."

I rose and tried without success to see what she was seeing on the x-ray sheet. "So he'll be okay?"

Jane tapped her tablet. "I'd say so, yes. With a little patience, proper feeding and handling." Her fingers ran along the tablet's screen. "I can give you the name of a local wildlife rehabilitator, if you're interested?"

"That would be great." An expert on bird rehabilitation was what the towhee needed, not somebody who sold birdseed. And definitely not Esther the Pester feeding him cookies. "Thanks, Doctor."

"Call me, Jane," she said, placing her tablet in one of her coat's oversized front pockets.

"Thanks, Jane." I picked up the cardboard box from the stainless-steel examination table. "How much do I owe you?"

Jane reached into the box and let the little towhee peck at her finger. "Nothing."

"Nothing?"

The vet nodded. "We like to do a little community service here at Buchman's. I'd say this little fellow . . . Sammy?" I nodded, and she continued. "I'd say Sammy deserves some of that charity."

"I can't thank you enough for your time and your help." I hesitated at the door. "If there's anything I can do for you . . ."

"Well . . ." Jane bit her lip.

"What is it?"

"I hear you've joined the cast of *Annie Get Your Gun*."

"You did?" It had been what, maybe twenty-four hours?

"Hey"—she shrugged—"life in a small town."

"Can I get you free tickets to the show?" I said with a laugh.

"Nah." Jane waved away the suggestion. "Pop and I have seats. Heck, he's a subscriber, gets us season tickets every year."

"What is it then?"

Jane's fingers touched my wrist. "I know it's a lot to ask, but Pop would be thrilled to meet Ava Turner."

My brow shot up.

"I know it's a big imposition. It's just that Pop's such a big fan of hers. Even though she's been living in town for years, as you know, she is quite reclusive." Jane stopped and laughed. "Too bad she doesn't have a pet. That way, Pop could at least see her when it was time for its checkup."

"Of course," I said without thinking. "I'm sure I can arrange for that." Why not?

"Personally, I mean, I know Miss Turner's a big star and all," Jane said, following me out to the front counter, where I signed a couple of papers. "But I don't see the big deal. Maybe I'm not the starstruck type."

Jane asked her receptionist for the wildlife rehabilitator's card, which she then handed to me. "Be
with you in a minute, Mr. Langstrom," she called to
the man with the collie. The vet held the door as I
juggled the cardboard box outside. "Then when you
add all Ava Turner's sordid history, the drug and alcohol addictions, the love affairs, the murder—"

I stopped on the sidewalk. "The murder?"

"Don't you remember? Gosh, it must be twenty
years ago." The vet explained how Ava Turner had
returned home from an L.A. film studio to discover
her daughter being attacked by her boyfriend. Ava
had shot and killed him. The court had ruled it justi-
fiable homicide.

I sighed. "I do remember. How horrible." I set the
box back in my van. "Isn't that about the time she
moved here to Ruby Lake?"

"Yeah, then, not a year later, the daughter committed suicide. Shot herself."

6

I arrived at TOTS five minutes late, parked quickly, and ran to the front door. "Locked," I mumbled, rattling the door and seeing no one inside. "Of course."

I ran all the way back to the parking lot and the side entrance. Crawford's Harley was parked beside the dumpster at the back corner of the building.

I was huffing and puffing like a sad old spinster by the time I was standing on the stage with the rest of my cast.

August Mantooth crossed his arms over his expansive chest. "How nice of you to join us, Miss Simms."

"Very disrespectful, if you ask me," said Amy Harlan, looking sideways at me. Not that anybody *had* asked her.

"Sorry." I waved to everyone, then leaned over, pressing my hands against my thighs as I fought to calm my breathing. I nodded to Ben Harlan. The attorney was chatting offstage with a Native American named Nathan Longfellow, whom I had been introduced to earlier in the day. He was playing Chief Sitting Bull. I'd heard he was part-Cherokee. The director definitely seemed to lack imagination.

Dick Feller, Amy Harlan, and T-Bone Crawford were missing. Were they off in a corner somewhere playing skat, Germany's most popular card came for three persons?

The afternoon had been a flurry of activity, from taking Sammy the towhee to the wildlife rehabilitator—who lived well outside of town, in the countryside—to dealing with customers, then wolfing down a quick supper with Kim and Randy at Ruby's Diner, where they battered me with talk of load-bearing walls, the benefits of laminate over hardwood, and whether to go with granite or quartz kitchen countertops.

I should be home, kicking my feet up on the sofa, watching the Hallmark Channel and sipping Chablis. But no, I was rehearsing my unasked-for role in *Annie Get Your Gun.*

Oh, sure, I'd always imagined I'd make a great Broadway star. But, unlike Cousin Riley, I knew better than to think I actually had what it took to be one. Like talent. And the ability to sing. OMG, were they going to ask me to sing?

The ancient Romans and Greeks had eaten songbirds, particularly nightingales, in the belief that it would improve their singing voices, but I wasn't up to testing the theory.

"It's bad enough that the police were here earlier asking questions," moaned August.

"The police?" I said.

"And Lance Jennings." This from Rhonda. For the

first time, I wondered where Riley was. It wasn't like him to be far from his sister.

Lance is a reporter for the *Ruby Lake Weekender*, the town's newspaper. Lance is no ace reporter. Not that it mattered. His father, Monty, owned the paper.

"The police and Lance were asking questions about the earlier incident involving Miss Turner," answered Ben.

"How did they find out?" I wondered. After all, I knew I hadn't said anything. That had been my deal with the director.

"It was that stagehand fellow," August Mantooth said, his jaw tight. "I fired him."

I remembered how he'd taken the movie star's picture as well.

"I explained to the police and that nosy reporter that it was all a simple accident."

I wasn't sure what about clobbering a woman in the head with a board with a nail in it was simple or an accident, but wasn't surprised that Jerry Kennedy, our chief of police, had bought what August Mantooth was selling.

"Where's Miss Turner?" demanded the director.

"I left her in her dressing room," Rhonda answered.

"Somebody please go get her!" August Mantooth ordered, clearly exasperated.

"Miss Turner told me she didn't want to be disturbed," Patsy said, staring the director down. She wore a white shirt with long white fringe along the undersides of each arm and a buckskin skirt.

"She always tells you that," muttered the director, rubbing his left wrist.

"She told me to stand in for her." Patsy smoothed down her billowy skirt. "I know all the lines."

So she wasn't only a member of the crew; she was a stand-in. That explained the costume.

"Nonetheless," August Mantooth backpedaled, perhaps fearing the great woman's wrath, "we'll give her a few minutes." He cleared his throat. "We can start without her."

I unbuttoned my tan cardigan and handed it to Patsy Klein, who occupied my personal space and held up, by a wire hanger, a second buckskin cowgirl costume with way too much fringe.

"I took in the bosoms," she snapped, a little too loudly for my taste. "The top might be a little loose yet."

Patsy shot the director a look. "Mr. Mantooth likes to see the female form." She slipped the costume off the hanger and pressed it to my shoulders "But it'll do." She frowned. "I suppose."

"Thank you," I said, not sure exactly what I was thanking her for.

Amy Harlan put her hand to her lips and giggled.

"Try it on and let me know," Patsy ordered.

"I think you'll look great!" I heard a man's voice call from behind. "Why don't you go slip it on? Give us a first look."

I turned, gripping the hanger by the hook end. Paul Anderson stood there, looking like something straight out of a Wild West show, which was fitting because that was exactly what we were supposed to be doing. The real-life Annie Oakley toured with the famed Buffalo Bill in Buffalo Bill Cody's Wild West show. That's the story the Irving Berlin and Dorothy and Herbert Fields musical is based on.

He turned to the director. "This is supposed to be a dress rehearsal, isn't it?"

Mantooth nodded for my benefit.

Paul Anderson tugged at his shirtsleeves. "You've done a great job with my costume, Patsy." He cradled the woman in his arms. She was clearly thrilled with the attention.

Paul released her and sauntered toward me. "I'll bet you're surprised to see me again."

"Surprised isn't the word." I held him at bay as he attempted to hug me, too. "You're playing Frank Butler?"

Paul smiled and nodded. "If I'd known you were going to be playing Winnie, I'd have asked to switch roles with Eli." He glanced over his shoulder. "That way, I'd be the one getting to throw knives at you." He placed his hands on his hips as he laughed, deep and hard.

"Sorry, Paul, that's my job," said the man with the baritone voice behind him.

"Throwing knives at me?" I turned toward the man Paul Anderson had been addressing. He had jet-black hair and a day's stubble across his square jaw. His broad shoulders bulged from a less flamboyant buckskin jacket than my own.

The stranger stepped in front of Paul, his hands brandishing a knife. When he saw the expression on my face, he brightened. "Don't worry," he said. "This is just a prop knife. See?" He grabbed the knife by its sharp tip and it bent easily.

I gulped.

"I'm surprised you weren't aware of the knife-throwing bit," Ben said, obviously noting the look on my face. "Your cousin Riley mentioned you're quite the Broadway buff."

I remembered now. There was a knife thrower in the original 1946 Broadway musical. In the revised 1966 Broadway book, as in the movie version starring Betty Hutton and Howard Keel, that character and mine had been written out. "Slipped my mind," I confessed.

The man before me chuckled. "Eli Wallace." He stuck out a strong, calloused hand. "I'm playing Tommy Keeler." He pantomimed throwing the knife a couple of times. "Knife thrower extraordinaire."

"And you throw them at me?" I pointed to my chest.

"That's the idea," Eli said with a shrug.

I was about to say, "Over my dead body," but didn't want to give the man any ideas.

The director's telephone started ringing, and he whipped it from his coat, soured as he looked at the number, then answered. August Mantooth held his hand over the phone as he said, "Take five, everyone!"

Cast and crew dispersed as the director bounded down the stairs into the orchestra pit with his phone pressed to his cheek, then disappeared through the heavy brocade curtain.

"Where did everybody go?" I said to Riley, turning around and noticing that the stage had emptied quickly of everyone but the two of us.

Cousin Riley had opened his mouth to reply when we heard the shot.

7

I dropped my costume, hurried down the narrow hall, and turned toward the sound of the banging.

"Miss Turner!" Lou pounded on a white dressing room door with a yellow star painted at eye level. His forehead glistened with sweat. "Are you in there? Are you all right?" He banged some more.

August Mantooth was right behind him. He hitched up his trousers. "Out of the way," he barked. "Let me try." He jiggled the door handle.

"I already told you it was locked."

"Ava!" shouted the director. "Open the door, my dear!"

"Don't you have the key?" I asked the stage manager.

Lou's brow shot up. "Of course. It's in my desk. I'll be right back!" Lou's heavy steps pounded down the hall, the sound dwindling as he disappeared.

August Mantooth sagged against the door, shaking his head. "I can't believe she really did it."

Riley and I looked at one another. "Did what?" I said.

August moaned some more.

"Did what?" I repeated, struggling to find his chin buried under all that beard and turning his face toward me. "What did Miss Turner do?"

"Shot herself!" huffed Lou, running along the hall, a thick ring of keys jingling in his hand.

I turned. "Shot herself?" A chill ran along my spine.

"I received her text telling me what she intended to do mere moments ago," the director said with a trembling voice.

"Me, too," wheezed Lou.

"Incredible," whispered Riley, his face white. "Are you certain?"

"Will be in a minute," replied Lou. He nervously tried one key after another until alighting on one that fit the antique doorknob. Lou glanced my way, as if steeling his nerves.

"Open it," hissed August Mantooth, waving his hands.

Lou gulped and complied. The sweat was literally pouring off him now. His shirt was soaked through, and I could see the outline of his undershirt. "Miss Turner?" His fingers twisted the knob. "Ava?" The door opened with the tiniest of squeaks, then held. "The chain's on."

"Break it!" urged the director.

Lou hesitated, then put his shoulder into it. The chain gave way and Lou practically fell inside. "No!"

The director and Riley hurried to the doorway. "I don't believe it!" shouted August Mantooth.

"What the devil is going on?" Ben Harlan demanded from the hall.

I pushed between the two men. Lou stood over the body.

Only it wasn't Ruby Lake's own Ava Turner.

It was Patsy Klein.

She sat facing us with surprised, dead eyes, her arms at her sides, her long legs stretched straight out. A large red blotch spread across her white shirt.

A revolver rested on the floor below her extended right hand.

"Is that a real gun?" August reached for the gun.

I clamped my fingers on his arm. "No," I said. "Don't touch it." I fought the urge to vomit. The shocking sight of the bloody corpse had left me nauseous and light-headed.

He looked at me quizzically. "Surely it's only a prop gun."

"She looks pretty dead to me," I replied. "So I'd say the answer to your question is no." My arms had broken out in a cold sweat.

"Amazing," remarked Lou. "It does look exactly like one of our prop guns."

"Like it or not," I explained to the men, "this is a crime scene."

August Mantooth nodded.

"I'm calling the police," said Lou, reaching into his pocket for his cell phone.

"No need to," replied Mayor Mac MacDonald, suddenly filling the doorway. "Chief Kennedy is already on his way."

"I need some air," gasped a white-faced August Mantooth. I caught a pungent whiff of spice as he brushed past me and shoved the mayor aside in his effort to escape the confined space.

The director did look bad, but not as bad as Patsy Klein. Her buttery-yellow flounce skirt rode above her bare ankles. I spotted a small blue butterfly tattoo above her left heel.

I looked around the small, cramped dressing room. A round-backed raspberry-colored settee sat along the right side. The director's chair Patsy Klein was sitting in faced the door but was clearly intended for the cluttered makeup table behind. A tall six-drawer wardrobe chest and dressing screen took up most of the left side. A bank of lights above the three-sided mirror cast a friendly glow in a now decidedly unfriendly-seeming space. One small window high on the back wall gaped open mere inches.

Aged framed photographs of past occupants of the dressing room peppered the walls, including several more recent shots of Ava Turner.

Out the window, I caught the sound of a motorcycle springing to life, then quickly fading in the distance.

"What was Patsy doing in here?" I asked Riley and Lou. Looking beyond them, I could see what looked like the entire cast and crew squeezing into the narrow hallway, hoping to catch a glimpse inside. Several had their cell phones out and were talking in clipped tones and shooting pictures of the deceased. Deep furrows formed on my brow. "Isn't this Miss Turner's dressing room?"

Both men nodded.

"Out of the way, everybody. Move aside!" The sonorous baritone voice reverberated along the hall, and I knew it could only be Eli Wallace. "Right this way, Chief." The actor burst through the door with Chief Kennedy and Officer Dan Sutton close behind.

"Lord a-mighty," Chief Jerry Kennedy said, taking in the corpse. He turned to Eli. "I thought you said Ava Turner shot herself? This sure as hell isn't Ava Turner!"

Eli looked befuddled. "I-I thought it was. I mean"—his eyes searched the crowd—"that was what I heard." His face had gone deep red. For the first time, I noticed his bloodshot eyes. Had he been drinking?

Officer Sutton's toothpick worked up and down like clockwork as his eyes also fell on Patsy Klein's dead body. "Who is she?"

"Get all those people out of here!" snarled Chief Kennedy, with a backward wave of his hand. He bent to inspect the revolver. Jerry Kennedy's rather boyish looking, especially with that crew-cut blond hair of his that's always sticking up. Match that with a fleshy, squat nose, an uneven smattering of freckles, and dark jade eyes, and he looks like a big kid playing dress-up. He fills out his brown uniform as well as ten pounds of Idaho potatoes fill out a sack.

"You heard the chief!" Officer Sutton began pushing everyone out. "Move it, people!" The officer, a stocky fellow who obviously knew his way around a weight room, was far younger and fitter than the chief. Dan Sutton was half Hawaiian on his father's side. Each time I saw the officer, his big brown eyes seemed to dart all around like a skittish woodpecker watching for a lurking hawk.

Riley tumbled out. Ben took my arm and escorted me to the door.

"Hold on," Chief Kennedy ordered.

"Yes, sir?" Officer Sutton wiped his brow with the back of his hand, knocking his brown cap to my feet. I handed it back.

"Have everyone wait for me down in the theater. I'm going to want a word with everybody who was here." The chief of police extracted a pair of latex gloves from his jacket and slipped them on before lifting the gun from the floor.

"Call Larry and tell him to bring the camera, Dan." Larry would be Larry Reynolds, another of Jerry's officers. I'd seen him around town now and again. "Has somebody called Greeley?" Andrew Greeley was a sweet old fellow who looked about ninety, but Mom told me was only seventy-one. He owned the local mortuary and doubled as Ruby Lake's coroner.

"I spoke to Anita. She called him up and said he'll be straight over."

I wondered how long "straight over" might be. Old Andrew moves at sloth speed, and that's on a good day. His daily driver is a hundred-foot-long black hearse with frilly white curtains. He'd owned that vehicle for as long as he'd owned Greeley's Mortuary, which he'd inherited from his father and his father before him. As a girl, I always got a chill whenever he drove by. Still do.

"Why do we have to stick around?" demanded Nathan Longfellow. I hadn't seen him enter. "The woman killed herself. And since we are obviously not going to be rehearsing this evening, I'd like to get home. I have work in the morning."

"Who are you?" Chief Kennedy rose, holding the gun by its trigger guard, its barrel pointing forward.

"Nathan Longfellow," the big Cherokee answered.

"Well, Mr. Longfellow, it's only a formality." His right hand rested atop his holstered service revolver. "Rules are rules."

Longfellow frowned and exited.

Chief Kennedy frisked Patsy Klein and she didn't seem to mind one bit.

Officer Sutton returned and said, "EMTs are on their way in, Chief."

Kennedy nodded. "No hurry. No hurry at all." Then Jerry saw me standing at the door. Jerry Kennedy and I have a bit of history. We'd had a date in high school. He had tried to frisk me then and I'd rebuffed him.

Things had gone downhill from there.

"Why are you still here, Simms? Everybody else left like I asked."

See what I mean?

The corner of his mouth turned down like he'd swallowed a piece of bad cheese. "Grab a seat with everybody else."

"Sorry." I ran my finger along the edge of the doorframe. "It's just funny, is all."

"You find something funny about suicide, Amy?"

I made a sour face. "Of course not, Jerry. Don't be ridiculous."

"So?" The chief laid the revolver on the dressing table. "Spill it." He stroked his thumb across his five-point silver badge.

"Ava Turner texts Lou and August—"

"Who?" Kennedy squeezed his eyebrows together.

"The director," I filled in. "Apparently, she texted

them both that she was about to kill herself." I stepped to one side as a couple of paramedics bustled into the small quarters.

"So I heard. What's your point?" Jerry scratched the tip of his nose with this right thumb.

"What happened to Ava Turner?"

8

"**M**iss Turner!" I couldn't believe the actress was sitting at The Coffee and Tea House on the square. I spied her as I headed up the sidewalk, head bent in response to the cool breeze coming in over Ruby Lake. She looked so calm, complacent, and relaxed, her hands gripping an oversized mug of some steaming beverage.

I pushed open the door to the café and crossed over to the counter. My friend Susan Terwilliger was rearranging what was left of the day's pastries inside the glass display case. "Hi, Amy." She wiped her hands on her black apron and placed her palms on the countertop. "A bit late for you, isn't it?"

She was right. With a business to run, I wasn't out late most nights. "We had some commotion at the theater. I've got a part in *Annie Get Your Gun*, in case you haven't heard."

"Oh, I heard." Her brown eyes danced.

I made a face. "I should have known."

"You'll get used to it."

"If you say so," I replied. "Kind of late for you, too, no?"

"One of my employees called in sick." She looked around the fairly quiet room as she knotted her brown hair into a bob. "I couldn't find anyone else, so here I am." Her brow went up. "Like a part-time job?"

I threw up my hands. "No, thanks. I've got more than enough on my plate at the moment."

I ordered a cup of the Serenity blend, a pleasant mixture of chamomile, valerian root, lavender, and lemon balm. Susan swore by its ability to help with sleep. With her "brood of four," as she fondly called her three boys and a girl, keeping her running all day, she should know.

"So, what was all the commotion over there?" Susan nodded toward Theater On The Square, which was visible from her storefront window.

I blew across my mug, took a careful sip, and surveyed the seating area. Besides Ava Turner, there was a small group of high school-age kids and two couples at separate tables. "Someone died," I said softly.

"Oh, no," Susan whispered back. "I wondered what the police cars and ambulance were doing there. I just figured somebody else got hurt."

I nodded. The ambulance and most of the other vehicles were now gone. Only Chief Kennedy's car remained, parked at an odd angle directly in front of the theater. Sure, if I'd tried parking like that, I'd be cited with a parking infraction.

"You heard about the other accidents?"

"Oh, yeah," Susan said, nonchalantly wiping a rag across the countertop. "The little incidents, like petty theft. Your cousin Riley claiming somebody purpose-fully tried to run him off the road." Susan rolled her eyes toward the ceiling. "Personally, I think that was probably a lost tourist not paying attention or some-body texting and driving."

I'd been meaning to ask Riley about that. "Two people were seriously hurt."

"Robert LaChance and Coralie Sampson, wasn't it?"

"It was," I replied.

Susan pointed to my cup. "Want anything to go with that?"

I smiled. "I thought you'd never ask." I pointed to one of the almond and raisin bear claws and bit into it greedily.

"Pretty weird," Susan remarked as she rang up my purchases. "All these accidents and now somebody dies." She sighed heavily. "The theater's troubles keep piling up."

"I guess it may not be long until TOTS does close its doors for good," I commented, thinking of Cousin Riley's remarks.

"I hope not," Susan said, eyes widening. "I count on them being open summer evenings. We get a lot of extra business when the series is running." She poured herself a cup of decaf. "So who died?"

"A woman working with the show named Patsy Klein."

Susan's eyebrows drew together. "I don't think I know her."

"I didn't either," I admitted. "And now she's dead."

I must have said that a little too loudly because one of the high schoolers shot me a very funny look.

Susan pulled me to the corner. "How did it happen? Another accident?"

I shook my head slowly. "It looks like suicide." I looked her in the eye.

Susan sucked in a breath and made the sign of the cross over her chest. "Oh my god."

"Yeah." I described how we'd all heard the shot and gone running and found her in one of the dressing rooms.

"How terrible for you," Susan said, pouring me a refill.

I yawned. Another cup of Serenity and I'd be out like a proverbial light. "The funny thing is . . ."

"Yes?"

"We all thought it was her." I turned my head slowly toward Ava Turner. The actress sat almost unmoving at the small table beside the window. The actress sipped slowly from her mug, then set it quietly on the place mat.

"Ava Turner?" Susan looked puzzled. "Why would you think that?"

"Not me personally," I replied. "But, apparently, Lou Ferris and August Mantooth—he's the show's director—received a text message from Ava saying she was on the verge of killing herself."

Susan looked amused. "No way," she said with a toss of her head.

"Then we break down the dressing room door." I paused for dramatic effect. "Ava Turner's dressing room door." *Breaking down* sounded so much more interesting than *getting a key and unlocking*.

Susan's eyes grew even wider.

"And there was Patsy Klein."

"Spooky." Susan bit down on her lower lip. "I think I've heard enough." She fluttered her hands. "Let's stop. You'll be giving me nightmares."

I managed a small smile. "That's why I decided to drop in for the tea." Of course, the umpteen grams of sugar I'd also consumed were likely to counteract any soporific effects of the herbal beverage.

"Have a good night," Susan called over my shoulder to a couple heading out the door.

"Tell me something," I said, pointing my chin toward the front window. "How long has she been here?"

Susan tilted her head in thought. "Miss Turner? I'm not sure. A long time. Since before the police cars and ambulance. That I know."

"Huh." Why had Ava Turner left the theater? Had she left before or after Patsy Klein killed herself? "You're certain?"

Susan opened her mouth, then shut it again. She looked at the actress. "I think so. I mean, it's not like I was taking notes or anything."

I set down my nearly empty mug. "I think I'll go say hello."

I steeled my nerves and approached the actress. "Miss Turner?"

Ava looked up at me, adjusting the dark brown and grey fox stole around her neck. Damned if it didn't look real. "Yes?"

"I'm Amy Simms." In response to the seeming lack of recognition in her eyes, I added, "I'm in the show." Still nothing. *"Annie Get Your Gun?"*

She allowed herself a small smile. "Yes, of course, you are." Miss Turner motioned for me to sit.

"Did you know the police are looking for you?" I said, wasting no time as I scooted my chair closer.

Her green eyes appeared amused. "Are they?" she remarked out of the side of her mouth. I smelled bourbon. She must have been lacing her coffee with it, and she must have brought it in herself. The Coffee and Tea House didn't sell liquor or alcohol of any kind.

"Yes, they are. Or at least they were." I knew Chief Kennedy and his men had searched the theater from top to bottom without finding a trace of her. I think we'd all been expecting to find the actress's corpse in some dark corner.

"He sent someone to your house to see if you were there and if you were all right," I added. There was a long pause during which Ava Turner's finely manicured fingers played along the sides of her mug. "Don't you want to know why?"

She turned her gaze away from the window and toward me. I took that for a yes.

"We all thought you committed suicide." I laid my hand atop hers, but the look she returned me told me to remove it. I did. "Everyone went crazy looking for you. Lou had to break into your dressing room."

She said nothing and so I continued. "Once we were able to get inside, we discovered you weren't there at all and found her sitting in your chair. Dead."

Miss Turner lofted her mug to her lips and sipped silently.

"Why *did* you send that text?"

"What text?"

"The one to Lou and August threatening to kill yourself."

"I can assure you I did no such thing. I rarely text," she said with evident disdain. "Besides, my cell phone has gone missing."

"You're saying you did not send Mr. Ferris and Mr. Mantooth a message stating that you were going to commit suicide?"

For the first time, I saw amusement work its way onto her face. The actress drew herself up as she said, "Why would I kill myself?"

She plucked her purse from the place mat at the seat to her left. "People would kill to know me." She stood, bobbled a moment, and then cinched her stole around her neck. "People," she said rather forcefully, "would kill to *be* me."

Without another word, she departed. I watched in fascination as Ava Turner crossed the dark square. For a moment, I thought she intended to return to the theater, but she avoided TOTS and instead headed diagonally up to the intersection of Main Street and School Drive. I had no idea how she was planning to get home. I didn't give it much thought either.

I was too busy thinking about how I had failed to mention, and how Ava Turner had not asked me, the name of the dead woman in her dressing room.

9

"How can I help you?"
"I'm Amy Simms. I'm here to see Floyd Withers, Miss . . . ?"

"Millicent Bryant," the woman said. The lobby of Rolling Acres, the senior living facility, was way fancier than I'd been expecting. The fortyish woman sat at a desk to the right of the main doors. She exuded an air of quiet confidence and a scent of flowery perfume.

I told her I was happy to meet her, but she seemed unimpressed.

There was a traditional-style oxblood leather-trimmed blotter with a calendar atop the desk, along with one fancy black pen and one number-two pencil, its point clean and sharp. Nothing more. No desktop nameplate. Not even a mug.

The elegantly dressed brunette rose from her ornate walnut desk, smoothed down the skirt of her eggplant and charcoal knee-length flocked jacquard dress and floated over to a computer monitor. The dark monitor rested atop a buffet table, which was nestled along the paneled wall, toward the back of the quiet lobby.

Ms. Bryant tapped the space bar, bringing the PC to life. "Are you family?" she inquired, turning from the computer screen to me.

"Friend." I folded my hands and waited as she did her thing on the computer.

After spelling my name and showing her my driver's license, the woman looked at her slender gold watch and said, "You'll find Mr. Withers in the activities center."

"Okay." I wondered how she knew that. Did they track all their residents?

She handed me a self-stick nametag and pointed to my chest, and I affixed AMY SIMMS to my shirt. "Thanks."

"Follow the hall to the second door on your right." She pointed, waited until I'd nodded to show I'd understood, and then walked wordlessly back to her seat.

The dense carpet muffled the sound of my footsteps as I meandered down the long hall. Eventually, I came to a pair of open glass doors leading to a room that was identified by its overhead signage as the ACTIVITIES CENTER. Bingo.

Though there wasn't a whole lot of activity going on at the moment. Some residents sat in tall, spindle-backed rockers and plush chairs soaking up the afternoon sun. Two gentlemen and three women sat around a card table. I had no idea what game they were playing. The only chips I could see were potato.

Others seemed to be snoozing. Two Ping-Pong tables sat unused, except that someone was using a corner of one as a spot to rest his or her inhaler.

I spied Floyd Withers sitting by himself near a large plate-glass window, looking out onto the lush grounds. He was dressed comfortably in brown trousers and a beige cardigan over a button-down shirt the color of creamed corn.

"Floyd?"

Mr. Withers slowly turned his head.

"It's me, Amy."

His eyes trembled for a moment; then recognition seemed to come. "Hello, Amy." His voice came out a whisper.

"It's good to see you again." I patted his arm. "How have you been?" Like most men his age, at least those who didn't use hair dyes or toupees, Mr. Withers had thinning white hair and a well-trimmed yet bushy mustache.

"So-so." He pulled himself up straighter. "Really good," he said then. *"Really good,"* he repeated more firmly, as if to convince himself. He waved to the chair beside him. "Have a seat."

I gazed out the window panes with him. The trees were leafing up nicely now. There was a clear view of the mountains in the background. "I hear you've sold your house."

Floyd nodded. "The old place was getting to be a bit much for me to take care of on my own."

At his age, and with his wife gone, it was no wonder. He'd been mugged recently, too. An event like that, added to everything else that had happened in his life, probably weighed heavily on him.

"Is there anything you need?" I asked. "Anything I can get you?"

"Nah." The old man waved away my offer. "They give me everything. Food, TV, books."

I watched his eyes spark to life as a northern flicker attacked a dead oak limb in search of hidden insects. "This is a nice place to bird-watch," I remarked.

His eyes never left the northern flicker. "Yeah. It's okay. Not like home though," he said with a touch of sadness creeping through, "like it was with Della's feeder."

Della had been Floyd's wife of nearly fifty years. She'd been the one who was an avid bird-watcher and feeder. Floyd's trouble trying to fill her feeder had been the impetus for our meeting. He'd been one of my first customers at Birds & Bees.

I had a sudden thought. "Why don't I bring you a new feeder?" I suggested. "From the store?" There wasn't a bird feeder in sight.

"Thanks," he said, turning his rheumy eyes to me after the bird had flown. "But I can't ask you to do that." He sighed heavily. "Besides, it wouldn't be the same."

I thought about that beat-up old feeder of his wife's. No, it wouldn't be the same. New is not always better, lacking the character, the history, the memory that some objects can hold, like hidden, priceless treasure.

"Who's the girlfriend?" cackled a stooped man with dazzling grey eyes and a shock of white hair on his shiny bald head. He pointed his wooden cane at me with an arthritic hand. His brown trousers were held up with red suspenders. His checked shirt pocket, I noted with surprise, held a cigar.

"Girlfriend is right," said Floyd with a smile. "So I guess you're going to have to get your own girl."

The second old man hooted. "Karl Vogel"—he swapped his cane over to his left hand and extended his right—"at your service." Thick, black-rimmed glasses balanced on his nose.

"Vogel." I tapped my cheek. "Why does that name sound familiar?"

Floyd chuckled. "Old Karl used to be Ruby Lake's chief of police for some years." He shot his friend a look. "Still thinks he is sometimes."

"Couldn't do no worse than that colt Kennedy!" Floyd snorted. He pulled up a chair and joined us.

"Of course," I said. "I remember." I patted his knee. "Not that I ever gave you any reason to remember me."

Karl Vogel laughed too.

"Did you know that Vogel is the German word for bird?" I told him.

"You don't say?" He turned to Floyd and said with a wink, "Your girlfriend's got brains and looks."

I blushed. "So you reside here at Rolling Acres, too?"

"Yep." He plucked the cigar from his pocket, rubbed it under his nose, and inhaled deeply. "Got a bungalow in the West Village."

"West Village?"

The corner of Floyd's mouth turned up. "That's this place's fancy name for the bungalows down that way." He pointed to his right.

"He's jealous," Karl said with a heavy wink.

"I've got a one-bedroom condo in the main building," Floyd explained. "Karl here thinks I'm jealous just because he's got a two-bedroom bungalow."

"And a prettier housekeeper," added the ex-chief of police.

"Yeah," Floyd admitted grudgingly, "I've got to give you that."

"So you're the famous bird lady, eh?" Karl stuffed the cigar between his lips.

"What do you mean, famous? And is that thing even legal?" I pointed to the fat cigar dangling from his face.

He extracted the cigar and looked at it with what I took to be a combination of love and frustration. "Just so long as I don't light up." He shot a dirty look at the white uniformed orderly clearing dirty dishes from a small snack and beverage station along the far wall.

Karl returned the damp, tattered cigar to his lips. "Floyd here told me all about what happened at your store a while back and that dead kid."

My brow went up and I shot Mr. Withers a look.

"What?" said Floyd. "It's not like it was a state secret or something."

"Besides, I hear you were responsible for catching the guy's killer." The cigar bounced with every word.

"Well, I wouldn't say that exactly."

The former chief shrugged. "Give yourself credit. You couldn't do any worse than our fair town's current chief. Like now." He looked from Floyd back to me. "Damn fool calls in a suicide, then has to backtrack when he finds out it's murder!" Karl hooted and slapped his knees.

The hairs on my arms stood up. "What?"

"I may be retired," Karl said, plucking the wet cigar from his lips and stuffing it back in his shirt pocket. Now I understood the dark brown stain. "But I have my sources." He winked at me. "I'm retired, but I'm not dead."

"Are you talking about Patsy Klein?" I said, struggling to keep my voice down. It seemed wrong, somehow, to be speaking about death in a senior living facility. Besides, such talk might get me thrown out.

Karl and Floyd bobbed their heads.

I leaned closer. "Do you mean to say that Patsy Klein did not shoot herself?"

Karl barked out a laugh and everybody turned our way. "What are you all looking at?" he said loudly. "Can't a man spend a little time with his girlfriend without everybody sticking their noses in?"

Everybody went back to what they were doing, or at least pretended to, while I waited for the red to drain from my face. Though my mouth was dry, I managed to blurt, "About Miss Klein, are you certain she didn't shoot herself?"

Karl Vogel grinned from ear to ear. "Young lady, nobody shot Miss Patsy Klein." This time it was Floyd who was the recipient of his wink. "Greeley told me himself." He held a finger to his lips, intimating that his communication with the coroner-slash-mortician was to be kept in confidence.

"But that can't be," I stuttered. "I saw the body with my own eyes." I'd seen the gun. I'd seen the blood. I cast a beseeching look at Floyd, thinking maybe he could make sense of his friend's words. But it was to no avail. I was beginning to suspect the dear old man might be senile.

Karl was shaking his head from side to side. The cigar left a growing brown puddle in his shirt pocket. "Nope. Nobody shot Patsy Klein."

Vogel leaned in so close our foreheads were a hairbreadth from touching. His breath came out smelling of wet tobacco. "Patsy Klein was stabbed to death."

10

My brain was reeling. Was it true? Why would Karl Vogel lie? The former chief of police had nothing to gain by telling me a falsehood. Besides, Mr. Withers would never be a party to such a thing.

So Patsy Klein had not committed suicide. And she had not been shot. She had been stabbed to death. In Ava Turner's dressing room.

Ava Turner's locked-from-the-inside dressing room.

While Ava Turner had texted that she was about to kill herself. Which she'd claimed she had never done. She'd also implied that she would never commit suicide. Did that mean she hadn't sent the text?

Nothing made any sense.

Were Lou and August lying? I rather doubted it. Surely, Jerry Kennedy would have asked to see their cell phones as evidence. Did I dare ask them to show me the same? Did I dare ask Jerry?

No. He'd never share any information related to the investigation with me. At least not on purpose.

And, according to Mr. Vogel, a murder investigation was exactly what Patsy Klein's unusual death had become.

And what had Patsy been stabbed with? A knife? Or maybe something more obscure like a sword or a screwdriver? For all I knew, there might have been swords around the theater, used in some play or other. There were certainly plenty of sharp tools lying about, including screwdrivers.

I explained all this to my mother over dinner at Ruby's. Not only was the food excellent, the location was unbeatable, being directly across the street from Birds & Bees.

Mom had the open-face roast beef sandwich with gravy. I'd opted for the homemade chicken pot pie. I could have used a glass of wine, but the diner does not have a license to serve alcohol.

"What do you think, Mom?" I slid my empty casserole dish toward the center of the table. Had I really eaten the entire dinner pie? It had been my intention to eat half and save the other half for tomorrow's lunch. I groaned, feeling my jeans dig into my belly. I really needed to start watching what I ate. Perhaps I should switch to birdseed? Maybe three times a week. I could call it the Birds & Bees diet. You don't see a lot of birds flying around with love handles, I realized, surreptitiously pinching my waist under the table.

"I don't know what to think," Mom replied, carefully sipping her coffee. Personally, if I drank coffee this late in the day, I'd be up all night. Mom scrunched up her brow. "The name of the dead woman doesn't sound familiar. Was Ms. Klein from around here? Does she have family?" Mom prided herself on knowing almost every family in town.

I shook my head in frustration. "I don't know if she has family or not. I suppose she must." I was certain the police would discover that soon enough. "I heard she wasn't from around here."

"Do you suppose they will cancel the show?" She wiped a spot of gravy from the table with her napkin. Mom doesn't like to leave behind a dirty table, even when that table isn't her own. "I was looking forward to your debut," she remarked, with a mischievous glint in her eyes. She was wearing a comfy pair of dark blue slacks with one of our Birds & Bees V-neck T-shirts. I'd ordered a small quantity in each of three colors, blue-jay blue, cardinal red, and raven black. Mom was color-matching in the blue.

I tilted my head at her. "Personally, I wouldn't mind if they did pull the plug on it. On the other hand . . ." I paused for a defeatist sigh. "I know how important the theater is to the community." It created jobs, sure, but it went further than that. The theater brought in locals and tourists and, as my friend Susan at The Coffee and Tea House reminded me, also supported other local business owners.

"Speaking of the community," Mom said, shifting gears, "are you prepared for tomorrow's meeting?"

I sipped my orange soda. "If by prepared you mean, 'Am I ready to butt heads with those jerks on the planning commission,' then yes." I crumpled up my used napkin and tossed it into my empty casserole dish. "If you mean, 'ready to kowtow to a bunch of conniving crooks out to—' "

"Maybe I should go with you tomorrow, Amy," Mom interrupted my tirade, placing her hands over mine. I felt the tension that had been building inside me begin to subside.

"I'll play nice, Mom." I smiled. "I promise." All of a sudden, I felt myself being slammed sideways in the booth.

"Shove over."

"Riley!" I blurted, loudly enough to cause heads to turn. "What are you doing?" I shoved back, and he was stuck with one half of his backside in the booth and the other dangling over the edge. Mom shot me a look of disapproval so I grudgingly made room for my cousin.

"Hi, Aunt Barbara." Ever the fashion plate, my cousin wore a baggy black BEER MAKES EVERYTHING BETTER T-shirt, droopy jeans, and dirty work boots.

"Hello, Riley," Mother said very graciously. "How nice of you to join us." She kicked me under the table. I wasn't sure if it was an accident or on purpose. "Isn't it, Amy?"

I pasted on a smile. "Yes, nice of you to join us." I gave my cousin one last hip shove for good measure. Some things never do change. We'd behaved the same way when we were kids. "Why are you joining us?" If he was here to mooch a free meal, he was a little late. We were finished eating.

Riley laid his hands on the table and nervously pulled on the ring on his left hand, glancing anxiously at first me, then Mom. "It's about Rhonda."

Mom straightened. "What about Rhonda?"

Riley licked his lips and leaned across the table. "Well, you see—"

Tiffany LaChance, once married to my pal Robert LaChance and now working as a waitress here at the diner, chose that moment to approach. She grinned as she pulled out her ticket book and pen. "Hi, Riley. Can I get you something?"

Tiffany's a buxom, green-eyed blonde a few years my senior. If the guys didn't come here for the food, they came here because of her. She is very easy on the eyes, and I don't even think she realizes it.

Riley was clearly under her spell. "Hello, Tiffany. Good to see you."

She smiled in reply. "Do you know what you want, or do you need to see a menu?"

Riley looked greedily at my mother's plate, now bare except for the merest hint of gravy. "Open-face roast beef sandwich?"

Mom nodded, and I waited impatiently for Riley to order his food and drink before prodding him to continue. His eyes followed Tiffany's departing backside, as if he might ever have a shot at her, and I called him back to the real world. "You were saying something about Cousin Rhonda?"

Riley turned his head in my direction, looking as if he'd forgotten I was there. "Oh, yeah." He cleared his throat. "Kennedy's got her."

My mother and I shared a look across the table. "What exactly do you mean when you say Kennedy's got her?" I finally asked.

Riley gulped down half my glass of orange soda before answering. "He's talking to her down at the station. He seems to think she might have had something to do with Patsy Klein's stabbing."

So, apparently everybody now knew that Ms. Klein

had been stabbed to death, not shot. That really had to be getting under Jerry Kennedy's skin.

"What on earth makes him think that?" My mother was first to ask.

Riley ducked back as Tiffany slid a plate of hot, gravy-slathered roast beef under his nose and departed. "That idiot Nathan—"

"Longfellow?" I said.

Riley nodded. "He went and told the chief when he interviewed him that Rhonda and Patsy had been going at it." Cousin Riley scooped up his fork and cut into his dinner, quickly shoving a big chunk in his mouth and chewing loudly.

I waited for him to get the lump down to a manageable size. "And were they? Going at it?"

"I suppose you could call it that," admitted Riley. "Patsy was a pain. Always nitpicking Rhonda about the hair and makeup." He snorted. "Like it was any of her business."

"That doesn't sound like a reason to kill a person," my mother said.

I agreed and said so. "Not even for Jerry to think so."

"Well," Riley said, his mouth full of bread, gravy, and beef, "there may have been a little shoving."

The corner of my mouth went down. "Just how little?"

"Sort of a catfight, really." Now he was beaming from ear to ear.

"You really ought to go down to the station," Mom said, "and see what you can do to help."

"Yes, Riley," I said with satisfaction. "You should."

Mom arched her brow my way. "I was speaking to you, Amy."

My face fell. "Me? Why me?"

"You are her cousin," Mom replied.

Riley watched our conversation as if it were a tennis match.

"Riley's her brother," I retorted. "And you're her aunt." Hey, I'm no slouch in the debate department.

"Amy . . ." Mom drew my name out in a way that I'm sure she'd practiced in the mirror a dozen times or more. Per day.

I gave Riley a shove. "It's not fair," I said. Getting up, I grabbed my purse from the end of the booth and headed for the exit. "Hey, Riley," I yelled back across the dining room. A question had come to mind. "What do you know about Miss Turner's cell phone?"

"Don't look at me!" he hollered with a look of alarm, bringing his right hand to his chest. "I didn't take it." He blushed as the other diners looked at him with renewed interest.

"So it is missing?"

Riley lowered his head and shoveled a chunk of dripping sandwich into his mouth, but that didn't stop him from replying. "I guess so."

Moire Leora Breeder, the café's owner, stood by the cash register and grinned as I approached. "Everything okay tonight?"

"Terrific," I said. I nodded to our booth. "They're paying."

"That's cool." Moire Leora is older than me by a few years. She's of Scottish and Italian descent and lost her U.S. Marine husband in a training accident half a dozen years ago. Still, she remained remarkably optimistic.

The diner had once been Ruby Lake's first gas station. Moire couldn't resist adding the hand-painted slogan in the window that read EAT HERE, GET GAS in a nod to the diner's previous incarnation. The tall neon sign with the big green dinosaur on it still stood proudly in the parking lot at the edge of the street. Moire Leora serves up her own take on a bronto burger as an homage to the corporate apatosaurus.

There's a row of stools running the length of the counter along the back. The cash register's up near the door. A lot of the original gas station décor and fixtures remained, giving the diner a pleasant small-town, days-gone-by sort of ambience.

In addition, all Ruby's Diner employees, including Moire, wear khaki slacks and kelly-green shirt uniforms with white name patches, stylistically reminiscent of those worn by old-school gas station attendants. Tiffany elevates that look to a whole other level. I couldn't begin to count the number of times Riley had quipped that she could pump his gas anytime.

Moire Leora reminds me of a slightly plumper version of Jennifer Aniston with blue eyes and naturally blond shoulder-length hair with a touch of gray, which she normally parts over her left eye. At about five-four, the diner owner is several inches shorter than me.

"I heard what happened at the theater," Moire began. "Do you think the show will go on?"

"I don't know if that's been decided or even discussed yet." It seemed like everyone in town was interested in knowing if the show would continue. Then it hit me—was there anyone in particular who might want the show to close before it opened? Somebody who might gain by seeing TOTS shut down?

One of the line cooks called Moire's name, and she told him she'd be right over. She eased the cash drawer closed. "If I were Ava Turner, you wouldn't get me to go back there."

"Why not?"

"Are you kidding?" Her right eyebrow arched in question. "If somebody was trying to kill me and missed and got the wrong person or something," she said in a hushed tone, "I'd be afraid they'd try again." She gave me a meaningful look. "And what if they succeeded?" The line cook sounded more flustered this time as he called his boss's name a second time. "Gotta go!"

Moire twirled and headed for the kitchen.

The woman had a point. What if the killer did try again? I decided it might be worth trying to talk to Ava Turner once more. Her life could still be in jeopardy.

Speaking of jeopardy, I had my cousin to deal with.

As luck would have it, for once, I didn't have to enter the police station to see what I could do for Cousin Rhonda. Pulling my van up to the curb outside the Ruby Lake Police Department on Barwick Street, I found her sitting on a bench outside the drugstore up the block.

I crossed over. "Rhonda? Are you okay?"

"Oh, hi, Amy." Rhonda sat slumped on the bus

stop bench, clutching her large black purse in her lap. Her eyes were red and her mascara blotchy. Seeing my cousin in such disarray was a rare sight. I'd sooner expect to find a bald eagle roosting in my fireplace than discover my cousin with her makeup smeared.

"Riley said Jerry had you over at the police station." I looked up the street. Jerry Kennedy's vehicle sat right outside the station.

"Yes," Rhonda sniffed. I dug around in my purse and came out with a travel pack of tissues and handed it to her. She slowly pulled one out and blew. "He-he considers me a *person of interest*." Her voice shook.

I squeezed in beside her. "Your brother mentioned that you and Patsy had had some . . ." I paused. "Conflicts, shall we say?"

Rhonda's face hardened. "I hated that woman." She squeezed the tissue in her hand into a tiny ball.

"Sure," I said, forcing a laugh, "but not enough to kill her."

Rhonda looked at me funny.

"Right?"

Rhonda blew her nose again. "Right."

"From what I hear"—I watched a group of sparrows dancing in and out of the branches of a pear tree not ten feet away—"she could be difficult to work with." The truth was, I hadn't heard much. But it was beginning to look that way.

"She tried to tell me my job." Rhonda scooched my way and our knees banged. "I know my job, Amy."

I nodded. "Of course, you do." I cleared my throat.

"I did hear the two of you got into a bit of a shoving match?"

Rhonda frowned. "Wherever did you hear that?"

"Riley."

Rhonda bit her lip. "You know, Amy"—she rested her fingers on my sleeve—"as much as you like Riley, I have to tell you, my brother can be quite the pain in the patooty sometimes, too."

It was hard, really hard, but I resisted the urge to burst out laughing.

Rhonda talked. "We did have a few physical altercations. But nothing that ever escalated to—" Rhonda stopped herself.

"Stabbing her?"

Rhonda shivered. "It's simply too awful to think of it, isn't it?"

I agreed. "Have they found the murder weapon?"

"No," said Rhonda. "At least that's the impression I get. I did hear the chief and a couple of his officers talking about how the gun really was one of our, I mean, the theater's prop guns."

I stiffened. "The gun on the floor beside Patsy? It wasn't a real gun?" Though we'd definitely heard a shot, so the weapon was at least capable of firing blanks.

"No, I don't believe it was." Rhonda pulled out a pack of gum and offered me a stick, which I declined. She popped a piece of spearmint in her mouth and chewed. She looked at me through red-tinted, makeup-smeared eyes. "I may not have liked the woman, but I certainly didn't kill her."

I patted my cousin's knee. "Of course not."

"Not to speak ill of the dead, but I do think she was the one who was stealing things around the theater though."

"Really?" My brow shot up.

Rhonda nodded and wiped her red nose. If she kept rubbing, she'd be ready to play the part of Rudolph in the annual TOTS Christmas production.

"I can't prove it though."

"Do you suppose someone she was stealing from might have killed her because of it?"

My cousin seemed to give my suggestion some serious thought before she spoke. "I can't see why. It was mostly small stuff. Nothing very valuable or irreplaceable. A person would have to be crazy to kill over a missing mug or a jacket."

"So who do you suppose might have wanted her dead?"

Rhonda thought some more. "I have no idea."

"What about someone who might want to see the show canceled?"

"Gosh, Amy, why on earth would anybody want to do a mean thing like that?"

I told her I didn't know.

The bus pulled up, coughing out a cloud of diesel fumes in our faces. Rhonda stood and clutched her purse.

"Are you sure I can't give you a lift?"

The bus door opened with a soft whoosh. Rhonda placed her foot on the first step. "No, thank you. The bus goes right to my place." The driver waved to us both.

"Don't worry," I called, coming to a stand. "I'm sure everything will work out." I watched as Rhonda trudged down the aisle and took an empty seat.

She waved me over to her window and slid it down. "There was one person she really made see red."

"There was?"

Rhonda nodded. "Patsy did make quite the fool out of Nathan Longfellow."

"But he's the one who said he saw the two of you fighting."

"He did?" Rhonda's face screwed up. "Well, I don't care what that jerk said." She sniffed. "He's got some nerve. Serves him right what she did to him."

I stood on my tiptoes and leaned my hands against the side of the bus for support. "What did she do?"

Rhonda managed a smile. My cousin explained how Patsy and Nathan had been close from the beginning. "Like a couple, you know? Then, one day, Patsy came stomping backstage with Nathan at her heels. She was mad and he was madder."

"What were they arguing about?"

Rhonda shrugged. "I never did figure it out. Only Patsy told him she wanted nothing more to do with him."

I scrunched up my face as the bus's engine revved. A cloud of diesel fumes belched out the muffler. "And you think he might have murdered her simply because she rejected him?"

Rhonda shrugged. "Patsy poked fun of him in front of everybody every chance she got after that. Nathan was furious. Patsy told everybody how he was chasing after her and that she'd sooner date a sow."

The bus shuddered and lunged forward. I was forced to step back from the curb. Patsy Klein had told everybody she'd rather go out with a female pig than Nathan Longfellow?

Maybe Chief Sitting Bull had decided to exact his revenge.

11

I popped two aspirin and swallowed a cupful of luke-warm tap water. The noise from the construction next door was nearly unbearable. Whatever my new neighbor, Paul Anderson, was up to, he seemed to have ratcheted it up a notch. Or twenty.

I eyed the aspirin bottle, wishing I hadn't opted for the time-release formula. I was also keeping an eye out for my ex, Craig Bigelow. From what Anderson said, it was only a matter of time until the louse showed up.

I was alone in Birds & Bees except for a couple of children wandering loose. Mom was out somewhere, and Kim was off with Randy. Apparently, they planned to do some demolition over at Mr. Withers's old house this afternoon. Kim had also mentioned something about a tile delivery. I'd helped Kim retile her guest bath once. The tile guy we both paid to redo our redo got quite a kick out of that.

The floor started shaking and the hanging bird feeders commenced swinging as whatever instrument of destruction was being employed at the beer garden kicked into high gear.

The racket was probably scaring away my customers as much as it was spooking the birds that normally hung around the feeders out front. There's a song in the musical *Hairspray* called "You Can't Stop the Beat."

Sadly, that was true, but not in the way the tune's writers had meant it.

I looked forward to the remodel of Brewer's Biergarten being completed so my life could get back to semi-normal. It had been a couple of days since Patsy Klein's murder, and the town was still buzzing with the story.

"Please stay out of the storeroom, kids!" I called in my friendliest tone to the boy and girl. "Can I help you find something?"

The boy met the girl's eyes, then spoke for them both. "We're just sort of looking," he muttered. The girl reminded me of someone, but I couldn't think who.

"That's fine," I replied, brushing a strand of hair from my eyes. "Let me know if you need anything."

I yawned and stared at the front door, willing a customer to walk in. None obliged. I had managed to sell one of my Aaron Maddley bluebird houses earlier to a tourist couple. Glancing at the shelf, I saw that I was getting low on inventory. I'd have to give Aaron a call and let him know how well his houses had been selling and that I'd be needing more. I only hoped he'd agree to provide me with some. He seemed to be holding a grudge.

Figuring there was no time like the present, I

picked up the store phone, then set it down again when I noticed the police cruiser pulling up outside the store.

Officer Dan Sutton stepped out and adjusted his cap on his head, pulling the visor down low over his eyebrows, then walked over to my new neighbor's camper.

Call me nosy. I crossed from the sales counter to the front window for a better look. Officer Sutton walked once around the battered vehicle. He then came around again, stopping beside the door of the camper shell. He knocked several times.

There was no answer, and Officer Sutton looked up and down the street. I could have told him that Paul Anderson was probably inside Brewer's, but whatever was going on was none of my business.

Sutton sucked on his toothpick. A minute later, he reached into the passenger side of his squad car and pulled out what looked like a ticket book. I should know. I'd been on the receiving end of it myself. I blamed that on a squirrel that failed to signal before crossing the street. Sutton popped the top of his pen off with his teeth and began writing.

I watched in fascination as he tore the sheet from the pad, walked to the front of Paul's monstrosity, and slipped the ticket under a windshield wiper blade. Yep, that had definitely been a ticket book.

"That's them!"

"Oh!" I spun around. "Esther!" I clutched my heart. "What are you doing sneaking up on me like that?" I gasped for breath.

Esther the Pester rolled her eyes. "I'm trying to

tell you, Simms. That's them." She nodded her head toward the back of the store.

I followed her gaze and squinted. "Them who? All I see are two kids." The boy and girl marched around the main staircase that led up to the second floor. I'd attached a sign to a chain asking customers not to go the steps. Those were private quarters. Esther's apartment was up there.

"What are you doing here, anyway?" Probably come for the food and drink. She certainly never bought anything. I turned back to the street. Officer Sutton was gone. I frowned at Esther.

"Those are the youngsters who brought the toe heel."

I gaped at the old woman. The toe heel? Was Esther finally losing her mind? "What toe heel?" Had she lost a shoe?

"Sammy," Esther whispered loudly. "The bird in the box. Your mother's pet."

"Oh." I studied the boy and girl. "The towhee."

"That's what I said, didn't I?" Esther crossed her arms over her chest. I suddenly realized she was standing in the middle of my place of business in a tatty pink bathrobe and threadbare slippers, with her hair up in curlers.

"I'll handle this," I said. I grabbed Esther gently and walked her to the stairs. "You go get dressed."

"I ain't had my coffee yet."

I looked down my nose at her. So, she had come down for the coffee. "I'm not running a restaurant here, Esther. The coffee is for customers and employees only."

"Are you offering me a job?" Esther asked enthusiastically.

"Heavens no! Look, there's a perfectly good café right across the street." I pointed at Ruby's Diner.

Esther paused on the second tread. "I don't feel up to going out."

"Fine," I acquiesced. "Give me a few minutes and I'll bring you a fresh cup." I waited for Esther to work her way up to her apartment, then searched out the children.

They were in the storeroom once more, despite my instructions, tiptoeing around behind the boxes of merchandise warehoused there.

I planted my hands on my hips and smiled. "If you're looking for the bird, he isn't here."

The two kids looked at me, guilt and apprehension written on their tiny faces.

"Don't worry," I said. "The towhee is fine. I took him to a wildlife rehabilitator."

"The what?" This from the girl.

"Towhee." I gave the two the short version of the identity of the bird they'd left on my porch. "How about if I get you some cookies and juice?"

They agreed and we retreated to the kitchenette. "I'm Amy," I said, offering the cookie jar.

"I'm Will," said the boy. "This is Maeve." He waved toward his friend. "She found that bird on the side of her house."

Maeve nodded.

"Pleased to meet you both." I poured a round of apple juice. I explained how the bird's wing had been injured. "I'm grateful that you brought him to me. The vet told me he'll be fine. All he needs is a bit of nursing."

"At the wildlife rehabilitator's?" Maeve asked.

I nodded. "That's right." I thought for a moment. "You know, I could take you to see Sammy," I suggested.

"Sammy?" Will said.

I smiled. "That's the name my mother gave him."

"I like it," said Maeve. Will nodded his agreement.

"Anyway"—I extended the jar of cookies for a second round, but both declined—"like I was saying, we could go visit Sammy. If you get your parents' permission."

"I can get mine," Will said quickly. "After all, Mom's the one who said we should bring the bird here."

"Me, too!" Maeve said with delight.

"You aren't brother and sister?"

"Nah." Will made a face. "We're friends."

"We'd best be going." Maeve tugged Will's arm. The boy concurred.

I held open the front door and watched them bounce down the steps. "Wait," I said. "Who are your mothers? Maybe I know them."

"My mom's Sofia Quiroz," shouted the boy. The name was unfamiliar to me.

"And my mother is Amy," said the girl, a bright smile on her face. "Like you! Wait till I tell her you both have the same name."

"Amy?" I said with a cock of my head. My grip tightened on the door handle.

The girl nodded briskly. "Amy Harlan."

Amy Harlan, I thought, resting my back against the closed door and shutting my eyes. Derek Harlan's ex. The woman who had threatened to kill me if I had anything to do with him.

How would she take it once she found out I'd also befriended her daughter?

12

I gunned the van as hard as I dared. I was late, but I was also less than two hundred yards from Ruby Lake Town Hall. No point tempting fate or traffic patrol officers. Besides, I could see two empty spaces at the very back of the parking lot that extends from the road to the south side of the building. Plenty of room.

I drummed my fingers across the steering wheel, waiting for the traffic in the opposite lane to clear, then gunned the motor again. "Hey!"

Paul Anderson's mammoth old camper hit the curb with a thump and a scrape, then bounced into the lot. The heap filled about a space and a half.

I slammed on the brakes behind him and tooted my horn.

"What's the trouble?" Then he stuck his head out the window. "Oh, it's you. Hiya, neighbor!"

"What do you think you're doing?" I glared at his vehicle. "I was about to pull in."

"Sorry." He smiled and batted his eyes at me. "Guess I beat you to it."

I leaned out. "Can't you move over a bit?" I gestured with my open hand.

He looked barely contrite as he said, "Sorry, this baby takes up a lot of space." With those words, he climbed out of his cab and rapped the hood of my van. "Besides"—now he tapped his watch—"running late. See ya!" The brewer tossed his hand in the air and turned his back to me on his trot to town hall.

"Great," I muttered, along with a hundred cuss words of many colors and syllables. "Now I've got to find another parking space, probably the next block over." That was where the first off-street free parking lot was located. I threw the van into reverse and backed into the street, much to the consternation of the cars heading toward me.

"Yeah, yeah," I said, yanking the wheel hard to my right. "Give me a minute, please." It figured that *Les Misérables* would be spinning in the CD player, because *trés misérable* was what I was feeling.

Having secured a spot in the public lot, I slammed the door and locked the van. I braved a look at my watch. Wonderful. Now I was twice as late.

This public hearing was important to me. It was the first step in the town's plan to possibly tear down my home-slash-business and widen the intersection of Lake Shore Drive and Serviceberry Road. For whatever nefarious purposes they had in mind.

Birds & Bees sits on what is known locally, though unofficially, as Upper Lake Shore Drive, the part of

Lake Shore Drive that diverges up from the lake and intersects farther up with Airport Road on the west edge of town.

Serviceberry Road is so named because of the wonderful century-old serviceberry trees that the town's early inhabitants had planted as ornamentals. I loved the thin, ashy gray bark. Drooping clusters of white flowers appeared in early spring. The small dark purple-black fruit the trees bear was attractive to birds.

I ran into Paul Anderson wetting his lips at the drinking fountain outside the meeting room. Water splashed carelessly onto the worn marble floor. "I thought you were in a hurry?"

He licked his lips. "Apparently they're running late." He looked at the sheaf of papers in my hand. "What's all that?"

I frowned at the jumbled stack of papers I'd sandwiched into a manila folder that wasn't anywhere near big enough for the job. "Statistics, rules. Legal precedents." Mostly it was notes about how long the house had been there and what it meant to the town historically, but he didn't need to know that. "Thanks for driving that tank to the parking lot."

His eyes danced. "Hey, I had no choice." Paul folded his arms across his chest. "I got a ticket for living on the street. I was told to move it or get it impounded." His eyes bored into mine. "It seems somebody must have reported me to the police."

I stepped back. "Don't look at me. I didn't report you." I turned my back on him as a lanky clerk called from the door that the meeting was about to begin. "Not that I didn't want to."

I started for the door and bumped shoulders with Paul Anderson. "What are you doing?"

"Going to the meeting."

I cocked my head. "This is a meeting concerning the fate of my house," I explained. "My business."

"I know."

Paul looked like somebody with a secret, and I desperately felt like squeezing it out of him. "You care what happens to Birds and Bees?"

"Something like that." He squeezed my elbow and headed up the row of folding chairs. I counted about a dozen people and three dozen chairs. I took the first empty seat in the middle row. I watched in quiet fascination as the bar owner sauntered up to the long table set up at the far wall with a row of microphones and chairs. With luck, the clerk would toss him out on his ear.

Paul shook hands with a man I recognized as a member of the town's planning commission, then sat beside him, waving to the rest of those already seated.

A slow dread crept over me like a cold fog.

A hand squeezed my shoulder from behind and I spun my head around. "Derek!" I twisted in my chair and whispered, "What are you doing here?" I looked wildly around for his ex, the other Amy. Harlan.

"Hi, Amy." Derek was in his go-to lawyering attire: dark charcoal suit that his shoulders filled out nicely, crisp white shirt, and a deep red tie. Though a lawyer, with his rugged looks and trim physique, he looked like he could just as easily have been a lumberjack. Or a firefighter.

"I heard about the meeting and wanted to lend my support." Was it my imagination or were his perfect blue eyes sinking into mine?

I felt myself flush. He did? Derek Harlan wanted to lend me his support? My eyes scanned the seats. There was no sign of Amy Harlan. That was a good omen. Getting into a shouting match—or a wrestling match—while trying to make a case for saving my home and business was probably not a good move.

I also realized that Aaron wasn't there. Not that I'd expected him. There was nothing at stake for him in this matter. But still, Derek had come and I hadn't exactly treated him in the nicest fashion. He'd asked me out once or twice, and I'd turned him down cold. I'd also told everyone, including Kim and my mother, that the man was dirt.

In my own defense, that was because I had thought he was married.

Now I knew better. Now I knew he merely had a crazy ex-wife.

"Mind if I join you?"

I shook my head no and scooted over to the next chair to make room. Derek came around, and I caught a whiff of woodsy cologne.

"If everyone is present," Howard Mooney, the head of the commission, said, looking to his left and right, "we can begin."

"Don't worry," Derek said out of the corner of his mouth, unbuttoning his coat. He patted my thigh in what I'm sure he meant to be a chummy fashion, but I felt the tingle all the way down to my toes. "You'll do just fine."

"I can't believe it," Derek said, guiding me out of doors by the arm less than an hour later.

I couldn't believe it either. I felt numb inside. I watched as Howard Mooney, the chair of the planning commission, left the town hall in a huddle with Mayor Mac MacDonald, Robert LaChance, and Gertie Hammer—the Terrible Troika.

I realized Derek had been speaking. "What?"

"I asked if you'd like to get some dinner."

Gertie climbed into her big old Oldsmobile Delta '88. It had started its automobile life as beige but had slowly turned to rust. Black smoke poured from her muffler. Robert and the mayor left together.

Paul Anderson was still inside somewhere. Mooney had explained to those present tonight that the brewer had accepted a last-minute seat on the commission when old Ira Planer and his wife, Erma, retired to Louisiana's Cajun Riviera. Louisiana is also known as the Pelican State. If I was forced out of business, maybe I'd take my early retirement there. Though I'd never been, I'd read that Louisiana was great bird-watching country.

"What I could really use is a drink," I quipped.

Derek smiled, showing a set of perfect white teeth. "I know just the place."

My jaw tightened. "Don't look now, but I think we're about to have company."

Howard Mooney ambled toward us. Like a fla-
mingo's, his legs seemed longer than his body. I pictured him napping on one leg. His fuzzy black hair
clearly was held up with a strong gel or some sort of
super glue. "Ms. Simms, I'm sure you understand the
position the town of Ruby Lake is in." His smile was
broad and fake. "But we can't fight progress now,
can we?"

"Yes," Derek Harlan said, his voice hard, "we can."
He placed his hand against the flat of my back. "Shall
we go, Amy?"

Derek Harlan was right. He did know just the
place. Located on Main Street, a mere block from
the square, the interior of Byblos was all soft yellow
tablecloths and blue seating, modern yet cozy.

"I must have driven by this place a dozen times or
more since returning to town, but never tried it." I
swirled my cabernet and took a sip. Who knew
Lebanese food could be this good?

"You like it?"

"Very much."

"I hear the family is from the city of Byblos, which
they tell me is near Beirut." Derek beckoned our
waiter, then turned to me. "How about some dessert?"

"Oh, no," I begged off. "I couldn't." I'd stuffed
myself on falafel and vegetables. Derek had chosen
the sea bass. I'd grabbed a forkful of that, too. Not to
mention polishing off my share of the appetizer,
something called warak anab, which consisted of
grape leaves stuffed with a mixture of rice and vegetables.

"An order of the baklava," Derek told the waiter, who nodded and departed. "You're not going to make me eat it all by myself, are you?" He had removed his coat and rolled up his shirtsleeves, revealing strong forearms. He reached over and refilled my glass.

"I was surprised to see you at the hearing," I said. We had refrained from talking business over dinner by mutual agreement. Neither of us wanted to spoil the meal. But now that I'd had time to get my blood sugar level up and my rage down, it was time to get down to business.

Derek shrugged like it was nothing. "I know how difficult these things can be." He leaned back as our waiter settled a mouthwatering plate of pastry between us.

Derek slid the plate my way and I settled a couple of pieces of the baklava on my small dessert plate. The filo dough was light and flaky and filled with a delightful mixture of walnuts and pistachios and a sweet rose water syrup.

"In fact," Derek continued as I chewed, "sometimes I think small-town politics can be more brutal than big-city."

I nodded my agreement. I knew Derek had practiced in Charlotte, a city of about a million people, before coming to Ruby Lake to be nearer to his daughter. "Thank you. I don't think I could have contained myself if you hadn't been there." More than once, he'd had to lay his hand on my knee to keep me from jumping up and interrupting the proceedings.

I helped myself to a third slice of baklava. The way

things stood, my house looked destined to become a public parking lot. The planning commission had agreed that there was sufficient data to proceed with a recommendation for eminent domain, though at Derek's insistence, they had agreed to allow fifteen days for further public review and comment. I never thought I'd say it, but thank goodness for lawyers.

"I don't know what I'm going to do now." If public opinion remained against me or even disinterested, Howard Mooney, as chairperson, would be making that recommendation formally to the town's officials. That meant he'd be making his recommendation to Mayor MacDonald and the town council.

How cozy.

"You've got to get the public on your side," Derek replied. He helped himself to dessert, probably afraid I'd steal it all before he'd gotten a single taste. "The good part of living in a small town is that once people get to hear your story, you can win them over."

"If I can get them to care at all," I said with a frown. I tossed my napkin over my plate to keep myself from eating any more sweets. "I sure wish I knew what the mayor, Robert LaChance, and Gertie Hammer are getting out of all this."

Derek rubbed his jaw. "Let me see what I can find out."

"Would you?"

"I'm not making any promises, but I'll ask around. I know a few people." He paused with a smile on his face. "And Dad knows lots of people."

I grinned too. "Your father is quite popular."

Derek chuckled. "Tell me about it." He leaned closer. "Do not tell him I told you this. . . ."

I raised my brow and met him halfway. "What?"

"I think Dad likes your mom."

"What?!" Heads turned. I dropped my chin. "I mean, are you sure?" I whispered.

"I think so."

I nodded. That made sense. Mom had been seeing more and more of him of late.

"He also said he's having a blast acting in that musical you all are doing. You know, he's never acted before."

"Well, from what little I've seen, I'd say he's a natural." I stopped talking as Derek settled the check. He returned his leather wallet to the top inside pocket of his suit coat, which he'd draped over the back of his seat. "Too bad the show's been canceled."

Derek's face twisted up, not that it still didn't look handsome. "Canceled? What makes you say that?"

I shrugged and grabbed my purse. "It's been a couple of days. I haven't heard anything since the murder. I assume they've shut the production down."

Derek shook his head as I spoke. "Not at all. In fact," he said, twirling a very expensive black watch around his wrist, "it's nearly time for rehearsal." He stood. "Can I give you a lift?"

"Rehearsal?" I grabbed the edge of the table. My mouth went dry.

"Yes." Ever the gentleman, he came around and stood by my chair. "Didn't you get the message?"

"No," I replied. I rose and stood beside him.

"That's funny." Derek rubbed his neck. "Dad got a call from some guy who said he was the director."

"August Mantooth," I interjected.

Derek nodded. "Yeah, that's the guy. Anyway, Dad said he told Amy." We walked to the exit. "And Amy said she'd call you. . . ."

13

I silently cursed Amy Harlan all the way to the the-ater.

"Sorry I can't stick around and give you a ride home," Derek said as he pulled to a stop. A light driz-zle was falling. The rain was silent, but the silver Civic's wipers chugged slowly from side to side, pro-viding a rhythmic, almost musical soundtrack to our conversation.

"That's okay. I'm sure I'll be able to catch a ride with someone."

"Ask Dad," Derek replied. "He'll be happy to oblige."

A blast of cold air hit me as I entered TOTS via the side entrance. I heard the muffled chorus of "There's No Business Like Show Business" coming from the other end of the building. Ava Turner's voice rang out above all others. The woman could still belt out a tune.

Lou stepped out of the shadows holding a red-handled monkey wrench. "Heater's on the fritz again," he said, mopping his brow. "I did what I could, but—" He shrugged heavily. Running the theater, as much as keeping the theater physically running, appeared to be taking a toll on the out-of-shape man.

That explained the frigidness of the air. It wasn't the iciness of the recent murder. It was the night chill creeping in through the old building's thin walls. Though summer was around the corner, it could get chilly up here at this elevation come nightfall. Even in the apartment, there were nights I still needed the heat and a heavy blanket.

Lou told me everybody was on stage, and I headed that way.

As I rounded the dimly lit hall leading up to the wings on the left of the stage, Nathan Longfellow stepped into my path. He was the size of a small truck, with a dark complexion, shiny black hair swept back in an extravagant pompadour, and bushy black sideburns. He wore a blue and black checked shirt and loose-fitting blue jeans. His fists were clenched.

I gulped. "What are you doing here?" I could hear the sounds of the other actors coming from the stage, along with the occasional bark of August Mantooth as he gave his cast direction. For the hundredth time, I pondered the wisdom of getting involved in community theater. "Shouldn't you be rehearsing?"

Nathan's deep blue eyes were bloodshot. "Yeah. So what?" His lips twisted sideways. "We'll never open anyway. Like Mac says, this play, this place"—the big man waved his fist in the tight quarters—"is cursed."

"I don't know," I said, looking around wildly. There was no way past Longfellow. What if I turned and ran? Would he chase? "The show must go on, right?"

My heart jumped as Nathan slammed the side of his fist against the flimsy wall. "Not this one!" He leaned in close. I smelled alcohol on his breath. "Do you believe in ghosts?"

I shivered despite myself. I'd had some recent experience with ghosts, or at least the possibility of ghosts. I found the subject discomfiting. I pulled my face away. "Are you saying you do?"

Longfellow looked over his shoulder before replying, "It's like *The Phantom of the Opera*, you know what I mean?"

I thought for a moment. "Are you trying to say that you think there is somebody or some*thing* haunting TOTS?" What was it with actors, even part-time amateur ones, that made them so nuts?

In Gaston Leroux's original novel, *The Phantom of the Opera*, the mysterious phantom haunted the Paris Opera, sending mysterious messages and performing malevolent deeds. Lon Chaney had played the deformed phantom in the original silent movie version. Was Nathan Longfellow suggesting a similar situation here at TOTS? That was absurd. Besides, this was *Annie Get Your Gun*, not *The Phantom of the Opera*.

"I think," Nathan said, his voice low and coarse, "that somebody has wanted the show to fail from the beginning."

So I wasn't the only one thinking such thoughts. "I had heard there were a number of accidents and other incidents."

Nathan's snort filled the hallway. "If you ask me, a lot of that was Patsy's doing."

"Patsy's? Why do you think that?" Could she have been responsible for Robert LaChance's broken arm and Coralie Sampson's busted foot? It seemed rather unlikely.

"Because she was a wicked woman." He glowered at me. "And, in case you haven't noticed . . ." He paused, then said, "The accidents have stopped." His face was an ugly rictus. "Now that Patsy's dead."

Rhonda had suggested the same thing.

He wagged his finger at my nose. "Like I said, she was a wicked woman."

I couldn't resist a smirk. "Is that why the two of you stopped dating?" His mouth fell open as I continued. "I heard she dumped you." I was on a roll as I planted my hands on my hips and added, "In front of everyone."

"The woman was using me. I do not like being used." He hovered over me. "By anyone," he said darkly.

"How exactly was she using you?" I asked, trying to hide the fear this guy was instilling in me.

"Why don't you ask her yourself?" he said with a sneer. "Oh, that's right. You can't. She's dead."

Nathan surged past me. "Good riddance to her and to you both." He spun around, gripping the wall at the corner. "If you don't think she was evil, just ask our dear director," he spat. "I bet he could tell you a story or two about Patsy Klein."

Nathan stomped around the corner toward the wardrobe area. "If he has the guts."

I hurried in the opposite direction, putting as much distance between myself and the volatile man as I could. At the next corner, near where I knew the dressing rooms were located—not that I had one, being too lowly a member of the cast to warrant my own quarters—I spotted a door slightly ajar.

I crept closer. No light spilled out. All was black. In fact, it smelled smoky, like burnt rubber. I inched the door open and peered inside. I discovered a tiny room, with barely enough clearance to turn around. Pipes and wire skirted up the walls and crisscrossed the ceiling. A dented metal mop bucket, with a splintered wooden handle protruding, sat dully in the corner. An electric panel stood open. It was charred, with scorch marks fanning out from the fuses. A fire extinguisher lay tipped over on its side against the baseboard.

I searched my brain. Who had said something about an electrical fire? This had to be where it had occurred. Unless there had been more than one.

I also realized what was on the other side of the room's back wall—Ava Turner's dressing room. Was that a coincidence or had someone intended to somehow burn her to death?

That was a scary thought. I didn't feel like being charred to a crisp while performing *Annie Get Your Gun,* decked out in some long-forgotten Hollywood designer's idea of a Native American costume. How would that look on my tombstone? Lame, that's how. I reached out and ran my fingers along the metal sides of the panel. It was cool to the touch.

"Careful, Amy."

I turned with a gasp. "Eli!" Eli Wallace, the actor playing the expert knife-throwing Tommy Keeler, blinked at me.

He nodded his chiseled chin at the open circuit breaker panel. "That thing could be dangerous." Eli was in full cowboy costume. He looked very handsome and very devilish. And not just a little scary with that knife attached to his belt. Rubber prop or no.

"I-I guess you're right." He stepped aside as I moved to leave the cramped space. The handle of his knife brushed my hip as I passed. Patsy Klein had been savagely murdered with a knife. And Eli Wallace, aka Tommy Keeler, was the show's expert. Was he an expert in real life?

"Trust me," Eli said.

I brushed down my slacks in the hallway. "What are you doing here?" I heard the sounds of dancing on stage, and the dull thud of my heart beating against my ribs. "Shouldn't you be out there?"

"I'm off stage for now. Mantooth sent me and your cousin Riley looking for you. He went one way," Eli said with a jerk of his thumb, "and I went the other." He smiled lasciviously. "Looks like I found you first."

"Tell me," I said, as we walked side by side in the narrow hall toward the others, "are you an expert with that thing in real life?" I stopped and tapped the tip of the knife.

"This?" Eli rubbed the handle. "You might say so," he bragged.

"What do you do for a living?"

"Taxidermy."

I shuddered. "Taxidermy?"

"You shoot 'em and I stuff 'em," he said with a flash of big white teeth.

"Interesting."

"Come by the studio sometime and I'll show you around." Eli waved me forward as we approached the short flight of stairs leading up to stage level.

"I'll keep that in mind," I said. "But between the show and running Birds and Bees—"

"Patsy loved it," Eli interjected before I could complete my planned graceful refusal.

I paused. Alarms went off in my head. "Patsy visited your studio?"

Eli puffed up his chest. "Yep. Patsy was real interested, too. She said she might have a job for me." He tipped his head meaningfully. "A real big one."

"You know," I said, "I'd love to take you up on your offer. How about tomorrow?"

"Great," said Eli, a giant smirk on his face. "It's a date. Maybe we can even rehearse our lines." He eased his arm over my shoulder. "My character is supposed to be in love with yours. We should work on that."

"Amy!" Riley said. He laid his hands on his hips as he looked down on us. "I've been looking all over for you."

"Coming!" I couldn't remember ever being so happy to see Cousin Riley.

Eli held me back. "I like you, Amy. You're not like the rest of them."

"The rest of them?" I asked, uneasily.

He waved his hand. "Yeah, like Patsy. Always fawning over me. I mean, I get it. I'm a good-looking guy. I've got my own business. But a man wants to do the chasing, not be chased. You know what I mean?"

"Are you saying Patsy was chasing you?" I couldn't resist smiling.

"Yeah, but I put a stop to it."

My eyes grew. "You did?"

"Amy! Now!" Riley hollered. "Director's waiting!"

14

"Did somebody really try to run you off the road, Riley?" I asked as I followed behind. Both Aunt Betty's kids were prone to hyperbole.

He looked over his shoulder at me. "I admit I thought so at first, Amy. But then Patsy told me she'd dropped her cell phone under the passenger seat of her car while she was driving. She was bending down trying to reach for it because it was ringing."

"Patsy? She's the person you thought tried to run you down?" If what Patsy had told my cousin was the truth, it was pure stupid. She could have been killed.

Then again, she had been killed.

He nodded. "She apologized and everything." Riley pointed to the makeup station. "So I guess it was an accident after all. But when I saw that car coming straight at me and Miss Turner, I was sure we were both going to be goners!"

"Miss Turner was with you?"

"I was giving her a ride to the theater." Riley gave me a push. "Now get moving. Rhonda's waiting for you in makeup. She's got your costume and every-thing."

Sure enough, Rhonda was tapping a hairbrush against her palm when I arrived. I'd have to digest Cousin Riley's words later. What he'd said about Patsy had been interesting, but his mentioning that Ava Turner was in the car with him was especially in-triguing.

And confusing enough that I got a headache just thinking about thinking about it all.

"Rhonda," I exclaimed. "I'm so glad to see you."

She made an *ooh that's icky* face that I usually saw only on three-year-olds. "What's that sticky stuff all over your cheek?"

I rubbed my face and studied my fingers. Baklava. Great. Why hadn't Derek mentioned I was covered with dessert? "It's—"

"Never mind," snapped Rhonda, a wad of gum bouncing atop her tongue. "Let's get to work on you." My cousin pointed to the makeup chair and I plopped myself down. "Darn chief of police hasn't stopped hounding me." She yanked the brush through my hair.

"Ouch!" I winced.

"Sorry." Rhonda slowed down.

I patted my scalp, testing for blood. "Hounding you how?"

"Coming around to the salon, asking questions." Rhonda worked in a local beauty parlor called Spring Beauty. "Spooking our clients."

I grunted an acknowledgment.

"Misty was fit to be tied." Misty Spring was the salon owner.

"I'm sorry to hear that," I replied. "I'm sure the police will find Patsy Klein's real killer soon enough."

"Huh!" Rhonda sniffed, attacking my head with a bottle of hair spray that smelled like wet latex paint and geraniums. "You know he's been poking his nose around here all day. He might still be here as far as I know." She looked to see if anyone was listening, then brought her lips to my ear. "Though I don't get tired of looking at Officer Sutton, I don't mind telling you."

"He is a handsome fellow."

Rhonda nodded. "And I didn't see a wedding ring on his finger."

"Maybe you ought to ask Sutton to interrogate you next time," I teased.

Rhonda giggled. She pressed her finger against my chin, turning my head from side to side, with a frown. "You'll do." She pointed to a rolling clothes rack. "There's your costume. Put it on and join the party."

I snatched the hanger holding my outfit and scooted toward the ladies' dressing room. There was a large common room with a row of battered lockers without locks, which were available for us to stash our street clothes and valuables, like purses and such. With all the petty thievery that had been going on, Lou might want to rethink that no-lock policy.

The separate communal dressing rooms for the men and women were located off this main room. I changed quickly, bundled up my clothes, and went in search of a free locker.

Each locker seemed to be identical, with a small

upper metal shelf and a metal hook on each side of the larger compartment. The first several I tried were jammed with clothes and shoes. I thrust my street clothes and purse in the first empty locker I could find, down near the end of the line. At least it was nearly empty.

A gray, soiled towel lay coiled atop the shelf of this one. I wrinkled my nose and reached for it with two fingers. "Disgusting." There was no way I wanted my clothes soaking up the rancid smell of perspiration and stage fright coming from that towel.

As I lifted the towel by its corner, I heard a muffled metallic clatter. There was something in the towel. As much as I dreaded touching the towel, curiosity got the best of me. I palpated the clumsily folded towel.

There was definitely something inside. As I carefully unwrapped the old towel, a knife tumbled out, bounced off the inside of the locker, and landed point down in my slacks, where it held.

I stared at it, my mouth gaping. This was definitely no prop knife, not the way it had penetrated my slacks. My fifty-dollar pair of slacks.

I had no doubt this knife was real. I leaned closer for a better look. The solid-looking weapon was about eight inches long from end to end. The question was: Was this the knife that killed Patsy Klein?

"You're telling me," whined Chief Kennedy, "that you found this thing right here in your locker?" He looked from the knife sticking into my jeans to me.

"We searched every inch of this place the other day. It sure as hell wasn't here then."

I hovered over his shoulder. "In the first place, it's not my locker. Look around," I admonished, with a wave of my hand. "These are communal lockers."

"Get some pictures before I bag all this stuff," Jerry Kennedy ordered Officer Reynolds. Unfortunately for Rhonda, the chief had brought one of his other subordinates.

I stepped aside as Officer Larry Reynolds got busy. "I assume by *all this stuff* you mean the knife?" I asked, hopefully.

"I mean everything in this locker." He moved his gaze from me to Officer Reynolds. "Bag it all. The knife, that rag thing, all those clothes."

"My clothes? Come on, Jerry. You don't mean it," I pleaded. "I mean, take the pants, sure," I offered. They did have a fresh hole in them, after all. "But leave me the rest."

Looking me in the eye, Chief Kennedy said to the officer, "And the shoes, Larry."

I fell onto one of several wobbly wooden stools scattered around the common room. I was feeling a little unsteady myself. "Fine." I ran my hands through my hair. I'd have to go home in costume. That would be perfect if this was Halloween night. Which it was not. "Can you at least tell me how the murder investigation is going?"

The corner of Jerry's mouth turned down. "I could, but it's got nothing to do with you." He placed a hand on his leather belt. "Right?"

I quickly said that I agreed. "I'm concerned about

Rhonda. She's nervous as a sparrow in a room full of ravenous red-shouldered hawks."

"She's got good reason to be," Jerry said, rather ominously. "Rhonda Foxcombe and Patsy Klein were mortal enemies."

"Please." I shot to my feet. "They had a disagreement or two. Besides . . ." I paused as Officer Reynolds turned and snapped a picture of me. What was that all about? "If you ask me, Patsy Klein was never the intended victim. Somebody wanted Ava Turner dead. Ms. Klein had the unfortunate luck of being in the wrong place at the wrong time."

"Maybe." Jerry chewed at his bottom lip. "But you want to tell me who wanted to kill Ms. Turner?" I started to form a reply, but the chief kept talking. "And why?"

"I haven't figured that out yet."

Chief Kennedy waved toward the door. "And you aren't going to. Number one, it's none of your concern. Number two, Ava Turner is a beloved movie star."

"Maybe it's a relative after her money."

"She's got no living relatives."

"Really?" I said, nonplussed. "Well, there must be somebody who inherits."

"It all goes to a charitable foundation," retorted the chief. "I already asked her."

I was surprised. Kennedy actually appeared to be doing his job.

"Anything else, Sherlock?"

"Yes," I shot, from the door. "No matter what you say or think you know, it's clear that somebody out

there would love to see Ava Turner dead. Look
around. Patsy's already dead, but something is still
going on, isn't it?"

Chief Kennedy made no reply, but the troubled
look he and his officer shared told me I'd rattled
him.

Good.

15

"I think it's a lovely idea," Mom said.

"Very cool," agreed Kim.

Mom enveloped me in her arms. "I'm so proud of you, Amy. What you've done with the store and now this."

I shot Kim a warning look. While I had told Kim the bad news about the eminent domain issue, I'd made her swear not to discuss it with my mother. I didn't want to worry her any more than necessary. I still intended to fight this battle with the town and would do everything I could to win. I didn't know how long I could keep word of yesterday's meeting from spreading and reaching Mom's ears, but I wasn't going to be the one to burst her bubble.

I tacked the sign to the wall: DONATE HERE FOR THE SENIOR SEEDS PROGRAM. I'd made the paper sign and a couple of dozen brochures on my computer and printed everything on pale green paper.

The sign now hung at the front of the store, beside the double row of bulk bins that contained an assortment of loose birdseed. Customers could purchase the seed by the pound or buy custom prepackaged mixes that I put together. So far, the bins had been a hit with my customers. The brochures rested atop the shelf above the bins. I'd added a small plastic bucket for donations.

I hoped the new program I was instituting would be popular. The idea had come to me in the night. I needed to think about something positive rather than the murder and my fear that Ava Turner was in danger still. I already planned to get the feeder that Mr. Withers and his wife had used at their old house and deliver it to him at Rolling Acres.

I had no doubt he'd be glad to see the old feeder again. I'd be taking a sack of unshelled sunflower seeds, too. Whether the crusty old fellow wanted to admit it or not, he was as hooked on bird-watching as his now deceased wife had been. Perhaps his pal ex-chief Karl Vogel would learn to watch the birds as much as he seemed to like to watch the ladies.

Then the thought had hit me. Why not try to get other people involved as well? I couldn't afford to do much on my own. But if a few other folks pitched in a few dollars' worth of birdseed or money toward more bird feeders, we might really make a difference in the lives of some of our senior citizens. And not just Rolling Acres. We could expand the program to other senior living facilities in the area. Bird-watching and bird feeding could give the retirees something new and interesting to see and do. I could even arrange talks, if enough of the residents were inter-

ested and management agreed, and teach them a little about the various birds in our region.

I drove the last tack into the sheet on the wall. "It's
worth a shot."

"Maybe you could pay a couple of kids to hang a
few flyers around town?" Mom suggested. "I'll bet
some of the other shopkeepers would be happy to
oblige."

"Good idea." Here at Birds & Bees, we were con-
stantly hanging announcements for a local event of
one sort or another in the windows. "But where are
we going to find the kids?"

"School's out," Kim said. "How hard can it be?"
She snapped her fingers. "Hey, I know. Get that boy
and girl that dropped the towhee off."

"The boy, maybe," I replied. "But the girl . . ." I explained that the girl was Derek and Amy Harlan's
daughter.

"That could be tricky," agreed Kim.

"Nonsense," Mom said, untying her store apron. I
knew she had planned a shopping trip with one of
her friends. They were driving down to the mall in
Charlotte. "I'll talk to Ben. I'm sure it will be fine."

I sidled up to my mother and draped my arm over
shoulders. "About Ben."

She looked at me quizzically. "What about him?"

I wriggled my brow suggestively. "Anything going
on that I should know about?"

"Amy!" Mom's cheeks reddened. She tossed her
apron under the front counter and headed for the
door.

Kim laughed. "Barbara's got a boyfriend," she sang.

Mom shot her the evil eye, then shook her head. "You girls are bad!" She shook her finger at us and departed.

"Looks like it's just you and me today," Kim said.

"No," I replied, as I headed for the door myself. I had several extra flyers and brochures in my hand. "It's just you."

"Where are you going?" whined Kim, following in my tracks.

"To see a few people so I can learn about Patsy Klein's murder and figure out a way to save Ava Turner from becoming our killer's next victim." I told Kim my theory of how Patsy had been in the wrong place at the wrong time.

"That's horrible." Kim stepped aside as two women entered and headed toward the gift section, which contained items such as mugs, socks, and chimes. "But do you really think anybody is going to talk to you about murder?"

"Number one, this is a small town," I replied. "People love to talk."

Kim grinned. "You're right there."

I waved the papers concerning the senior seed project in Kim's face. "And this seeds thing is going to be my entrée to get them to talk. One of them could be our killer."

"Our killer?" Kim said, her voice rising in question. "Since when did this become *our* killer, and why would you want to confront them? Are you crazy? That isn't safe."

"Until Patsy's killer is caught, none of us are safe. We could be collateral damage."

"Maybe," agreed Kim, with reluctance. "But maybe it was a stranger passing through. We don't know the murderer was local."

"I still believe the killer's intended victim was Ava Turner," I said stubbornly. "That means it wasn't a stranger passing through town. It's someone who knows her."

Kim frowned. "Shouldn't you leave this to Jerry?"

"Probably," I said. "But Ms. Turner could be dead by the time he finds *our* killer."

Ava Turner's house was unlike any other in Ruby Lake. Even if you didn't know she lived there, you would know somebody special did. The modern concrete and steel house sprawled atop a rounded hill set back from the road. A long, paved drive wound around and up. A pair of elaborately patterned steel gates hung open.

The grounds grew more controlled and elaborate as I neared the house, with untouched woods turning to fancy Italianate gardens with terraced Tennessee fieldstone walls, statuary, and a couple of matching four-tiered marble fountains at either end of a large reflecting pool.

The architect who had designed the estate had clearly meant for the house and yard to stand out rather than blend in with the surroundings. Floor-to-ceiling plate-glass windows ran along the front, letting in all the sunshine in the world. I drove up the travertine circular drive, fully aware of how shabby my old van must look to anyone watching, and shut off the engine.

I grabbed my purse and the papers I'd brought with me, scooped up my nerve, and approached the door. There wasn't a doorbell in sight, so I rapped on one of the two dark walnut doors that served as a focal point as much as they served as a point of entry. Those doors probably cost more money than I earned last year.

An elderly woman with white hair and an elven complexion answered. Her eyes were the palest blue I had ever seen. "Yes? May I help you?" A plain navy-blue dress fell straight from her shoulders to just below her knees.

"Hi. I'm Amy Simms," I began. "I know I should have telephoned first, but I was hoping to have a word with Miss Turner?" Not calling had been a tactical decision. It would have been far easier for her to say no to me over the phone than in person.

"Miss Turner is on a call." The woman looked down her nose at me, though she expressed no emotion. She held out a slender hand with prominent veins. "Do you have a card?"

My lip turned down. "No, I'm sorry, I don't. I have these though." I held out a copy of my flyer and a brochure. She eyed them wordlessly from a distance.

"I could jot my name down on the back of one." I cleared my throat. Why did this woman make me so uncomfortable? "If you like?"

She slowly drew the green flyer from my fingers. "That won't be necessary." The door closed quietly. I took that for a good sign. She hadn't slammed it shut in my face.

I shifted from foot to foot and admired the garden in the center of the drive as I waited. A pair of goldfinches, the male bright yellow and his companion female a duller shade of yellow, hopped among a patch of thistle. Some minutes later, the woman returned.

"Miss Turner will entertain you in the conservatory."

Entertain me? Would the former movie star be honoring me with a song and dance routine or perhaps a solo reenactment of one of her most famous film roles?

She waved me inside and I scurried in behind. The woman's simple, unadorned low black heels made no sound as she led me to the conservatory.

The single-story house was vast and endless seeming. It was as quiet and imposing as a fortress and as pristine as a museum. The walls were white, the floors a medium-toned, narrow-planked hardwood. Subdued artwork hung on the walls, and relatively simple sculptures of stone and metal sat atop white plinths.

I caught a glimpse of myself in a passing silver-framed mirror and groaned. Why hadn't I thought to change out of my Birds & Bees red V-neck T-shirt and slacks?

"Your guest, Miss Turner."

"Thank you, Gail." I felt the woman's eyes crawl over me, assessing me carefully.

My guide bowed and retreated.

The great lady sat in a tall wingback chair in the

far left corner of the conservatory. Not a hair on her head was out of place.

A glass of tea and a delicate teapot rested on a wood table beside her. Like everywhere else, the floor was narrow-planked hardwood. I hadn't noticed a single rug. The walls on three sides were floor-to-ceiling plate glass, affording an incredible view of the western Carolina mountains rising in the distance.

A girl could get used to living like this. If a girl won the lottery . . . or was a famous movie star. Music spilled out from hidden speakers at a low volume. I recognized the song, "The World Belongs to the Young." I pointed to where the sound seemed to be emanating from. "It's from *Coco*, isn't it?"

"Yes. The story of Coco Chanel." She paused and smiled. "As imagined by Andre Previn and Alan Jay Lerner, that is to say.

"Katharine Hepburn won a Tony for that," the actress added as the song wound down. "I starred in a West End production some years later." Miss Turner motioned for me to sit in her chair's companion. She set down her tea and laid her hands delicately in her lap. "Miss Simpson, is it?" She wore a snow-white dressing gown over a fuchsia pant and shirt. Her feet were coddled in thick wool socks.

"Simms," I replied. "Amy Simms." I noticed my flyer on the tray beside the teapot. "Thank you for seeing me." When she made no reply, I grasped for something to say. "We're doing *Annie Get Your Gun* together." I laughed nervously. "Well, not *together*, of course." I ran a hand through my hair and glanced at the green mountains. "You're the star. I've only got the teeniest part." I held my thumb and index finger out in a pinch formation. In fact, my character had not even made it into the movie version of the musical.

Those intelligent brilliant green eyes followed me like a pair of stage lights. Miss Turner batted a pair of thick, perfectly shaped eyelashes. "You were at the coffee shop the other night."

I had the impression that she was not nearly as dull or uninformed as she appeared.

"The Coffee and Tea House on the Square." I nodded. "That's right." That she remembered, but she couldn't seem to remember that I was performing in a Broadway musical with her? Nonetheless, I took this as the opening I'd been looking for—an opening that might not soon come again. "It was the night Patsy Klein was murdered."

"Did you know I once played Eliza in *My Fair Lady*?"

"Um, no." My brow formed a V. "I didn't." Nor did I know what that little non sequitur was supposed to mean.

Miss Turner nodded slowly. " 'I Could Have Danced All Night.' " She looked at me as if I should know what she meant. I didn't.

"That was my favorite song in the show." She smiled for the first time. "I was in love with him, you know."

"Who?" I was surprised to notice that my voice had come out a whisper.

"Rex," she answered. "Rex Richardson."

That was a name I hadn't heard since I was a child.

He'd been a famous star of stage and screen himself. "Miss Turner," I said, shifting in my chair to face her more directly, "if you don't mind my asking, have you given any more thought to what I asked you the other night?"

"What was that, my dear?"

"If you could think of anyone who might—" I struggled. "How can I put this?"

"Want me dead?" she said with a wan smile.

I nodded.

"As I told you the other night, as I explained to the police as well, there is no one."

"I can't help thinking you are mistaken, Miss Turner," I said, shaking my head. I explained my theory of Patsy Klein being in the wrong place at the wrong time.

The actress didn't argue with me. "So?"

"Don't you see?" I argued. "That means you were the intended victim."

"Oh, dear." Ava Turner stood and walked slowly to the window. She stared out quietly, hands folded behind her back. I caught a faint scent of floral bouquet. "I assure you, I am perfectly safe here."

"Were you and Miss Klein friends?"

"Not in the least." The words spilled out like venom.

"And yet, she was assisting you at the theater—"

"And doing a very poor job of it," Ava Turner said with unmasked derision.

"Then why would you—" My phone rang. "Sorry." I pulled it from my pocket. I recognized the number.

Derek Harlan. Whatever he wanted would have to wait.

The actress pulled open the drawer of a side table and bid me to look inside. "Regarding my safety, I assure you, I am perfectly safe here." Inside was a black gun.

"I hope so," I said in earnest, though the nearness of the gun creeped me out a little. Her house did seem to be secure enough. But it was isolated. Far from help. Did she even know how to shoot that thing? No, wait. From what I'd heard, she'd shot a man once before. A chill swept over me, and I fought it down.

"Don't forget," I said, distancing myself from the weapon, though she had shut the drawer, removing it from sight. "Someone attacked you the other day in the theater. With a dozen or more people around."

"What?" Her head turned my way.

I patted the side of my skull. "When you got struck in the head by that board with the nail in it."

"Yes." She nodded. "Of course."

"Are you certain you didn't see or hear anyone before it happened?"

The actress lowered her eyes. "No. Chief Kennedy asked me that very question. I'm afraid I didn't see or hear anything. In fact," she added, "I'm beginning to wonder if it was an accident, after all. Perhaps I bumped into the shelf. I have been rather clumsy lately." Ava smiled apologetically. "So it could have been an accident, like that nice young man suggested."

"Aaron," I filled in. "He's wrong." I gripped her

hand for a moment. "Maybe you could ask Chief Kennedy for police protection?" It was a big house. Plenty of room for a killer to get in without being seen.

"There is a state-of-the-art alarm system all throughout the house," she replied as if reading my mind. The actress turned toward me. "And I am not alone. I have Gail."

Gail? The sweet if stolid woman who had shown me in? A poodle would provide more protection.

And speak of the devil, the woman appeared out of nowhere. "Miss Turner, that policeman is here to see you."

"Chief Kennedy?" asked the actress.

Gail nodded. "That's the one." She looked at me. "Should I show him in?"

"Yes, of course, Gail."

Like a great horned owl caught in the beam of a flashlight, I stood by, nervously awaiting Jerry Kennedy's entrance. He was not going to like finding me in Ava Turner's house, butting into his police investigation.

The surprised, ugly look on his face told me I was right.

"Simms?" Chief Kennedy stomped toward me, his boots banging loud and clear on the hardwood, upsetting the tranquility of the space. "What on earth are you doing here?"

I struggled for words. "I—that is, Miss Turner and I were discussing *Annie*." I threw Ava a *rescue me* look.

"That is correct," the actress replied with authority. "Amy and I were discussing acting techniques." She squeezed my arm. "Don't worry, dear. I have confidence in your performance." Ava held me in her gaze. "Don't worry," she insisted. "Everything will be just fine."

I nodded.

"Yeah, well, if you ladies don't mind," Chief Kennedy grumbled, his angry eyes fixed on me, "I would like a word with you, Miss Turner. If it's no inconvenience?"

"Certainly not." Miss Turner waved to the sofa, and the chief parked himself in the center.

"I'll be off then." I slid past Gail. "Thank you for seeing me, Miss Turner." I half bowed. Why, I didn't know. It seemed the thing to do.

"You must call me Ava."

"Yes, ma'am. I mean, Ava."

The actress settled into her chair. "Can we get you some refreshments, Chief Kennedy?" I heard her ask Jerry as I backed out of the room.

"I could go for some sweet tea."

"Oh, Amy!"

I stopped and turned. "Yes, Miss Turner?" She tilted her head. "I mean, Ava."

"Aren't you forgetting something?"

I thought for a moment. "I don't think so."

"Your money?"

"Money?" I pulled at my chin.

She lifted my flyer from the table and held it toward me.

"Of course. How silly of me."

"I think it's a wonderful idea." The actress told the confused-looking chief about my plans to provide bird feeders and seed to senior centers. He didn't appear impressed.

"Gail has prepared a check for you."

"Thank you," I replied. "Thank you very much."

Gail walked me to the door. From a silver salver on a small oval table beside the door, she silently lifted a folded pink check and handed it to me.

"Thank you."

She closed the door behind me without a sound. The woman could give church mice lessons.

On the way to the van, I unfolded the check. It was made out in my name for five hundred dollars.

16

Eli Wallace dwelled on a pleasant, nondescript middle-class street about a mile from the town center. I didn't know what I had been expecting, but it wasn't the modest yellow bungalow with the detached garage out back. I'd been imagining something more eldritch, less Middle America.

A small wood sign planted in the grassy swale was the only indication that the house did double duty as a business. The sign read: E. WALLACE, PRESERVATION SPECIALIST. Very quaint.

I pulled into the gravel drive and gathered my courage and patience. I figured I was going to need both to deal with Eli Wallace and his ego.

"You came," Eli said, opening the front door to me. A black T-shirt hung loose over his blue jeans, but its sleeves clung tightly to his muscular upper arms. He looked me over like I might be his next project. His eyes were so dark that on first glance I'd thought they were black. A German shepherd nuzzled his leg. "Easy, Tramp." He patted the dog's snout. "Come on in."

"Wow," I said, my eyes darting around the small living room. Dead animals were everywhere. Hung on the walls, sitting on tables, standing on the mantel. A large stuffed beaver posed with its upper legs braced against a short, thick river maple branch. Together they held up a glass top, forming an odd side table in the corner between the brown sofa and chair.

I crossed to the fireplace, where the cold ashes of a fire lay beneath the grate. Atop the solid mahogany mantel, a row of stuffed birds stood like silent soldiers. There was a cardinal, a crow, a blue jay, and a screech owl. I picked up the owl by its wooden base.

"That owl's one of my favorite birds," Eli said, coming closer.

"It's a screech owl," I explained.

"An eastern red screech owl."

I turned in surprise. "You know your birds."

"I know my animals." He threw out his hands. "Animals are my business, after all."

I nodded thoughtfully. "A couple of children dropped an injured towhee off at my store the other day."

"Bring it by. I'll preserve it for you." He took the owl from my hand. "My treat."

"The bird's still alive. I took it to a wildlife rehabber."

"Well, if the bird doesn't make it, bring it to me. I can memorialize it in any pose you like." He rubbed his fingers over the screech owl's wing feathers. "You could give it to the kids as a gift."

I forced myself to nod rather than wince.

Eli placed the stuffed bird back on the mantel. "Come on, let me show you around."

I listened dutifully as the taxidermist took me through to the back of his house, which he'd turned into his preservation studio, as he liked to call it.

I learned more about taxidermy than I'd thought possible and far more than I wish I did know.

"So, that's the lot." Eli thrust his hands in his jeans, looking smug and handsome and knowing it. He jerked his thumb over his shoulder. "I do have a couple of larger pieces, brown bears, out in the garage, if you're interested."

"It's all very fascinating," I said, following the taxidermist to his kitchen in the back. "Tell me, what was it that Patsy Klein wanted *memorialized?*"

He poured water in Tramp's steel dish near the back door and offered me a beer from the fridge. I declined. "She never did say."

"Just that it was something big," I reminded him.

"So she said." He chugged, and I watched his Adam's apple bounce up and down. "She might have just been leading me on."

"Leading you on?" Patsy Klein had sounded like a strange bird, but who leads on a taxidermist?

"You know." He glanced toward his loins. "Trying to get in my pants."

"Did she succeed?"

His smile filled his face. "A gentleman never tells. Besides, she isn't—wasn't really my type." The mouth of the bottle tipped my way. "You are."

"What's your opinion of Ava Turner?"

"She's a little old for me."

"But what do you think of her?"

"She's okay, I guess. A little full of herself." He sipped. "The great actress. Doing the folks of Ruby Lake a big favor by agreeing to appear in our little production." He ran the back of his arm over his full lips. "I'd like to stuff her sometime," he grunted with unexpected viciousness.

"You are not a fan, I take it?"

His face clouded. "The old hag tried to get me fired."

Now we were getting somewhere. "Why?"

"She said I couldn't act." He knotted his arms over his chest. "Can you believe it? I've been acting in community theater for more than ten years. I've got good reviews from the *Weekender*," he boasted. "I can show them to you. You want to see? They're in my desk."

"I believe you," I said, holding up my hands. "I've watched you in rehearsal. You're good." Placating the taxidermist seemed critical. Eli seemed ready to boil over. Had he boiled over the night Patsy died? Had she paid the price intended for Miss Turner?

"Someone hated Ava enough to want to stab her to death," I said.

"What are you talking about? It was Patsy that got killed."

I explained how it was clear that Patsy had not been the intended victim. "She was in Miss Turner's dressing room. Sitting in Miss Turner's chair."

"So somebody stabbed the wrong woman," Eli voiced my conclusion. He nodded, then stopped. "Wait just a minute. Are you trying to imply that I killed her?" He jabbed his chest with the bottle. "Is that what you're saying?"

"No." I took a step back. A bulky, oak block on the counter was loaded with black-handled knives.

Eli caught me looking at them. "Because it was a knife? That's it, isn't it? You think because Patsy was killed with a knife that I did it?"

"No, no, no." My head swung side to side. "You've got me all wrong. I know you wouldn't hurt a fly." He might stuff one and mount it on a plastic flyswatter though. "Besides"—I smiled as if to say, *We're all friends here*—"you weren't anywhere near Miss Turner's dressing room, right?"

Eli hesitated before replying, as if fearing a trick. "Yeah, so?"

"So you couldn't have killed her." Careful to control my voice, I asked, "Do you remember where you were at the time of the murder?"

"Enough bull." Eli settled his half-empty bottle of beer on the kitchen counter and swaggered toward me. "What do you say we get to rehearsing those love scenes of ours?" His voice came out a throaty, wolfish growl.

I tried to take another step backward, but there was nowhere to go. My spine banged against the kitchen wall and I bit my tongue, tasted blood. "Sorry, but I really have to get back to work. They're expecting me."

"Too bad," Eli replied. "I have a feeling we could really light things up." His arm rested on the wall above my shoulder.

I dipped and rolled free. I had no intention of lighting things up with Mr. Hands and every intention of shutting things down with him.

"Before I go," I began, pulling the papers from my purse, "I was wondering if you might be inter-

ested in helping out a good cause?" I handed him a
flyer and brochure.

Eli's jaw worked from side to side as he read.
"Sounds good," he said finally. "How much do you
need?"

I shrugged. "Whatever you feel comfortable giving. Birdseed is very inexpensive. Even twenty dollars
would make a big difference."

Eli reached into his back pocket and brought out
a black leather wallet. "What if I give you a hundred
bucks as a starter? How many bird feeders do you
think that would buy?"

"A hundred dollars?" I said with surprise. I thought
quickly. "Four or five. No, wait," I amended. "At least
half a dozen. I can get them wholesale."

The taxidermist handed me a hundred-dollar bill.
"There you go. Is there any way I can get a plaque
put on them?"

"A plaque?"

"Yeah," Eli explained. "A small metal one with my
company's name on it." He wrote in the air with his
index finger. "Donated by E. Wallace, Preservation
Specialist." He winked at me. "What do you think?"

"I don't see why not."

"Great." He rubbed his big, calloused hands together. "I'll get a few made up at the engravers and
drop them by your place."

"I hate to see you go to any trouble. I'll handle it
for you." I didn't need Eli showing up at my doorstep.
He walked me to the side door and followed me out
to my van. I hurried inside, seeking the safety of my
vehicle. I twisted the key in the ignition. I couldn't

get away fast enough. Eli rapped a knuckle against the glass and motioned for me to open the window.

I lowered it halfway. "Yes?"

The taxidermist looked up and down the quiet street. "If somebody wants the great lady dead, there's not a thing you can do about it. In fact," he said, kicking the van's front tire, "half the cast and probably all the crew would love to see her go. I don't care what Lou or August Mantooth say about how she's good for the show and the town." He spat on the grass. "In my book, Ava Turner isn't worth spit."

"Anybody else?"

"Anybody else what?" His eyes pulled together like they were being held in a vise.

"Anybody else feel that strongly about Miss Turner?" I could feel my heart pounding against my chest.

"Like I told you, nearly everybody." A smile played over his face. "Maybe Longfellow, most of all."

"Nathan Longfellow?" He was the big fellow playing Chief Sitting Bull. "Why would he have any particular animosity toward Ava Turner?"

"You don't know?"

I shrugged to make it clear I didn't.

"Nathan used to be a theater critic for one of those big Chicago newspapers. He wrote a rather unflattering review of one of Her Majesty's films or something, and she got him fired."

"Really?"

Eli nodded. "Folks say he's been bumming around from town to town ever since."

"What does he do for a living?"

"Nathan's a butcher down at the Lakeside Market."

That was quite a fall from having once been a theater critic for a major newspaper. It wouldn't be the first time a man had killed in revenge.

"Did you know that Patsy and Nathan were once an item?"

"Everybody was an item to Patsy."

"What's that supposed to mean?"

The taxidermist grinned. "It means Patsy cared about people the way I care about animals."

That was a disturbing thought. I muttered goodbye and drove off with my head filled with more new questions than it had answers.

If Eli was telling the truth.

He might be throwing Nathan under the bus to divert suspicion from himself. I was dubious about a lot of what the taxidermist had had to say about himself, Patsy Klein, and everybody else involved in the show.

I wondered if Mom was in the mood for steak, because a trip to the supermarket was in order.

17

I was having a hard time concentrating on the road. There were an awful lot of persons in Ruby Lake working with knives. I remembered seeing a big one in a sheath attached to T-Bone Crawford's waist, too.

Under normal circumstances, that wouldn't mean much around these parts. But these weren't normal circumstances. I wondered if the police had identified the knife in the dressing room as the weapon that had been used to kill Patsy Klein yet. If so, had they found any prints that would identify the killer? And why had the knife shown up now?

There was one more nagging question remaining: Why had Patsy Klein fired the prop gun? Had she forgotten that it was a toy in her fear and confusion when she confronted her attacker?

Maybe she'd fired the weapon to draw help. After all, it was the gunshot that had brought us all running.

The next thing I knew, I was at TOTS. Rehearsal went by in a blur. I didn't know if it was my imagination or not, but it seemed that a lot of the cast and crew were giving me the cold shoulder. Even August seemed a bit annoyed with me. Of course, that might have been due to hearing me sing for the very first time.

Only Ben Harlan, Eli Wallace, and Lou Ferris appeared cordial. I'd hoped for a moment alone with Ben. I was curious to learn if he'd picked up any news on the killing through the grapevine. I was even more curious to see if I could pry anything out of him about him and my mother. Unfortunately, the moment had never been right.

I spent my night stumbling over my lines, fending off ugly looks, and fearing a knife in the back from Derek's ex, Amy, at any moment.

Back home, I fired up my laptop on the sofa and searched on Nathan Longfellow's name. Sure enough, the man had been a popular theater critic in Chicago. He had been fired due to some controversy involving Ava Turner. It seemed things had gotten ugly and very public. Nathan had made some unflattering and unprofessional remarks that had cost him his job.

And now he was selling packaged meat by the pound.

My cell phone rang and I grabbed it quickly, knowing Mom was asleep in the next room. "Hello?"

"Hi, this is Tiffany LaChance."

"Hi, Tiffany. Everything okay?"

"I hope it's not too late. I mean, me calling you like this. But I saw your light on."

"Yeah, not too late at all. What's up? Wait." I rose. "You're here?" I peeked out the curtains.

"At the front door."

"I'll come down and let you in."

I squeezed my tired feet into a pair of slip-ons and headed downstairs, flicking on store lights as I went. The creaky, old house still spooked me, and I preferred to see where I was going, where the ghosts were or were not hiding, and all lurking and poised to attack killers.

I thumbed the lock. "Hi, Tiff. Come on inside." I glanced up and down the street. Things were quiet now, after nine. Though a handful of cars sat in the diner parking lot across the street.

"Are you sure you don't mind? I just got off shift." She wiped her feet on the mat and ran her hands down her nearly spotless uniform. I didn't know how she managed that trick, hustling coffee, gravy-soaked dinners, and everything else on the menu around the busy diner for hours on end.

On the second-floor landing, Esther's door opened with a nuthatch-like squeak. "A little late for people to be visiting, isn't it?" She was swaddled in her old heron-blue robe and gave us a curious look.

"Sorry," Tiffany said rather demurely.

I was sure I smelled cigarettes and cat but was in no mood for an argument. "Good night, Esther."

Tiffany wiggled her fingers good-bye to Esther.

"Please," I said, "don't encourage her." Sometimes I wondered if the *old pest* they were singing about in "Master of the House" from *Les Mis* was my tenant.

We settled into the living room. I offered Tiffany something to drink, but she declined.

Tiffany kicked off her shoes and folded her legs up under herself on the sofa. "Jimmy was with Robert today and—" She must have noticed me roll my eyes because she changed gears. "Hey, believe me. I know what he's like. You're lucky you've never been married."

"I don't know how lucky I am," I replied. "And I know my mother would take issue with that statement. I did come close once. And I'm glad close is as real as it got." Even today the thought that I might have married Craig Bigelow scared me. I'd think twice, three times, before I ever let myself get that close to a man again.

Tiffany edged forward. "What happened?"

"You really want to hear this?"

The waitress smiled. "I have time. I've got the babysitter booked until eleven, but Moire let me off early."

"Then we're going to need to grease the wheels." I rose. When I returned from the kitchen, I was carrying two glasses and an open bottle of Chablis. "Craig Bigelow was his name," I began. Even now, it hurt to say his name. "He was an MBA student and I was an English major."

"How did the two of you meet?"

My mind went back to those early college days, filled with good memories and bad. "I started working part-time at a local bird supply store to help cover college expenses." We drank.

"And Craig was into bird feeding?"

I chuckled and tipped the bottle. "No. Craig was into the waitress working at the pizza shop two doors down in the strip mall the shop was located in."

I dug in the freezer and pulled out two pints of chocolate mint ice cream. I grabbed two spoons from the drawer and pushed one down in each container. "When wine won't quite cut it, only ice cream will do."

Tiffany looked unconvinced. She twisted the spoon around the carton and took a bite. "It's good." I noticed she rested the carton atop a bird-watching magazine on the coffee table. Sure, you couldn't keep a figure like Tiff's if you downed gallons of ice cream and liters of wine.

I spooned a big glob and swallowed it whole. She might be watching her weight, but I was more concerned with my mental health. While they were perhaps not technically AMA approved, I knew from experience that ice cream and wine cured just about anything.

"Don't keep me hanging, Amy. How did you meet Craig?"

"Sorry. Craig was into the waitress. I was into the pizza. I'd see him there now and again. Eventually, we started talking. The next thing I knew, we were dating."

Tiffany nodded thoughtfully. "And then he broke your heart?"

"Not at first," I admitted, grudgingly. "Little by little, over the course of six years, on-and-off-again engagements." A yawn exploded out of nowhere. "And don't get me started on the cheating."

I jammed my spoon into the melting pool of ice cream and came up with a fist-sized blob. It was too big for my mouth so I worked around the edges, mindful of spilling on my clothes and/or the chair.

"Did you love him?" Tiffany asked between sips.

"Not as much as he loved himself. And you know what the worst part is?"

Tiffany's eyes grew wide. "What?"

"The new owner of the place next door—"

"Paul," she said.

My brow went up. "You know him?"

"He comes in the diner now and again." She ran a finger along the edge of her glass. "He's cute, don't you think?"

"I suppose." I did not want to go there. Besides, if she was interested in the man, who was I to splash cold water on the idea? "Anyway, it seems he's partners with my ex."

"You're kidding!"

I shook my head. "Nope. That's how he learned about Ruby Lake. I guess he liked what he heard so much that he decided to open a business here."

"Paul did mention a partner." Her brow formed a V. "I thought he said something about him being a silent partner though."

Silent? I drained my glass. "Maybe he's only coming to help Anderson get the business up and running. With a little luck, he'll hightail it back to Raleigh when he's finished." I reached for the bottle. It was empty. A *little* luck seemed to be all the luck I was having lately.

The corners of Tiffany's full lips dipped down. "He sounds a lot like Robert."

We nodded, kindred souls, birds of a feather.

"Speaking of Robert," Tiffany said, sliding down the sofa nearer to me. "Like I said, Robert had Jimmy most of the day."

I nodded and forced myself to set down my own carton of ice cream. If Tiffany could show some restraint, so could I. Jimmy was Tiffany and Robert's eleven-year-old son. Their only child.

"Jimmy said his dad was in a particularly good mood. He was bragging about some new restaurant he's planning to open, if everything goes according to plan."

"Bella Bologna!" I exclaimed, pulling the name out of my memory banks. Bella Bologna was one of those popular upscale Italian restaurant chains that cost a million bucks or more to franchise.

"You knew?"

"I saw the brochure one time when I was in his office." I'd needed a car rental desperately. Under any other circumstances short of desperation, I wouldn't go near the man or his business. "Say," I said with a little smile, "do you suppose he'll move to Raleigh if the deal goes through?"

Tiffany wrinkled her nose. "Raleigh? Why would Robert move to Raleigh?" She rose and returned both ice cream cartons to the freezer. I guess she was saving me from myself.

"To run the restaurant," I said. I mean, wasn't it obvious?

Tiffany stood over me. "Robert's not planning on opening a franchise in Raleigh."

"He's not?" Had I had too much to drink? It was only two glasses of wine. Why wasn't Tiffany making any sense?

"No, Amy. He and his partners are planning to open a Bella Bologna right here in Ruby Lake."

"Oh," I said. "Interesting." Not what I expected, but still, it was none of my business.

"You don't understand." Tiffany grabbed my hand. "Right *here* in Ruby Lake."

"Yeah, I get it. Right here in Ruby Lake." Maybe Tiffany had had too much to drink. At the very least, she didn't seem to be able to hold her drink. I might have to call a cab for her ride home, short though it was. Tiffany and Jimmy lived in a condo complex down by the lake.

Tiffany sat so close our knees touched. *"Right here."* She nodded to the floor. "At this corner."

"At this corner?" My brow furrowed. "But the only place that makes any sense at all . . . I mean, there's no room here for a place that size." The diner was across the street on Lake Shore Drive. There was no way Moire Leora would sell. A relatively new complex of shops and offices sat on this side of Lake Shore Drive and Serviceberry Road. That couldn't possibly be for sale. Serviceberry dead-ended at Lake Shore Drive and the Ruby Diner. To the west of the diner, separated by a paved walk leading to the lake, there was a strip of tourist-oriented stores and a small U.S. Post Office branch. That wouldn't be going anyplace. "You need parking and—"

"And he wants to tear down Birds and Bees and—"

"Turn it into a parking lot," I finished for her, my anger rising.

"Something like that. From what Jimmy told me, they plan on erecting the restaurant on the next street and using the land by Main Street for parking." She shook her head. "Or maybe it was the other way around."

"That land is privately held," I argued. "There are houses on all those lots." There were several older, small detached bungalows one street back, butting up against the back of my property.

"Guess who owns them?"

I cocked my head. "Who?" I voiced, glumly. "Your ex?"

"Gertrude Hammer."

"Gertie!" I leapt from the chair.

"Sorry," said Tiffany. "I thought you'd want to know."

I fanned myself. The room was spinning like a carousel. I felt woozy.

So that was what was behind this whole eminent domain business and Gertie Hammer's attempts to buy back my house. She, Robert, the mayor, and who knew who else, were planning to redevelop this whole corner.

And to put me out of business in the process.

18

"What are you doing here, Simms?"

"I thought I'd see if I could tape a flyer in your window."

Chief Kennedy had his hands in the file cabinet near the door to the police station. "This is a police station not a mini-mart." He slammed the drawer shut.

Officer Sutton looked up from the paperwork spread out on his desk.

Jerry waved his fingers at me. "Take your paper and go. You ought to know better."

I did know better. But sticking a flyer up in his window wasn't the real reason I'd come. "Okay, okay. Don't get your shorts in a bunch." I pressed my palm against the door. "Say, while I'm here . . ." I turned and followed Jerry to his desk near the back.

The police station still gave me the shivers. I'd spent more time in this place than I liked recently, and not of my own volition. "What's the word on the knife?" Chief Kennedy's mouth hung open. "Lift any prints? Test for blood yet?"

Jerry fell into his chair and crossed his legs and arms. "Do you have any idea how long these things take?"

"Long?" I said, with a half smile. A glare was his only response. "Whose knife was it anyway? It doesn't take long to lift a fingerprint."

"There were no prints on the knife, Simms." He pointed to the door. "Now go."

"Yeah, just like the gun," Officer Sutton put in.

Jerry sent his underling a look that clammed him up and got him moving paperwork again.

"No prints, huh? I'm not surprised," I replied. "Somebody planted that knife."

"In an empty locker," said Chief Kennedy. "Have you got an explanation for that?"

I admitted I didn't. "Don't you think you should be providing Miss Turner with security?"

"She told me she didn't want any. Not that I have the manpower to provide it if she did."

"I have a theory that our killer isn't going to stop until Miss Turner is dead." I loomed over Jerry like a bad shadow. "I also have a few theories on who might want to see Ava Turner cross to the other side." I arched my brow. "If you get my drift."

"I've got my own theories, Simms."

"Like who?" I scoffed. "My cousin Rhonda? The killer hairdresser? Why would she want Ava Turner dead? Both she and Riley adore her."

"No, smarty-pants. Though she is on my list. And you can tell her I said so." He leaned forward in his chair and his gut spilled over his belt. "I do believe I've narrowed down the suspects to a precious few."

Now he had me interested. "Such as?"

"Such as you can read about it in the *Weekender* once I get them in custody." Quick as a cat, Jerry sprang from his desk and marched me out of the police station by the elbow.

I'd finally reconnected with Derek yesterday, and he'd agreed to take the two children to see Sammy the towhee. That was fine by me. There was no sense causing a deeper rift between me and his ex, Amy. Kim was working at the flip house, Mr. Withers's former home, so I made that my next stop. I had another hour before I had to get back to the store. I'd left Mom and her sister in charge. I knew Aunt Betty was driving Mom for her checkup so I couldn't afford to be late getting back.

Randy and Kim were hard at work on the master bath. Rather, I should say Randy was hard at work demoing the old yellow ceramic tile that matched the yellow toilet, tub, and sink. Kim was on her cell phone.

"Hi, Amy." She held up a finger. "What's that?" she said into the phone. "Uh-huh. That's right."

I turned to Randy in exasperation. "How's it going?"

He lowered the claw hammer he held in his right hand and pushed damp hair from his white-powder-coated face. "Rough, but we'll get there. What brings you, Amy?" He extended the hand with the hammer. "Come to help?"

"Sorry." I coughed. There was a lot of grout dust swimming around in the tiny space. "I came to get Mr. Withers's old bird feeder."

Randy grinned. "Help yourself. It's out back. Kim told me what you're doing. I think it's great. I told your friend here"—he aimed the tool at my partner—"to put me down for fifty."

"Pounds or bucks?"

Randy's gap-tooth grin widened. "Whichever helps the most."

I told him thanks again and hurried out of the dust cloud and into warm afternoon sunshine. There were two bird feeders in the yard. I recognized the one hanging in the maple off the back porch right away. That was the feeder that had been giving Floyd Withers so much trouble the first day he'd walked into my store. It was a tube feeder. And it was empty. Poor birds. Not that there wasn't plenty of natural nourishment around.

The second feeder, a hopper with a gabled green roof, was attached to a black pole and sat close to the big shed near the edge of the property. There was a small cast-cement birdbath beside it. What water there was in the bowl was dirty, and a ring of scum surrounded the edges of the basin. I spotted a garden hose and gave it a good rinse before refilling it.

I got back to Birds & Bees in the nick of time. Mom was wrapping up a sale. She'd sold two varieties of seed, a hanging seed feeder, and a hummingbird feeder. *Yea, Mom!*

Mom reached behind her and untied her apron. I

took it and hung it on the hook behind the counter. Aunt Betty appeared from the back. "It's about time, young lady."

My aunt was dressed to kill in a red dress and black heels. You'd never know she was nearly twice my age. And with her hair now dyed a brilliant blond, you'd never take her for my mother's sister, let alone her twin. "We were getting nervous. You know how the doctors' offices are these days. They hate it when you're late."

"I know. Sorry, Aunt Betty."

"Leave the poor girl alone," Mom said with a smile. "Our Amy has a lot to handle." She picked up her purse and tucked it under her arm.

"Well, hopefully the extra money will help with that." Aunt Betty ran a tube of bright red lipstick around lips.

"Believe me," said my mother, "it will."

"Extra money?" That sounded good. "What extra money?" Though, as far as I was concerned, there was no such thing as *extra* money.

Something soft but massive bounced against my back. My hip ricocheted off the sales counter and I turned.

"Oops!" Paul Anderson smiled at me from around the side of a large bare mattress that he was holding up at one end. "Sorry about that." He turned to his partner, who was nothing more than a pair of arms and legs from where I stood. "Okay, let's go. One or two more trips and we're done!"

"Right!" came the muffled reply.

Anderson turned and angled the bulky mattress toward the stairs. He had the back end and his helper the front. I stood, mouth agape, as they traipsed up to my second floor.

"What the devil is going on?" My eyes flew from Mom to Aunt Betty and back again to my mother, who stood there with a funny look on her face and squirmed. Aunt Betty chose that moment to say she'd bring the car around, allowing me to focus on my mom. "Mother?"

Mom wrung her hands and glanced up the stairs, from which we heard the sounds of banging and slamming and not a little bit of cursing. "What is going on? Why is Paul Anderson lugging a mattress up my stairs?"

Mom sucked in her lower lip. Outside, Aunt Betty tooted her horn. "That's me," said Mom. "Gotta go!" Mom went for the door and I dogged her heels.

She stopped at the entrance. "I'm sure it will be fine. You'll hardly notice he's here. Besides," Mom said, planting a kiss on my cheek and starting down to the street, "Kim assured me you would be fine with it."

What had Kim done?

I slowly turned the lock and hung the closed sign. Then I counted to ten. Then I counted to one hundred.

Then I headed upstairs to have it out with Mr. Anderson. The door to the apartment next door to Esther's hung open. I heard voices inside.

Paul's elbow was resting on the kitchen island top. He was tipping back a beer. "Hey, Amy." He set his can on the counter and walked toward me.

I stood agog. The apartment was full of furniture. This was an empty apartment. At least, it was supposed to be. "What's all this?" I spread my arms.

"My stuff. I'm moving in." His smile was one-hundred watt. "I know Kim said tomorrow, but there's no time like the present, right?"

"Oh, no, you're not!" My voice went up a notch. "You need to get all this—this junk of yours out of here." Most of the furniture looked like it had come from a college dorm. The matching pair of keg-based tables most of all.

"What do you mean? Your partner said you were cool with this." He folded his arms over his chest. "In fact, she said it was your idea."

I closed my eyes for a moment. "Look," I began, trying desperately to stay calm, "I don't know what Kim—"

"We getting a new roommate?" Esther stuck her head around the corner.

"Yes," Paul said.

"No," I retorted simultaneously.

Anderson extended his hand with a smile. "I'm your new neighbor, Paul Anderson."

"Esther Pilaster." Esther fluffed her hair. "I'm right next door if you need anything, honey." She turned her eyes on me. "Or if you need any pointers on how to handle this one." She jerked a gnarly, long-nailed pink thumb my way.

Paul laughed. "I'll keep that in mind."

Esther said goodbye and returned to her apartment.

"Look, Mr. Anderson, like I was saying—"

"What's all the commotion?"

The blood in my veins congealed and my brain did a flip-flop. A gangly fellow in a sharp pair of blue jeans and a gray and blue UNC T-shirt appeared at the bedroom door. It was the guy who'd been at the other end of the mattress. It was also the guy I had once shared a mattress with.

"Craig?" I gasped.

The dimples in Craig's ridiculously handsome face deepened. "Hi, Amy! Long time no see."

19

"Craig?" I repeated, taking a step back toward the open door. My mouth went dry.

"So you do know my partner," Paul said.

"Yeah," Craig said, swaddling me in his arms.

I worked myself free. "You are not staying here, too." I looked worriedly from one man to the other.

Craig ran a hand through his hair. "Only for a couple of days." He punched Paul in the side of the arm. "Checking up on my investment."

"Well, the first thing I suggest . . ." I said, struggling to breathe. All of a sudden I was feeling claustrophobic and breathless. ". . . is that the two of you check into a motel."

"A motel?" Craig helped himself to a beer from the Styrofoam chest on the counter. Ice water dripped down the sides of the can and spilled all over my hardwood floors. "You wouldn't really make us sleep in a motel?" He popped the lid and took a long pull. "After all we've been through? We're friends."

"We've been through a lot, all right." I folded my

arms across my chest and scowled. "Cheating, lying." I shook my head. "After all we've been through together, I ought to make you sleep in the Dumpster. You are trash, after all."

Paul burst out laughing. A moment later, Craig joined in.

"Why not stay at your house?" I suggested, knowing Craig would never take me up on the Dumpster idea. "You did mention you had a house."

"No certificate of occupancy, remember?" Paul winked at Craig, who didn't look like he'd shaved in three days. The stubble added a certain allure, and he knew it.

"So park that camper thingamajig of yours in the driveway and sleep there."

"No power hookup. Besides, this is more convenient."

"Not for me, it isn't."

"Think of it this way," Paul said, "the sooner we get the build-out completed, the sooner we open for business."

"Yeah, and put me out of business," I mumbled.

"What's that supposed to mean?" Paul asked.

I narrowed my eyes at the two of them. "You know what it means."

Paul and Craig shared a look of confusion. I wondered if they shared a brain as well. "I'm talking about the eminent domain of my house and business."

"Oh, that," Paul said with a dismissive wave of the hand. "You worry too much. Besides, it could be good for business."

"Yours maybe, but not mine." How convenient for

Paul and Craig to own a brew pub next door to a well-known Italian restaurant franchise. There would be a lot more synergy between those two businesses than there would with a birding supply store.

I resisted the urge to accuse the entire commission of political corruption. "I'm going to fight it, you know."

"And you should, Amy," said Paul, rather glibly, I thought. "To tell you the truth, I don't know which way I'll vote on the matter."

I frowned at him. Was he trying to pull the wool over my eyes? Lull me into complacency? If he was, it wasn't going to work. I'd fight the rezoning all the way.

"I don't see what the big deal is, Amy," Craig said, putting in his two cents. "It seems to me you could re-open this little bird store of yours anywhere."

Had he been talking to Robert LaChance? "I've invested a lot in this place, Craig. You wouldn't understand that, would you?" A lot of time and a lot of money. Like all the time I had invested in my failed relationship with him.

I crossed to the wall where an old dumbwaiter had once held something I'd rather not think about. Okay, it was a dead body. That was one of the reasons I hadn't gotten around to renting the space out. First, I'd been busy. Second, folks in town knew about the dead body and, believe it or not, it discouraged renters. Craig, on the other hand, loved all that supernatural stuff and, if I told him the room's history, it would only encourage him to stay.

A four-foot-tall massive black safe now sat directly in front of the dumbwaiter. The name REMINGTON was stenciled across the top of the door in gold letters. "Is this a gun safe?" I asked in disbelief.

"Yeah." Paul crossed the small living room and placed his arm over the top. "You can never be too safe, you know?"

"No guns allowed."

Paul looked at Craig, who shrugged and said, "Don't look at me."

"Fine," Paul replied. "We'll move it over to the pub."

Craig groaned. "Do you have any idea how heavy that thing is?"

"I suggest you watch your toes on your way out," was my only reply.

"Wait," said Paul, grabbing my arm as I made to leave the apartment. "Does this mean you'll let us stay?"

"Well . . ."

"Come one, Amy. This is all your fault, after all."

My brow shot up. "My fault? How do you figure that?"

"You reported me to the police."

"I never reported you!"

"Whatever," Paul replied, clearly not believing me. "I got a huge ticket and was told I couldn't live on the street in my camper. I had to find someplace to live." He filled Craig in on his visit from the police. "So when your friend, Kim, told me you were offering this place and it was only eight hundred dollars a month—"

"Eight hundred?" I interrupted. I was only getting three hundred a month from Esther.

Paul nodded. "I already gave your mother my

check. She said she'd stick it in the register. Did Kim get the rate wrong?" He patted his pockets as if looking for something. "Not enough?"

I waved my hands at waist level. "No, no. Eight hundred is exactly right. Of course," I said, thinking quickly, "if Bigelow the gigolo is going to stay here, I'll have to charge an extra fifty a day."

"An extra fifty?" squawked Paul.

Craig pressed down on his friend's shoulder. "No worries." He pulled out his wallet and handed over five twenty-dollar bills. "Here's the first couple of days' extra rent."

"But fifty dollars," Paul began again.

Craig ran his finger along the edge of the damp beer can. "Worth every penny," he said, giving me one of his patented tall, dark, and handsome looks.

I made for the door before my body did something stupid, like swoon.

I microwaved some frozen mac and cheese with broccoli and washed it down with a glass of red wine. At least under the same roof I'd be able to keep an eye on them and whatever they were up to. Then I headed for Kim's house. I could have called first, but that would only have given her notice. I wanted the element of surprise.

Kim owned a craftsman-style bungalow on the opposite side of town. There's a full-width porch stretching from one outside end post to the other. Square posts rest atop chestnut red brick piers, which rise just slightly above the white porch railing. To my knowledge, the painted red flower box beneath the triple attic window has never held any flowers or living things of any kind, other than the occasional rooting chipmunk and squirrel.

Kim had maintained the home's classic color scheme: stone-colored weatherboard with white trim and a red door. Kim's car was in the driveway leading back to the single-car garage.

I knocked on the kitchen door. There was no answer so I let myself in with the spare key under the flowerpot on the back porch.

"Hey, Amy," Kim said, strolling into the kitchen in a puffy yellow robe. A bath towel was draped over her head. "Man," she began, pulling a couple of glasses down from the cabinet, "you wouldn't believe how dirty a job remodeling is."

I chuckled. I'd seen her remodeling efforts. They'd been mostly of the bystander variety. I took the glass of sweet tea she'd offered, drank, then set my glass beside the sink. "I hear I have you to thank for my new tenant."

"Isn't it great?" Kim said. She rooted around in the fridge and pulled out bucket of leftover fried chicken. "Want some?"

"No, thanks. I ate."

"Eight hundred dollars a month. Paul said it should be two months, maybe three."

"*Great,*" I said, drawing the word out.

"Something wrong?" Kim said, grabbing a greasy breaded leg and resting it on a paper napkin that she carried over to the kitchen table.

"What's wrong," I began, taking up a chair across from her, "is that you didn't ask me first."

Kim chewed and swallowed. "It just sort of came

up quick. I ran into him on the street, and he mentioned he was looking for an apartment." My friend smiled. "You were the first person I thought of."

"Lucky me."

"Hey." Kim wagged the half-eaten chicken at me. "I did you a favor. Not only do you collect some extra money, but you get to work on the guy."

"Work on the guy?"

"Yeah." Kim nodded. "You know, get him on your good side."

"Why would I want to do that?" I crossed my arms.

"To get his vote on this eminent domain thing." Kim reached into the bucket for a second piece. "You did say he was on the committee."

"Robert LaChance suggested I relocate Birds and Bees to a commercial property he owns. He said he'd give me a good deal."

"What did you tell him?"

"That I intended to stay right where I am."

"All the more reason to get Paul on your side."

I leaned back in my chair. "You may have something there."

Kim nodded quickly. "I know I do. It's only short term until he gets his house fixed up. You," she repeated, "need to get on his good side because you need his vote. That's why I suggested you to do the musical, too. Good community relations. Like the senior birdseed thing. We have to get people around here to know you, to like you." She grinned lopsidedly. "The way I do."

"Good idea," I grudgingly admitted.

"Not too many people liked Patsy Klein from what

Using my fingernail, I picked at the roll of tape I'd brought with me and affixed the flyer to the side of the ticket window. The window shades were up, and the street and square were teeming with tourists and locals alike.

Lou laid the box cutter on the wooden ticket taker's stool and grabbed a handful of playbills from the box. "Not that it matters now." He gave the *Annie Get Your Gun* playbills a straightening tap against the ticket counter and dropped them down beside the ticket slot. "Waste of money."

"Why do you say that?" I looked back toward the dark lobby. "Where is everybody anyway? Rehearsal starting late today?"

Lou twisted. "Didn't you hear?"

"Hear what?"

"It doesn't look like there will be a show."

"Why not?" I gasped.

"August pulled out," Lou said, wearily. He patted the stack of playbills. "You think if I set them out that folks will take some? Maybe like a souvenir or a memento?"

"I don't know, Lou." I tossed the roll of tape back in my purse. "But go back. August is pulling out?"

Lou nodded. "Leaving town."

"But he can't do that. Everybody is counting on him. They've all worked so hard."

Lou held open the door to the ticket booth as we passed into the quiet lobby. "Try telling him that. I tried, and he didn't listen or didn't care. He says this whole murder thing has changed everything."

"But Mr. Mantooth said he didn't believe in curses."

"I guess he changed his mind." Lou looked around the lugubrious, quiet space. "I can't say I blame him."

I tailed him to his cluttered office off the lobby. "Isn't there anything you can do?"

"Yeah." Lou looked at me from behind his desk. "If this theater season fails to open, I can look for a new job."

I told Lou how sorry I was to hear about everything.

Lou sighed. "It seems like nothing is going right around here." He picked up a sheet of paper. "Know what this is?"

I shook my head.

"The estimate on getting the electrical updates made and the repairs from the fire."

"You can't postpone the repairs?"

"Without them, we won't pass inspection. And without a passed inspection, the theater remains closed to the public."

Poor Lou. His troubles were mounting by the hour. "TOTS must be insured."

"Sure, but we've got a five-thousand-dollar deductible." He thwacked the estimate. "According to Mr. Calderon, repairs will run double that. And that's not counting the repairs to the HVAC and roof that he insists this old place needs."

I whistled. Cassius Calderon was a local general contractor and owner of CC Construction. He was the best in the area and, as they say, as honest as the day is long. So I knew whatever price he'd quoted Lou had to have been more than fair. Probably on the low side even. I'd had need of his services over at Birds & Bees, and any other contractor probably would have charged double what he had billed me for.

Lou crumpled the paper and threw it across the room. "Maybe I shouldn't even bother. With the show closing, this place is likely to follow."

"What do you mean?"

"The town treasurer told me there were no extra funds for the theater. The town's reserves for such things, as he put it, are tapped out." He frowned. "They'll probably turn this old place into a flea market." Lou looked like he'd swallowed a bug. "Or worse yet, bulldoze the place."

"No," I said. "They wouldn't do that, would they?"

Lou only shrugged dejectedly.

In truth, who knew what the town would do with the old theater? Look what certain town officials wanted to do to my house. What plans might they come up with for the TOTS location, perfectly situated as it was on prime town square frontage?

They might sell it to one of those drugstore chains or one of those other franchises that dotted the landscape everywhere you went.

"Without the theater," moaned Lou, "I don't know what I'll do." He gave me a forlorn baby-pelican look. "I don't know how to do anything else."

"Don't worry, Lou." I gave the theater manager a hug. "I'm not going to let *Annie Get Your Gun* die. I'm not going to let TOTS close either."

"That's nice, Amy, but I can't imagine what you can do to stop it." He grabbed a fancy letter opener carved to resemble a peacock feather and slit open the top envelope on a teetering stack of mail. "Bills," he muttered. "Bills and more bills."

"Cheer up," I said, "maybe there are some requests for tickets, season tickets even, in that pile." That reminded me that I had promised Dr. Buchman, Jane's dad, that I'd introduce him to Ava Turner. I wasn't sure now that I could deliver on that promise.

"One can hope," he admitted.

"All we need is for the show to go on, right? Keep the money coming in? That will keep the town officials happy?" I said, hopefully. "I'm sure we can work something out with Mr. Calderon, too."

Lou appeared dubious.

"A payment plan of some kind. That's what we need."

"He's a contractor—he'll never agree. What we need is a miracle."

I smiled. I explained how I'd been in a similar pinch and Mr. Calderon had worked out a payment plan that was acceptable to the both of us, one that I was still making monthly payments on.

"There's still the little problem of Patsy Klein's murder," Lou reminded me.

"And Miss Turner's safety," I added.

"Oh?"

I explained how it was likely the person who'd accidentally stabbed the wrong woman would try again to kill Ava Turner.

"That's a scary thought," Lou said with a shiver.

"Don't worry," I said again. "I've got a few ideas. I'll talk to Mr. Mantooth and see if I can get him to agree to stick with the show so we can open as scheduled. And," I vowed, standing in the office doorway, "I'll find our killer."

For the first time, I thought I saw hope in poor Lou's eyes. "Thanks, Amy."

I made my good-byes but hadn't gotten to the front door when I hurried back. I popped my head in the door as Lou sliced into another envelope. "Where exactly do I find Mr. Mantooth?"

"Ruby Lake Motor Inn." Lou savagely tore open the letter. His eyes scanned the page, and he muttered something about the high cost of electricity. Looking up at me, he said, "If he hasn't left town already."

21

I drove out to Rolling Acres the next morning. I didn't have an appointment, but I wasn't going to let that stop me. I'd come to do them a favor. They'd be thrilled to see me.

In the van, I had several selections of birdseed, one bag of fruit and nut mix, one bag of cracked corn, and one of straight-up unshelled black oil sunflower seeds.

I hadn't had time yet to have any donor plaques made for the feeders, like Eli Wallace had requested, but I had sourced a local jeweler-slash-trophy-shop whose owner insisted they could handle the work. He'd also said he'd give me the plaques at his cost once I had explained the nature of the program to him.

I also carried two bird feeders. I'd mount one on the pole I'd brought. The other I'd hang from one of those trees outside the activities center that I'd spotted the other day.

I found an empty space in the guest parking area

off to the side and checked my hair and makeup in the rearview mirror. Perfect, or at least as good as it was going to get.

I smoothed out the wrinkles in my tan twill skirt and matching blouse and walked to reception. I had wanted to wear something suitable to the occasion. Plus, I remembered how immaculately the woman up front had been dressed the first day I had shown up. I was determined to look as professional as she had. I'd even put on my pearl earrings and matching necklace. My folks had given them to me as a high school graduation present.

Cold air wafted over me as I entered, sending goose bumps up my forearms. The elegantly dressed brunette was behind her ornate walnut desk, hands clasped atop the blotter. She managed a small smile. "May I help you?" Her wavy locks were fashioned into a loose chignon today.

I matched her smile. "Hi. Ms. Bryan, wasn't it?"

"Bryant," she corrected, emphasizing the T.

"Oh, right. Sorry." I felt my face heat up. "I'm Amy Simms. I was here visiting Floyd Withers a few days ago."

Ms. Bryant-with-a-T pursed her lips. Her lipstick shade matched her plum dress. "I do remember." She rose. "Are you here visiting again? I'm not sure if Mr. Withers is available." She made for the computer.

"No," I said, following her steps. "I mean, yes. But what I'm really here for is this."

She looked at her elegant, manicured fingers a moment before taking the flyer and brochure from my hand. "I see. Are you here seeking a donation?"

"No, nothing like that. In fact, I'm here to give."

"Give?"

"That's right," I said quickly. I nodded toward the parking lot. "I've got birdseed and feeders and poles and stuff. Everything's ready to go!" I smiled broadly.

Ms. Bryant narrowed her gray-blue eyes at me. "Go where exactly?"

"Outside." I waved toward the back of the property. "I thought I'd set a couple of feeders out on the back lawn where residents can see them from the activities center. Of course," I said quickly, "if you can think of someplace better to put them, I'd be happy to oblige. They'll fit just about anywhere."

Tiny tsk-tsk noises came from the woman's throat, sounding like a sparrow twittering in the brush, as she shook her head no. "I am sorry, but I couldn't allow you to install bird feeders, Ms. Simms."

My face fell. "Why not?"

"Because there are rules." She paced silently to her seat and laid my homemade flyer and brochure carefully on the furthest corner of her desk. "I promise you, I will submit your idea to the board of directors."

"Then what happens?" I asked, looking down at my wrinkled papers.

Ms. Bryant sat. "If the board approves, you will be allowed to install your bird feeders on a trial basis."

I twisted my lips. "How long will that take?"

A highly polished fingernail traced an invisible path atop the desk blotter. "Ninety days is—"

"Ninety days?!"

She eyed me coolly. "Ninety days is typical, Ms. Simms." She leaned forward. "There are rules and regulations. These things take time."

"Not to be vulgar, but some of these people don't

have a lot of time." Were we really arguing over sticking a couple of bird feeders outside on their lawn? "It's only a couple of bird feeders, for crying out loud."

"All our contractors must abide by our written policies, Ms. Simms." Ms. Bryant's hand reached for the brochure and flyer. She silently pulled open her top desk drawer and dropped them inside. I watched them disappear as she pushed the drawer shut. I was beginning to wonder if they'd ever see the light of day again.

"But I'm not contracting anything," I said, trying unsuccessfully to hide the frustration I was feeling.

"I'll be sure to convey your thoughts to the board."

I decided to leave before I said anything else that she might convey to the board. If she and the board knew what I was thinking, they'd never allow the feeders. In fact, they'd probably ban me from returning to Rolling Acres.

I stood, fists planted on my hips, fuming, while the sun blasted me in the face. It had been like an icebox inside. I couldn't believe the woman had been so obstinate about a couple of bird feeders. I was trying to do her and, more importantly, the residents a favor, a good deed!

Well, I was not going to let Ms. Millicent Bryant and her precious board of directors stymie me.

I threw open the back doors of the van, took a quick and surreptitious look in the direction of Ms. Bryant's window, and got busy. It took me two trips, but I managed to haul the feeders, the pole, the baffle, and all three bags of seed out to the backyard of the retirement center without anybody noticing me.

If they did see me, they didn't care. Either way, I'd install the feeders first, then ask permission. If I waited for my request to go through proper channels, it could take months.

I found the perfect spot for the hanging feeder on a low, sturdy branch of an old pin oak. The feeder was squirrel proof, meaning that anything heavier than a medium-sized bird, like a blue jay, would cause the bar along the bottom to fall, shutting off access to the food.

I twisted the bird feeder pole into the ground in a soft spot near a field of petunias, then thumbscrewed the baffle to it before affixing the feeder atop. The baffle would keep squirrels and other critters, including snakes, from climbing up.

As I screwed the feeder to the base using a small screwdriver I'd brought for the occasion, I heard a banging noise. Startled, I dropped the screwdriver in the tall grass and glanced guiltily toward the main building.

Bright sun reflected off the glass. I couldn't see a thing inside. Hurriedly, I dug through the grass, grabbed the screwdriver, and finished the job. I shoved the screwdriver in my pocket as the side door beside the window eased open.

I gulped, fearing the wrath of Millicent Bryant and perhaps the entire board of directors of Rolling Acres.

A small, lightly dressed man stepped out on the paved walkway. He brought his hand up over his eyes. "Amy?" He tilted one way then the other. "Is that you?"

"Floyd?"

A second man came barreling out, propped up with a wooden cane. "I told you that was her!" bellowed the man with the cane.

"Karl?"

"Quick, bird lady!" Karl said something I couldn't catch to Floyd. I saw Floyd peek back inside, then wave. "Come on," urged Karl. "The coast is clear."

I scurried inside and took up a seat at one of the card tables with Floyd and Karl. I hadn't realized it, but I was out of breath.

"Breathe," Floyd said.

"Yeah," said Karl. "You look like you're about to croak."

I clutched my hand to my chest and forced myself to take a couple of regular breaths.

"Is that my Della's old bird feeder?"

I said it was and explained how the man who'd bought his house was dating a friend of mine. "I thought you might enjoy having it here." Floyd's eyes were drawn to the window. A couple of finches and a cardinal had already found the pole feeder.

Karl narrowed his eyes at me. He folded his hands across his chest as he leaned back in his seat. "You looked like a criminal out there," he said with a smile. The ex-chief of police touched a finger to the side of his nose. "And I know criminals."

I giggled. "I guess I am." I explained how Millicent Bryant-with-a-T had refused to let me install the feeders. "She insisted I go through the Rolling Acres board of directors."

"You're a hoot!" Floyd laughed and slapped the table. Faces turned our way.

"You won't turn me in, will you, Chief?" I batted my eyes at the retired law enforcement officer.

"Well now," the old dog said, "I might have to slap the cuffs on you."

"Karl!" barked Floyd. "Miss Amy is a lady."

"I know, I know." Karl waved a hand at his friend. "Me and the bird lady are just having fun." Karl gave me a wink. "Right?"

I laughed again. "Yes, in fact, I do believe that's the most fun I've had in some time." I leaned closer to the gents. "It was quite the adrenaline rush, if you know what I mean."

Floyd toyed with his mustache. "I hope they don't take them down."

I looked out into the yard. "Me too." I explained to Karl and Floyd my plan to provide feeders and birdseed to Rolling Acres and other senior living and retirement facilities.

"Sounds great," said Floyd Withers. "It looks like you've already made some new bird-watching fans."

I turned. Several seniors had taken up chairs near the window and were avidly watching the growing number of birds. I had an idea. "I'll bet I can get the *Ruby Lake Weekender* to write an article on the Seeds for Seniors program and the benefits of bird-watching as an activity."

"I like it," said Floyd. "A quality-of-life issue."

"Me, too," Karl admitted. "The administration wouldn't dare remove your feeders then, would they, Amy?"

It was my turn to wink. "That's the idea." I thought about the little towhee Derek's daughter, Maeve, and her friend Will Quiroz had brought to Birds & Bees.

Soon, from what the wildlife rehabber had recently told me by phone, Sammy would be free to fly again. Perhaps we'd see him here one day, foraging on the grass below the feeders, in search of fallen seed.

Floyd suggested refreshments and brought three sweating iced teas back to the table, along with a pile of sugar cookies on a plate.

Karl took a healthy swig. He banged the edge of a cookie against the tabletop. "Hard as a rock. Cook says they bake them, but I believe they dig them out of an old mine." Nonetheless, with a show of force, he bit the cookie in two and swallowed it with a look of satisfaction.

"Speaking of criminal behavior," I began, "did you hear *Annie Get Your Gun* has shut down?" Both men nodded. "In fact, the manager of the theater thinks TOTS itself may be permanently shut down by the town."

"We know," Floyd said, patting my hand.

Karl swirled his tea, watching the ice cubes dance. "Rolling Acres has a senior night once a year at TOTS."

"This year," explained Floyd, "we were going to see your show, *Annie.*"

"And you didn't tell me?"

"We wanted it to be a surprise," Floyd replied.

Karl added that they'd been informed of the canceled show just that morning. "It's a bummer."

"That it is," I agreed. "But it's probably a blessing that you don't have to see me act. Or hear me sing." I told them what I'd heard about the director quitting and leaving town and Lou fearing for his job.

Karl said he and Lou went way back. "I hate to see him or any man lose his job. Especially a vet."

I told the guys how I hoped to convince August to stay and find the killer.

"Well, Amy," said Karl, looking thoughtful, "while you do have a certain feminine charm, I would not recommend you go trying to find a killer." He flipped another sugar cookie from hand to hand. "You leave that to the professionals."

I arched my brow. "Even if that professional is Jerry Kennedy?"

Both men snorted in unison like a pair of pionus parrots.

"Kennedy's been working some with the state team on this one. You may have seen one or two of them around town." I said I hadn't. "Maybe they're gone now. I'll look into it." He popped the cookie he'd been toying with into his mouth and talked as he chewed. "I may be retired," he boasted, "but I do have my sources."

Floyd added, "Chief Kennedy often asks Karl's advice. Besides, Kennedy doesn't feel right withholding info from the old chief."

Karl nodded. "And from what I hear, our killer is either pretty smart or pretty lucky." He explained that there were fingerprints all over the scene, but those were all accounted for by the theater's staff, crew, and cast. "Not a print on that knife you found."

"Only Patsy Klein's prints on the gun," Floyd said, "from what the chief told Karl."

I told them that Chief Kennedy had told me that as well. "And that was a prop gun," I reminded them. "Why fire it?"

"Maybe the lady thought she could bluff her killer." That was Floyd again.

"And it didn't work," I said.

"And who was in that locked room with the woman, and how did they get out?"

I nibbled thoughtfully at a cookie. "You know, Nathan Longfellow thinks the theater is haunted."

Floyd replied. "Nathan Longfellow is crazy. He yelled at me once when I complained about a cut of brisket. I thought he was going to leap over the counter at me."

"Seriously?"

Floyd nodded. "The manager had to come calm him down. I'd stay away from him, if I were you."

"Yeah," added Karl. "He's a hothead, all right. The police have been called out to disturbances involving him more than once. It wouldn't surprise me if he was the one behind all this."

"Maybe." I told them how I'd learned that Nathan Longfellow more than likely had a personal grudge with Ava Turner. Both men agreed that gave him a pretty good motive.

"Sometimes these things fester in a man's mind," said the retired policeman.

"Funny that Nathan Longfellow and Ava Turner ended up living in the same town."

"Well, Ava is from town, as you know," Karl explained. "Nathan grew up on a reservation not far from here."

"What about T-Bone Crawford?"

"The ex-con?" Karl said, eyeing Floyd's remaining cookie. "Came to town a year or so ago. He hasn't caused any trouble that I've heard."

"Keep your hands to yourself." Floyd pulled his cookie to his chest as the old chief's hand approached within striking distance.

"Do you think Jerry can catch our culprit before he or she kills again?"

Karl shrugged heavily. "The thing with killers is"—he beckoned me closer with his finger—"that until you catch them, there is always the chance they may kill again."

I leaned back. The truth of the ex-chief's words was undeniable. Especially if that killer's intended victim was still walking and talking.

"Speaking of criminals . . ." Karl removed his spectacles and rolled his eyes to the left. "Don't look now."

"Uh-oh." Floyd twirled his mustache.

I set down my tea glass. "What's the big—" Then I saw Millicent Bryant down at the other side of the activities center chatting with an orderly.

"That's Ms. Bryant, the administrative assistant," Floyd whispered.

"I'm not sure she's going to be happy if she spots me here." My eyes pleaded with both men. "I didn't exactly sign in."

Floyd and Karl discussed strategies. So far, Ms. Bryant was facing away from me. But if she turned . . .

I didn't exactly fit the age group she was expecting to see.

"Karl is going to go keep Millicent busy," explained Floyd. "The kitchen is through that door behind me. You can go out that way."

I bit my lip. I felt ridiculous letting the woman run me off. Then again, I really did not want to get caught. "Are you sure it will work?" I had my doubts that the old chief could distract the administrative assistant long enough for me to make a clean getaway.

"Are you kidding?" whispered Floyd. "Have you heard the way this guy talks?" He jerked a thumb at his friend. "The man never shuts up."

I smiled. "You make a good point."

Floyd pushed back his chair. "Follow me."

I stood at a crouch. "Wait," I whispered. "What if she sees the bird feeders?" I glanced anxiously out the window.

"Not to worry," chortled Karl. "I'll tell her I made them in shop class."

"Shop class?" I said, dubiously.

"Okay, I'll tell her the bird fairy left them last night."

I didn't have time to argue. Floyd and Karl were on the move. And when I saw Millicent Bryant-with-a-T begin to stroll my way, so was I.

22

"**D**erek!" I dropped the mop I'd been using to clean up the pee my customer's Irish setter had left near the door. Derek looked immaculate in a charcoal-gray suit, expensive Italian loafers, and a crisp white shirt. Only the shadow of stubble along his firm jaw gave him an edge of intrigue.

I, of course, was a wreck. Filthy slacks, soiled shirt, smudged makeup, and tousled hair. Damp shoes.

It had been one of those mornings.

Derek smiled and took the mop from my hands. "It's good to see you." There was a small package in his other hand. He held it out. "I brought cupcakes." He leaned the dirty mop beside the umbrella stand at the door.

I relieved him of the treats. "How nice." I sniffed the flimsy cardboard box. "C Is For Cupcakes?" C Is For Cupcakes is a cupcake bakery located on the square. I tried to avoid it as much as possible—which wasn't often.

"Yep. I picked them up fresh on my way over." The lawyer diligently wiped his feet on the mat.

The man was adorable. His freshly polished shoes glowed while mine reeked of dog urine. Not to mention the floor was covered with dirt, leaves, and bits of birdseed. I was amazed how much loose bird food ended up on the floor each day.

"I hope you like chocolate?"

I laughed. "Come on, the shop's quiet." It was after noon, and there was generally a dip in traffic around that time as tourists and locals alike ate lunch. "I'll put on a fresh pot."

"So, did you hear the latest?" Derek asked, settling into one of the rockers in the kitchenette at the back of the store.

"No," I said, between bites of one of the best chocolate espresso cupcakes I'd ever sunk my teeth into. I'd tipped the cupcake over and started at the bottom, saving the buttercream top for last.

"There was a second attempt on Ava Turner's life."

I dropped the cupcake. It landed with a soft splat in my lap. I groaned and began wiping.

Derek laughed. "I'd offer to help, but, ah . . ."

I blushed. "I think I've got this." I grabbed a towel and washed up at the sink. Looking down, I noticed I now looked like I'd wet my pants. Could this day get any worse? I looked toward the stairs. "Maybe I should go change?"

"Sit down," Derek replied. "You look great."

I fluffed my hair, forgetting that my fingers were

covered in chocolate buttercream frosting and cupcake crumbs. Knowing further attempts to salvage
my looks were futile, I surrendered. I grabbed a fresh
cupcake and rested it carefully on a napkin I set atop
my knee. I cleared my throat. "Anyway, you were saying?"

Derek took a sip of his coffee. "It seems somebody
took a shot at the actress earlier today."

"Where?" I asked quickly. "Was she hurt? I mean,
she isn't dead, is she?" If she had been killed, I was
certain the Ruby Lake gossiping geese would have
spread the word by this time.

"No," Derek said, shaking his head. "She's fine."
He explained that Ava had been strolling in her garden after breakfast when shots had been fired. She
hadn't been hit, but a large ceramic ewer had been
shattered.

"I tried to warn Jerry that this was going to happen." I got to my feet. "More coffee?"

Derek nodded and I refilled his cup. "Well, it
seems you were right."

"I don't suppose they found the shooter?"

"No such luck. Jerry and one of his officers spent
hours out there digging for clues. So far, nothing."
Derek bit a cupcake in half and chewed. "At least,
that's what Dad says. And I guess he should know.
He's been in Ruby Lake for years."

Derek had only returned several months ago, to
be nearer his daughter and join his father in his
practice. Ben Harlan had been a practicing lawyer
for decades. Lawyers have a way of finding out
things.

"Does your dad have any idea if the police are any closer to finding out whoever our perpetrator is?"

"You know Jerry better than I do. According to Dad, he says he does. But Dad thinks it's all bluster."

I thought so too and said so. I filled Derek in on what I'd been able to learn myself.

"So you think Nathan Longfellow, Eli Wallace, and this T-Bone Crawford are the most likely suspects?"

I shrugged. "Any one of them could have done it. They certainly had opportunity. And the means." I explained about the knife connection and how one man was a butcher, the other a taxidermist, and the third a biker with a nasty-looking blade on his belt.

"All we need now is a candlestick maker," Derek said with a soft chuckle.

"Hey, come on," I said. "Don't make fun of me. Isn't that all it takes?" Heck, they could have all been in on it together, the same way the mayor, the sleazy car dealer, and the town coot were trying to get me kicked me out of my house.

"That's what all the cop shows and lawyers say," he said with a smile. "But what about motive?"

I admitted I hadn't quite puzzled that out. "And now August Mantooth is leaving town."

"Dad told me that the show had been canceled. Tough break."

I had a sudden realization. "Maybe that's the real reason why the director canceled *Annie* and is leaving town!" Derek looked at me questioningly. "Because he's guilty and trying to make his getaway." I slapped my knees. "I should tell Jerry."

"Go ahead if you want to, but it isn't much to go

on. I can't see him arresting or even getting Man-tooth to stick around without something solid to charge him with."

I frowned. "You may be right," I admitted, "but if—"

My words were interrupted by a very loud crash that shook the house.

Derek came to his feet. "What on earth was that?"

"Ignore that," I said, waving for him to sit back down. "That's the construction going on at the brew pub or, rather, *biergarten*," I said with a roll of my eyes, "next door."

"Ruby Lake's getting a *biergarten*?" He looked pleased.

"Yes, we are." I didn't share his enthusiasm and did not feel like going into all the machinations and permutations and problems the establishing of such a business was causing me. Nor did I want to discuss the other major problem it brought. My old boyfriend, Bigelow the gigolo.

There was a second bang and then silence. I scanned the wall my house shared with the business next door. No holes. No cracks. Always a good sign.

I set my mug in the sink and was giving it a quick rinse as the chime alerted me to the fact that I had a customer. Derek rose and stood close at my side. "Listen, Amy," he began, "I was wondering if you would—"

Craig appeared out of nowhere, dressed, as he fre-quently did, in designer jeans and a black T-shirt. "Hi, Amy," he said, throwing his arms around me. I caught a whiff of cologne and sawdust. "Sorry about the racket. I told Paul to try to get the crew not to put that slab for the fire pit so close to the wall."

Suddenly he stopped, seeming to notice Derek for the first time. Craig thrust out his hand. "Craig Bigelow."

I crawled out of Craig's arms and put myself well out of harm's way.

"Derek Harlan." Derek looked at me for some answers.

"Craig is one of the partners in the business going in next door."

"The *biergarten*." Derek smiled. "Amy was telling me all about it. I'll look forward to being a customer."

"Yeah," Craig said. "Did she also tell you that she and I are living together?"

Derek didn't blink, but I could tell the announcement had struck a nerve. It struck a nerve in me, too. "We are *not* living together," I said.

"Paul and I are living in the apartment on the second floor until we get things settled," my ex-boyfriend explained, though nobody was asking. "But Amy and I were together for six years, so who knows?" The idiot winked at me, then turned to Derek. "I might just end up sleeping on the top floor, right, Amy?"

"Not in a million years, Craig."

Derek made a show of looking at his watch. "I've got an appointment. Nice to meet you, Craig. Good seeing you again, Amy," he said rather stiffly.

"Wait," I said. "You wanted to ask me something?"

"It wasn't important."

I watched Derek walk out the door. "You drove him off, Craig."

"What?" Craig looked genuinely surprised. "Him? You're interested in that guy?"

"None of your business." I frowned as I watched Derek get in his car at the curb. What had he been about to ask me? Was he going to ask me out on a date? Now I might never know.

"Hey," said Craig, reaching a hand toward the cupcake box, "cupcakes. Mind if I—"

I slapped his hand away. "Those are for the customers. Go away."

Craig rubbed his hand. "But Amy—"

"Now," I insisted, "before I decide to raise your rent."

Craig stomped off in a snit, but there was no peace for me yet.

Riley rushed through the door. "Amy! Come quick!" He grabbed my arms. "Did you hear?"

"Calm down, Riley," I said, pulling myself free, despite the red marks his fingers left on my arms. "Yes, I heard. Somebody tried to shoot Ava Turner." I draped an arm over his shoulder. "Relax. She's fine." Riley's love for the woman knew no bounds. I wasn't sure I wanted to know what that was all about. She had to be twice his age.

Riley was shaking his head. "No," he spat. "Chief Kennedy arrested Rhonda!"

23

"I just brought the woman in for questioning." Chief Kennedy angrily pushed a mess of papers around on his desk, only succeeding in making the workspace look even more disheveled. "I didn't strap her to the electric chair." He glared at Riley. "What is it with everybody in Ruby Lake that they have to exaggerate so damn much?"

"I'm innocent!" cried Rhonda, wringing her hands. She was sitting on the edge of a chair at the end of the chief's desk. Her baggy khaki pants were wrinkled, and her pullover top was stained—with what, I didn't know. Even her usually perfectly applied and controlled makeup was a wreck. Her hair looked like a bird's nest somebody had dumped on her head. I'd never seen her look worse.

Riley stood behind her chair with his hands on her shoulders, like he was some sort of guardian angel. "Don't worry," he said. "I called Mom."

"I know, I know," I exclaimed in answer to my

cousin's plea of innocence. I turned to Jerry. "Why on earth would Rhonda shoot Ava Turner?"

"I don't know," his voice grumbled out. "Why don't you ask her? So far," he said, turning to my cousin, "she hasn't said anything that makes much sense to me."

"I will." I strode quickly across the room, grabbed one of the guest chairs at Officer Sutton's empty desk, and pulled up next to Rhonda. "Rhonda," I began, softly. "Please tell Chief Kennedy that you were not shooting at Miss Turner." I stroked her hand.

"I did not shoot Ava Turner," she said, her jaw tight.

"Then what were you doing out in the woods behind the woman's house?" Chief Kennedy asked.

My brow went up in alarm. "Ava Turner's house?" That couldn't be good.

"That's right," Jerry said, his tone smug. "She was seen by some hikers."

"You know I make my own natural hair products," Rhonda cried. "I was picking leaves and flowers." She narrowed her eyes at the chief. "Not shooting people."

I did know. Using such things as chamomile, elderflower, and rosemary, Rhonda mixes up natural hair and makeup products that she sells to her customers at the beauty salon. Some of it wasn't bad at all. Except for whatever it was she'd had me try for the holidays that had turned my hair shamrock green. That had been one memorable Christmas Eve party.

Jerry sighed and lifted a rifle beside his desk.

"Your rifle has been fired recently. How do you explain that?"

"I told you. I was shooting at squirrels this morning." Rhonda pushed her fingers nervously through her hair. The action did nothing to help.

I gaped at my cousin.

"Don't look at me like that," she snapped. "You know that I never hit them."

"It's against the law to shoot a firearm within town limits," Jerry said. "I could arrest you for that alone."

Rhonda pleaded at me with her eyes.

I was at a loss for what to say or do next and was relieved when Mom and Aunt Betty pushed through the door of the police station. Ben Harlan, Derek's father and, better still, high-powered attorney, stood between them.

Mom came quickly. "Are you all right, Amy? Are they hurting you?"

I assured her that I was fine. Mom had had the dubious pleasure of visiting me in the police station on more than one previous occasion, so I couldn't blame her for her mistaken concern.

Mom reached for my head and pulled at a lock of my hair. "Is that chocolate frosting in your hair?"

I pulled my head away. "It's nothing, Mom. Really."

Rhonda ran to her mother's side and took her hand. "Don't worry," Aunt Betty said with authority. "Nobody touches my baby." She aimed that last remark directly at Jerry.

I noticed him sink several inches into his chair.

"I hope you had a warrant for that rifle, Chief." Ben tugged at the sleeves of his striped shirt and winked at Rhonda.

"I didn't need a warrant. Officer Reynolds went to Ms. Foxcombe's home and she invited him inside."

"Is that true, Rhonda?" the lawyer asked my cousin.

"Y-yes," she stammered. "I don't have anything to hide."

Jerry snorted.

"Chief," Ben said, hovering over the desk, "I am very sorry to hear about Ms. Turner's troubles, but unless you have something more than the account of some hikers who saw my client in the woods . . ."

"She fought with the dead woman who was killed in Ava Turner's dressing room. She was seen in the vicinity of the attempted shooting of Ms. Turner at around the time of the shooting."

Ben looked down his nose at the chief. "Was she seen carrying a rifle?"

Jerry pulled a face. "No." He cast his eyes on his suspect the way a fisherman looks at his catch when he knows he's about to release it.

"Why would Rhonda Foxcombe want to murder Ava Turner, anyway?"

"I don't know." Jerry jerked his thumb at me. "Why don't you ask her? She's the one that seems to think there's some big deadly conspiracy going on around here. Personally," the chief said, thumping a stack of papers atop his desk, "I think this whole crime is based on jealousy or money or just plain orneriness." Jerry stood. "Or maybe Rhonda doesn't like the way her brother is fawning all over Miss Turner?"

I saw Riley blush.

"What?!" shrieked Rhonda, releasing her grip on

her mother. "I would never hurt a woman that Riley liked. I would never hurt anybody."

"My Rhonda is no more a killer than—than Amy here." Aunt Betty aimed her index finger at me and I took a step back. "My daughter is gentle as a lamb."

"Do you have any more questions for my client, Chief?" Ben rested the palm of his hand on Rhonda's shoulder.

Kennedy kicked back his chair and stomped to the coffeepot. He cursed when he discovered it empty and jabbed the carafe under the faucet. He turned and glared at the group of us. "What the hell are you all still doing in my office?"

Jerry ripped the top off a bag of ground coffee, spilling a considerable amount of it over his shoes and carpet. "Get out of here before I arrest the damn lot of you for loitering!"

Before leaving, I couldn't resist putting in my own two cents' worth. "You know, Jerry, you ought to be talking to some real suspects instead of harassing the fine citizens of Ruby Lake. The ones who pay your salary."

The chief opened his mouth to reply, but stopped when I put up my hand. "Like August Mantooth, the director, for instance. Did you know he was leaving town?"

I shook my head from side to side to express my disappointment in his job performance. "If he hasn't gone already. Did you ever think he might be the killer? Maybe he murdered Patsy Klein and then tried to kill Ava Turner when he got the wrong woman the first time."

The chief of police seemed unimpressed. "And now you figure he's on the run because he's afraid we might be on to him?"

"Maybe he doesn't know you as well as I do."

Jerry's face scrunched up like a plum left too long in the sun. "What's that supposed to mean?"

"Think about it!" I cried as Riley grabbed me by the arm and dragged me outside.

While Mom, Aunt Betty, and my cousins decided to go join Ben Harlan, who'd generously offered to take everyone out to celebrate, I begged off.

It was time to pay a visit to the Ruby Lake Motor Lodge and our dear director, August Mantooth—if, as Lou had intimated, the man hadn't already left town.

24

A local landmark since the fifties, the Ruby Lake Motor Inn is situated on what we locals consider Lower Lake Shore Drive, across the road from Ruby Lake. There is a big, popular public marina located at this edge of the lake as well. Permanent boat slips were available. There were also boat rentals, everything from kayaks to pontoon boats to cruisers.

Built in the so-called "neon era," the Ruby Lake Motor Inn was comprised of an L-shaped building that contained thirty rooms. It also housed the office and a small diner in the shorter line of the L. Behind the motel, eight studio-sized, rustic cabins with kitchens and wood-burning fireplaces had been added to accommodate those guests wanting a few more home comforts or planning an extended stay.

Rust-pitted thirty-foot-tall steel posts held up the motel's iconic giant ruby-red neon sign. A smaller amber sign braced high up between the posts proclaimed that there were no vacancies.

Dick Feller was sitting behind the front desk, sipping coffee and reading the newspaper as I came through the door. I smelled fried chicken coming from the diner, and my stomach pleaded with me to take a break and get something to eat. I ignored its plea.

A mother and daughter were thumbing through the postcard carousel near the newsstand.

Dick lowered his newspaper and looked up as I came in. His espresso-colored eyes were a stark contrast to his pasty white skin. Dick was skinny as a proverbial rail and went from point A to point B with an economy of moves. It had surprised me to discover that he had shown an interest in acting in the community theater. It seemed so contrary to his nature. But then, I barely knew the man.

"Hello, Amy. What brings you by?" His hair was short and brown and dull.

"I wanted to let you know that *Annie Get Your Gun* has been canceled."

The front desk manager folded his newspaper and set it at the edge of the counter. "Yes, I know."

"Oh, so Lou called you?" In truth, I was sure he had known, but I'd needed an opening.

"Mr. Mantooth himself told me." He clicked his tongue. "Such a shame."

I drummed my fingers against the counter. "Lou told me Mr. Mantooth has a room here. Is he still around? I was hoping to catch him if he is."

"I suppose so." Dick's eyes went to the computer. "He mentioned he would be checking out. Returning to New York City, I imagine. But he hasn't turned in his room key yet."

"Would you mind giving me his room number? I'd like to say good-bye." I knew from experience that Dick was a stickler for following the rules. One of those rules was never to give out a room number. I was sure there was a good reason for that. But that didn't mean the rule should apply to me.

Sure enough, Dick frowned. He swiveled the computer screen and his fingers glided over the keyboard. "Let me give him a call." After checking the computer, he dialed the director's room. "Sorry," he said, putting down the receiver. "No answer."

"That's okay," I said, grabbing my purse off the counter. "You tried, right?"

I stopped at the door. The mother and daughter placed two postcards on the counter: one a view of the lake and the other a shot of Lake Shore Drive as it wound through town. Both pictures had clearly been taken from the air. "Was Patsy Klein staying here, too?"

"That's right," Dick said. The little girl handed him a five-dollar bill and he popped open the register. "Room twenty-two. And I'll be happy when the police release the room. Todd and Angie are more annoyed with each day." Todd Carr and his wife, Angie, were the motel's proprietors.

He slid the two postcards into a slender brown bag. "Thank you very much," he said to the girl.

"Here it is, almost high season," Dick said, redirecting his attention to me, "and we can't rent out the room until Chief Kennedy gives us the go ahead. We're fully booked, too."

"Hopefully, things will get back to normal soon

enough," I said. Though, personally, I was beginning to wonder if there was such a thing as normal in Ruby Lake. Everything and everybody seemed a little . . . quirky, and hiding a secret or two. Had it always been that way? Had I been too young to notice before?

I held the door open for the girl and her mother, then headed down the covered walkway along which the motel's main guest rooms were located. I knew there was a passage around midway leading back to the cabins behind. August Mantooth was staying in Cabin 6. Yes, I'd been looking over Dick's shoulder. But what did it matter so long as I got results?

I was about to turn when I noticed a familiar shape step out of a room up ahead. He looked left, then right. I dodged behind a stainless-steel ice-maker and peeked. It was August Mantooth.

That was odd. I knew for a fact that he'd been staying in one of the cabins. What was he doing coming out of one of the motel rooms? Visiting another guest? That was always a possibility. Then why did he look like he'd been skulking? Was he having an affair?

A young couple walked past me holding hands. I smiled awkwardly. "Dropped something behind the machine," I said clumsily as they looked over their shoulders at me and whispered to one another.

The director shuffled off toward the cabins, and I walked quickly to the room he'd left. A scrap of tattered yellow police tape hung off the knob. I looked at the door. Room 22.

Patsy Klein's room!

So unless he was having an affair with Patsy Klein's

ghost, the affair theory had to go out the window. Had it been curiosity that drove him to enter a room that the police had quarantined or was he looking for something? If so, what?

I tried the handle. The door was unlocked. There was no seeing in the window because the drapes were pulled shut. Was anybody else inside? Or had August Mantooth been alone?

I dragged my teeth over my lower lip. I looked left, then right, and then out to the parking lot. The mother and daughter from the lobby were now climbing into a sedan with a man waiting behind the wheel.

There was no one else in sight. I knew the room was off limits, but what could I do? This was practically an invitation. The room was practically begging me to come inside.

I opened the door just wide enough to pass and quickly slid inside. The lamps were out, but there was enough sunlight seeping through the curtains for me to easily move around.

There was nothing impressive about the room. Two double beds faced a dresser with a flat-screen TV. A large, battered tan suitcase lay atop the bed farthest from the door. Its contents, mostly clothing and toiletries, spilled over the side and onto the flowery red and orange quilt.

A search of the night table and dresser drawers turned up nothing of interest, a Bible in the nightstand, some extra clothing and underwear in the dresser drawers, a light jacket hanging in the alcove that also held a portable ironing board. There was no sign of a laptop or other electronic devices like a cell phone or tablet. A page-curled copy of our script lay open on the floor beside an upholstered chair. It had been annotated in pencil.

The bathroom was empty, except for some used motel-sized shampoo and conditioner bottles and soiled towels. An open cosmetic kit sat in front of the dressing area mirror beside the sink.

The only other thing of interest was the small makeshift shelf that Patsy had built on the corner of the dresser. A row of books and DVDs were held in place by bookends comprised of an ice bucket on one side and the iron on the other. The DVD titles were a mix of Hollywood films and Broadway shows, including *Annie Get Your Gun.* The books included everything from popular fiction to a crime reference book—how odd—to Ava Turner's autobiography, *Ava Turner, With Love.* There was even a book on writing for the stage. Apparently, Ms. Klein had aspirations to be more than a backstage helper.

The Ava Turner autobiography was one I was tempted to take and read myself. I was beginning to think that the actress had led a very interesting life indeed. And, from what the vet, Jane Buchman, had related, that included a whole lot of love.

Why had Ava Turner returned to Ruby Lake? The town must seem terribly dull compared to the worlds of New York and Hollywood.

I peeked under the beds and I searched the suitcase and the clothes. All the while, my heart was racing. Each time I heard footsteps pass by outside the window, I feared discovery. Worse yet, the police might return. If Chief Kennedy found me snooping around, he'd throw the book at me.

I picked up my pace. I found nothing of note in the suitcase either. Moving to the alcove, I checked the pockets of the hanging jacket. Nothing.

Not that I knew what I was looking for or even expected to find anything. If there had been anything of interest, the police would have removed it days ago.

The jacket slid off the hanger. I bent to retrieve it and banged my head on the ironing board. The ironing board crashed to the carpet. "Shh!" My hands were shaking as I picked up the ironing board and stood it back in the alcove. As I did, I noticed a sliver of paper sticking out from under the ironing board cover.

The gray telephone on the nightstand started ringing loudly and I about had a heart attack. "Time to get out of here," I muttered, glancing over at flashing red light on the phone as it blinked on and off like a burglar alarm. I thrust the paper in my slacks and tiptoed to the door.

Peeking through the curtains, I saw Dick Feller speaking with August Mantooth. The director was throwing a suitcase into the trunk of a nondescript dark sedan. What were they conversing about? Did Dick know the director had been in Ms. Klein's room? Had he given him the key?

A moment later, Dick headed back to the lobby. Mr. Mantooth slammed the trunk down and disappeared, probably back to his cabin for more luggage.

I had to catch him before he left town.

Mantooth's cabin door was open so I didn't waste time on social convention. I marched up the front steps and went inside.

The director was hastily tossing clothes into a trunk on the floor. "Ms. Simms," he said. "What are you doing here?"

I noticed a slight red blush to his cheeks that his beard couldn't hide. "Hello, Mr. Mantooth. Are you leaving?"

"Show's over," he said, clumsily folding a hideous pink shirt and tossing it onto his growing pile. "Haven't you heard?"

I told him that I had. "Did you hear that somebody shot at Miss Turner this morning?"

He stopped in the middle of tossing a pair of trousers into his trunk. "Is she dead?"

"No," I answered. "Not even a scratch."

The director's face was inscrutable even as he said, "Well, that's good then."

"Yes. One murder per show is enough."

"More than enough."

Mantooth's Adam's apple bobbled up and down as I fiddled with the TV remote lying near his bed. "Tell me, how well did you know Patsy Klein?"

"Ms. Klein? Not well at all." The director blinked. "Why do you ask?"

"I saw you coming out of room twenty-two a few minutes ago." I watched August Mantooth's face carefully. "Ms. Klein's room."

The corner of the director's mouth turned down. "Are you spying on me, Ms. Simms?" He pulled at his mustache. "Shouldn't you be watching birds instead of people? Think you're James Bond, do you?" His tone was thick with mocking.

I shrugged as if to say, *What if I am?* He could hardly suggest that spying on him was worse than him being in Ms. Klein's motel room. "Did you know that the author Ian Fleming was an avid bird-watcher? In fact, he named his James Bond character after the name of an author-ornithologist of the same name."

"Fascinating, I'm sure."

"It is. James Bond wrote *Birds of the West Indies.* You might want to read it sometime."

"I'll wait for the stage production," August said with an unkind chuckle.

"What were you looking for in Patsy's room?"

Mantooth threw a pair of trousers, which he'd been holding and twisting savagely into a knot, down in the trunk. "Who said I was looking for something?"

I smiled. "Nobody. But the police might." I saw his ears perk up. "If somebody was to mention to them that you'd been fishing around in her motel room. A room that is officially off limits."

The director folded his arms across his chest. He wore a flowery red and blue Hawaiian shirt and billowing gray shorts. The knee-high white socks and open-toed sandals I tried not to look at. What was the man thinking?

"I-I was looking for some papers."

I raised an eyebrow, questioning.

"Ms. Klein worked as my assistant of sorts, too. She had notes not only on this show but on other projects as well. We"—he paused momentarily—"had a history together."

"A history?"

"That's right. She's worked on several productions for me over the years."

Realizing this was a good opportunity to learn about the deceased, I asked, "Where was she from?"

"I don't know." August rubbed his nose. "Buffalo, I think? Could be Moscow for all I know." The director plodded over to the compact kitchen tucked into the far corner of the cabin. He grabbed a bottle of scotch and poured a couple of fingers' worth into a plastic cup. He didn't offer me any.

"What about family? Where are they?"

He swallowed, then shrugged. "I have no idea where her family is or if the woman even had any. From what your chief of police says, no one has come forward to claim the body."

"It seems odd that you worked with her as much as you say yet know so little about her."

August Mantooth downed the rest of his booze and wiped the back of his arm across his face. "You didn't know Ms. Klein like I did."

I admitted I didn't.

"She was a quiet sort. She kept to herself. Patsy Klein was not one to share her personal life. She liked to keep her private life private. That's a trait I rather admire," the director said pointedly. "I didn't press her."

"Did you find what you were looking for?"

Mantooth's eyes were glassy. "What?"

"In Ms. Klein's room? Did you find your papers?"

"No," he said, forcefully. "I did not." August stepped around me and snatched some more clothes from the closet. The man had not packed light. "Now, if you do not mind, I have to finish."

"Of course," I said. "Though speaking of the chief of police, I wonder what the police will think of you leaving town so"—I tapped my index finger to my lips—"precipitously, shall we say?"

His brows pushed together. "What are you implying?"

I told him I wasn't implying anything. "I'm only concerned what the police might think. They may take your flight as a sign of guilt. Of course," I continued, "the police back home in New York could always interview you."

I ran a finger along the top of the lampshade on the table near the door. "I'd be careful those big-city news folk don't get wind of it though. You know how rumors spread."

The director's jaw worked back and forth, but no words were forthcoming.

"Look," I said, deciding to try a sweeter tack. "Won't you consider sticking around? Seeing the show through?"

August Mantooth paced like a trapped bear a moment. "There's a murderer loose, Ms. Simms. And apparently they have not finished killing. Or have you forgotten?"

"I haven't forgotten at all. But why should the theater suffer for it?" I told him how TOTS might close down completely if something couldn't be done to bring in some badly needed funds.

"Lou Ferris told me as much." He slammed the lid of the trunk. "Do you think I like abandoning a show? I lose money if the production shuts down. It's too late to find another show to direct on such short notice."

"So you'll stay?"

August Mantooth slumped on the edge of the bed. "I suppose."

I stood in the open doorway. "Why did you hire Patsy? I mean, not to speak ill of the dead . . ."

"You may speak ill of the dead all you like," Mantooth quipped.

"She did not seem to be a well-liked person."

"She wasn't."

"So why employ her?"

"I suggest you go feed your birds, Ms. Simms. Better yet, go rehearse your part." He pushed himself up from the bed. "I've said all I'm going to say to you about Patsy Klein."

He pushed me toward the cabin door. "And you need all the practice you can get!"

The construction noise was driving me crazy the next morning, so I asked Kim to run Birds & Bees alone while I paid a visit to more of the towns' shopkeepers, trying to convince them to hang flyers for my Seeds for Seniors program and sign the petition Kim, Mom, and I had put together to save the store.

Kim and Randy's renovation was on hold because they'd found termites in the foundation and were having the house tented and fumigated as a precaution.

I dropped in at Spring Beauty to tape a flyer in the window. Cousin Rhonda was busy clipping a client's locks. "Hi, Rhonda!" I called. "Okay if I put up a flyer?"

Scissors in hand, Rhonda waved. "Sure, you go right ahead. I'm sure Misty won't mind."

"What's it for?" asked a curious client in the chair at the next station.

"We're collecting donations to provide birdseed and feeders for senior living facilities. You know, to give residents something to do." I explained how I owned a shop specializing in such things.

"Like a hobby?" said the woman, with her hair up in big pink curlers. "I think that's wonderful. My mother used to be a bird-watcher."

"That's right. I'm supplying all my labor for free and materials at cost. I've already placed a couple of feeders at Rolling Acres, over by the lake." I hoped they were still there.

The stylist cutting the woman's hair said she'd be happy to donate.

"And you say you own a store?" The woman in curlers closed her eyes as the stylist's hand came across her forehead.

"Birds and Bees," I said again, watching her stylist deftly unwind the curlers from the woman's head. "We're at the corner of Lake Shore Drive and Service-berry Road."

She smiled. "By the diner. I believe I've seen it."

Since she'd been so nice, I asked if she'd mind signing my petition to keep the town from taking my store-slash-house. Not only did she agree, but every-one in the salon did too. Ka-ching, six more signa-tures!

I made my good-byes and headed for town square, where I got several more signatures. A number of shopkeepers, including Sherry at The Coffee and Tea House, let me put up my poster, too.

Coming back along Lake Shore Drive took me past LaChance Motors. On impulse, I pulled into the lot. A salesman came at me fast, like a shark smelling blood in the water.

I waved him off. "Sorry," I said. "I'm not actually looking to buy."

He gave my rust-spotted and dented van a look of disdain. "Are you sure?"

"I'm sure."

"My name is Juan Chavez." He handed me a black business card with raised gold letters. "In case you change your mind."

I dropped the card in my purse and thanked him. I might change my mind if I won the lottery. "I'm looking for Robert—Mr. LaChance. Is he around?"

Juan shook his head in the negative. "The boss and the mayor left on a hunting trip for a couple of days."

The corner of my mouth turned down. "That's too bad." It was also very interesting. What had the two men been hunting? Ava Turner, perhaps? And how was the car dealer planting and shooting with a broken arm? I was no hunter, but I knew that couldn't be easy.

Seeing the crestfallen look on my face, Juan added, "The boss should be back tomorrow. What's your name?" He tugged at the collar of his black long-sleeved shirt.

It seemed like an odd choice for such a warm day, but it wasn't my business to say so. "I'll tell him you stopped by."

"Actually, I'm here to hang an announcement in the window and drop off a few brochures." I pulled one of the flyers and a handful of brochures.

He looked a bit surprised but lost interest quickly as another car pulled into the lot. He eyed the blue coupe and its woman driver greedily. "If you don't mind?"

"Of course not," I said. "I'll tape this up and get out of your hair."

Juan attacked his new customer, and I made a bee-line for the small showroom. I would have loved the chance to snoop around Robert's office some, for evidence that I could use to show that he and the mayor were in cahoots against me, and maybe even tried to murder Ava Turner, for some murky reason. But I caught sight of his receptionist manning her desk in the front of Robert's trailer office. She was hard as nails and likely sleeping with him. She'd never let me past the front door.

I taped up the flyer inside the showroom window to the curious and amused looks of a couple of sales-men and got out before one of them, a slick talker with a thick Alabama drawl, talked me into an almost-new truck with zero down and only eighty-four low monthly payments.

I would have loved to have been a fly on the wall when Robert LaChance got back and discovered my flyer in his window! He'd probably have a cow.

I was on my way back to my own, paid-for van when I noticed the Harley. I only knew two men who rode Harley-Davidsons. One was Kim's boyfriend, Randy. The other was T-Bone Crawford.

And only T-Bone worked at LaChance Motors. The big black and chrome motorcycle with the stud-ded leather saddlebags had to belong to him.

I hitched my purse over my shoulder and walked

back to the garage, wincing with the noise my heels made against the concrete as I neared. I wouldn't be sneaking up on anybody.

The mechanic stood beneath a station wagon that was up on one of those hydraulic lifts. He wore short-sleeved gray overalls and work boots. I suppose they could have been motorcycle boots. They were big, black, and chunky.

His neck craned upward into the bowels of the car. A cigarette dangled from his lips. A cloud of smoke billowed around him.

I coughed.

T-Bone raked his eyes over me. "What are you doing here?" His voice was rough, like someone had sanded his vocal cords with gravel.

It took me a minute to come up with an answer. "Looking for Robert."

The mechanic narrowed his eyes at me. "He isn't here." A black and white skull-and-crossbones motif bandana was wrapped tightly around his long head. "You shouldn't be either. The shop is off limits to customers. That's the rules." He wasn't lying. I'd passed the No Customers Allowed sign on my way in.

We were alone in the service area. It must have been a slow day for auto repairs and maintenance.

He spat out the butt of his smoke and crushed it underfoot. That definitely had to be against the rules, too. Heck, it was probably against the law. I refrained from pointing that out to him. T-Bone Crawford did not, on first look, appear to be the sort who took criticism well.

I wasn't too certain he cared much for the law either.

I started to reply that I wasn't a customer but was also afraid T-Bone lacked a sense of humor. I slid my purse to my other shoulder and forced a smile. "Did you hear the news?"

T-Bone plucked a large ratchet wrench for a kit he had laid out on a cloth and did something to one of the front wheels. "What news would that be?"

"It looks like *Annie Get Your Gun* will go on, after all. I suppose we may start a day or two late, but still, good news, right?" T-Bone, much to my astonishment, did have one of the production's plum roles.

T-Bone tossed his ratcheting wrench back from whence it came and tugged at the wheel's brake calipers. A grunt was his only reply.

"Have you acted in other plays before?"

I took T-Bone's scowl for a no.

"Musicals?"

"Nope."

He grabbed a can of spray and attacked the wheel like he was bug-spraying a nest of hornets.

I waved a hand in front of my face and coughed hard.

"See?" T-Bone said, with a devilish look in his ever-changing green eyes. "It isn't safe around here."

I gagged and hurried to a foul-looking watercooler. I grabbed one of those ridiculous cone-shaped paper cups and swallowed a mouthful of lukewarm water that tasted like it had been piped directly from the septic system. "How do you drink this stuff?" I spat.

When I could finally speak again, I asked, "How did you wind up getting into acting?" Maybe he'd had his arm twisted, like I had.

T-Bone shrugged as if to say, *What does it matter?*

"The boss was doing it and he thought it might be good if I did, too."

That was a decidedly cryptic answer. Why had Robert wanted this surly and menacing mechanic to join him in *Annie Get Your Gun*? Was it so he could keep his hired goon close at hand?

The mechanic grabbed a small box from which he removed a pair of brand-new brake pads. He fondled them in his hands, the way I might a fine piece of jewelry. "Are you sure about the show being back on?"

"Pretty sure."

"Funny." He scratched his cheek with the edge of one of the pads. "I didn't think that Turner woman would want to go on, what with all the trouble."

Trouble? Is that what he called two attempts on her life? A nagging thought shaped itself in my brain. What if Robert LaChance, Mac MacDonald, and T-Bone Crawford were all in the musical because they wanted it to fail? Maybe, just maybe, they wanted the Theater On The Square to fail.

So they could take over the property like they intended to take over Birds & Bees! It was a crazy idea, but it might explain why the three of them were involved with the theater. What better way to make sure it closed down?

They might be plotting some sort of monopoly of half the town!

And if they murdered the show's star attraction, Ava Turner, the theater would likely shut down for good.

"Then again," T-Bone said with a laugh, "the woman does pack a mean right hook!" He cackled some more.

I took a measured step back. "You know this from personal experience?"

"Sort of," he replied, slyly.

"You want to elaborate on that?"

He grabbed a fresh cigarette from the pack of Winstons in his top pocket, took a long pause to light it with a silver butane lighter before speaking. "I saw her arguing with that guy who plays your boyfriend in the show."

"Eli?"

"Yep."

He took a drag of his cigarette, and we both watched the smoke billow out and dissipate in the smelly garage, where it would no doubt go undetected. "Well, not arguing so much as making herself clear."

Right then, I was wishing the mechanic would make himself clear. "I don't understand."

"The man came on to her. And the lady didn't care for it."

"Eli? Eli Wallace?" Were all theater people promiscuous, or was it something in Ruby Lake's water? "Miss Turner's old enough to be his mother!" Heck, maybe his grandmother!

T-Bone loomed over me, lit cigarette dangling inches from my face. "Lady, when she hit him in the face, I thought she was done for."

"Eli didn't take it well?"

T-Bone's grin split his face in two. "He about looked like he was going to rip her head off."

"So," I gulped, "why—why didn't he?"

"Lou showed up and Eli took off like a whipped pup with his tail between his legs. But I could tell his blood was boiling."

"Where did this happen?" I said.

"In one of the boxes."

"You mean one of the theater boxes?" There were several theater boxes on the left and right side of the stage. "And where were you while all this was going on?"

"Sitting down in one of the seats near the orchestra, taking a break."

"And you didn't think to intervene? What if Eli had hurt her?"

"I don't like to get involved." He tapped ash to the floor.

Didn't like to get involved or was happy to let Eli Wallace do his job for him?

"Besides, I'd seen the great lady going at it once with that lady that got herself killed. I figured she could hold her own."

"Miss Klein and Miss Turner were arguing?"

"More like a catfight, if you ask me," chuckled the mechanic, pulling the cigarette to his thick lips and inhaling once more.

"Did you tell your story to the police?"

T-Bone's eyes darkened and narrowed. "I don't talk to the police," he hissed.

Dick Feller had told me that T-Bone Crawford was an ex-con. It was understandable that he wasn't into sharing information with the local police. What was the mechanic's crime? Dick had clammed up before getting the chance to tell me what villainy T-Bone had been convicted of committing. Whatever it was, surely even Jerry Kennedy had learned of it. Hadn't he?

I decided there and then to make a point of learning what T-Bone had done and what Jerry did or did not know about the man's past.

The phone in T-Bone's pocket chirped and he dug it out. Thick, black grime coated the inside of his fingernails. He looked at the screen. "It's the boss."

He answered. "Yeah, Mr. LaChance?" T-Bone grunted, then said, "How's the hunting? Oh? Too bad." He listened a moment, nodded, and looked at me. "Yep. She's right here."

But I wasn't. I was halfway to my van.

26

I was nearly to town before I noticed the motorcycle behind me. First I saw it, weaving in traffic, passing cars with abandon. Then I heard it, a threatening rumble like an approaching thunderstorm.

I parked in front of my store, ran inside, and locked the door.

"What are you doing?" exclaimed Kim. She was holding an owl house up to a customer in a tank top and jean shorts.

"I thought we'd close early," I said, breathlessly. I took a quick look out the window as I heard the roar of the motorcycle approach.

"Are you all right, Amy?" Kim asked, leading her customer to the sales counter.

I nodded and waited while Kim rang up the sale. "Have a nice day!" I said, unlocking the front door and letting the young woman out. She looked at me like I was crazy. But I'd rather be thought crazy by a stranger than murdered by a motorcycle-riding ex-con.

"Are you sure you're all right?" Kim stood beside me now, clutching her purse. She explained that she and Randy were meeting at his place for dinner. I told her to have a good time and watched as she climbed into her car and drove off.

Over at Ruby's Diner, I saw T-Bone slowly dismount from his motorcycle. He removed his matte black helmet and hung it over the handlebars by its chin strap. He ran his fingers through his hair, then slowly looked my way. I dodged behind a carousel of bird-themed cards and peeked out.

There was no sign of him!

I ran to the back door and locked it. He might be sneaking around back to take me by surprise. After making sure all the doors and windows were secure, I dialed the police station on the store phone.

Jerry Kennedy picked up, and I explained the situation without mincing words.

"What were you doing down at LaChance Motors? You aren't finally planning to get rid of that eyesore of yours, are you?"

"I was hanging flyers," I snapped. "All perfectly innocent."

"Hanging flyers," he said, clearly skeptical, "or snooping into another murder?"

"Are you going to sit there arguing with me on the telephone, or are you going to get down here and arrest T-Bone Crawford?"

"Arrest him?!" snorted the chief. "Arrest him for what?"

I blew out a breath. "He is an ex-con, you know."

"Yes," drawled Jerry. "I do know."

"And?"

"And the man's done his time and he deserves to be left alone."

"Fine," I snarled. Jerry had finally made me mad. "I'm hanging up now. You can come by and take my cold, dead body to the morgue in the morning—if that would be more convenient for you."

"Wait." I heard Jerry sigh and his chair squeak. "You say Crawford followed you all the way from LaChance Motors to Birds and Bees?"

"That's right," I said, smugly. Finally, the man was listening to me.

"And you say he's parked over at Ruby's Diner?"

I said yes. "I can see his motorcycle even now. Who knows where he is?" Possibly sneaking up behind me with a knife or a garrote even as I was talking.

"Great, I'll be right over."

"You will?" I said, a little surprised and very hopeful.

"Yeah," Jerry Kennedy said, right before hanging up. "I'm hungry, too!"

I slammed down the receiver and retreated to my apartment on the third floor. If T-Bone Crawford wanted me, he'd have to climb three floors to get me.

Mom was out playing cards with her friends so I had the place to myself. I nuked a frozen pizza and uncorked a bottle of red. I wondered what Derek was up to. I wondered again what he had been about to ask me when that idiot Craig showed up and spoiled everything.

I poured a generous glass of wine. He'd spoiled six years of my life. I stomped my foot against the floor. Hard. Paul and Craig's apartment—temporary apartment—was directly below. I hoped they heard me. I hoped chunks of plaster from the ceiling fell on their heads and in their beer mugs.

I flopped down on the sofa with my wine and half the pizza and fired up my laptop. A search on Ava Turner brought up a million hits. I clicked on several but realized learning anything new about the actress that might pertain to someone wanting her dead was nearly an insurmountable task.

I searched for Patsy Klein, and the results were just the opposite. Plenty of Patsy Kleins. But none of them seemed to be the dead woman.

After my third slice of pizza and second glass of wine, with no sign of T-Bone breaking in to murder me, I searched the ex-con's name. After a half hour of excruciating digging, I found a decade-old article from a Pittsburgh newspaper that described a Thibodaux "T-Bone" Crawford having been arrested and convicted of aggravated assault on a store clerk.

I was a store clerk!

He'd been sentenced to seven years and was expected to serve a minimum of five.

Aggravated assault? That didn't sound good. I searched online for the definition. It wasn't good. According to the FBI's website, aggravated assault was an unlawful attack by one person upon another with the intent of inflicting severe bodily injury, often accompanied by use of a weapon.

I'd seen that knife T-Bone wore strapped to his belt. I'd definitely place it in the deadly weapon category. He'd had it with him in the garage, too. Maybe

Chief Kennedy didn't need to look any further than Crawford's belt for the knife that had been used to stab Patsy Klein. . . .

I heard the key turn in the lock and looked up. "Hi, Mom." I glanced at the clock on the wall. "You're home early."

"Ben wasn't feeling well."

"Ben?" I pulled my legs up under me on the sofa cushion. "I thought you were playing cards with the ladies?"

"No, Ben and I went to the movies."

I smiled. "You like Ben?"

Mom placed her blue purse on the edge of the kitchen counter beside the phone. "I like a lot of people, Amy." She poured a glass of water from the tap and took a couple of her pills.

"Yeah," I teased, "but you *really* like Ben. Right?"

Mom set the glass in the sink. "I'm going to run a load of laundry before bed," she said, in a not-so-subtle attempt to change the subject.

"This late?"

"What can I say? The sound of warm clothes tumbling in the dryer soothes me, helps me sleep." Mom had explained in the past that when she grew up, her bedroom had shared a wall with the laundry room. She'd grown accustomed to the sounds of laundry. "Give me those clothes you've got on, Amy. They look disgusting."

I tugged at my shirt and took a whiff. "Ugh. They smell disgusting too." Like a musty garage and cigarette smoke. I changed into pj's and settled back down on the sofa. I was nibbling at a fourth slice of cold pizza when Mom reappeared. She had changed from a simple yellow skirt and blouse to blue cotton pajamas and a rose-colored robe.

"I found this in your pants' pocket." She tossed me the scrap of paper, then headed back to the laundry room tucked into a small space off the kitchen.

I wriggled my bare toes and fingered the square of paper. "What is it?" I wondered aloud. Then I remembered, this was the paper I'd found tucked under the ironing board in Patsy Klein's motel room. I'd shoved it in my pocket and forgotten about it. It was probably one of those INSPECTED BY NUMBER 33 things, or some sort of note from the manufacturer about the care and cleaning of the ironing board's synthetic cover.

I glanced over it quickly, thinking to throw it out, but sat up straight when I saw it was an old yellowed newspaper article concerning a young August Mantooth. At least, from the grainy picture, it appeared to be August Mantooth, albeit a clean-shaven one. There was no mistaking that distinctive face. Only his name then hadn't been Mantooth. It had been Manfred.

Back in the eighties, he'd been the assistant to the director of a show at a small theater in St. Louis, Missouri. The show had closed abruptly when the theater's receipts had gone missing. August Mantooth, then Manfred, had gone missing too.

Authorities caught up with the young man in San Francisco, where he claimed no knowledge of the theft. Police were never able to prove otherwise and the case was closed.

I toyed with the old newspaper. I knocked on my

mom's bedroom door. She was sitting up in bed, reading a historical novel. I told her what I'd found.

Mom lowered her glasses down her nose. "So you think this director was being blackmailed by Patsy Klein, the dead woman?"

"It seems so." I explained how I'd discovered August Mantooth sneaking out of Patsy's room at the Ruby Lake Motor Inn. I held up the news article. "He had to have been looking for this. I'd bet anything on it."

"If he was being blackmailed by her, he doesn't have to worry about it anymore."

I rubbed my palms over my face. "But that would mean Patsy had been the intended victim all along. Yet she was killed in Ava's dressing room, while dressed like Ava's character."

"Plus," Mom said, lowering her book to her lap, "someone is still trying to kill Miss Turner."

I sighed. "None of this makes any sense."

"Murder seldom does," Mom replied. "You should tell Jerry about this."

I agreed. Mom held her hand to her mouth to cover a yawn. I fluffed her pillow and kissed her cheek. "Get some sleep." I turned off the bedside lamp at Mom's request and closed her door behind me.

It might have been the wine. It might have been my nerves settling down after my tangle with T-Bone Crawford, but I felt suddenly worn out and needed sleep as well. Before retiring, I dialed the inn's number and asked for Mr. Mantooth. There was no answer at his cabin, but at least he hadn't checked out and left town. I'd try to pin him down tomorrow and confront him with what I'd found.

Deep in thought, I brushed my teeth and grabbed my personal copy of the *Bird Watcher's Bible* for a little light bedtime reading. I had just turned down the covers when the front door started rattling.

Now what?

I threw on my robe and cursed as I went to the door. The store was closed, the house locked up. Who could it be at this hour?

"Miss Turner!" The actress was elegantly dressed in a flowing blue silk dress and low black heels. Despite the warmth of the evening, she wore the same fox stole—or its twin—that I'd seen wrapped around her neck the night I'd found her at The Coffee and Tea House. "What brings you to Birds and Bees?" I hadn't noticed a single bird feeder at her estate the other day. Not even a birdbath in the garden.

Then I noticed Esther standing behind the actress, swaddled in a cat-and-nicotine-scented terrycloth robe, her hair all lopsided like she'd been sleeping.

"I heard this lady banging on the front door," snapped my tenant. "She says she is a friend of yours."

I wasn't too happy with Esther inviting folks into my store after hours, but I was happy to see Ava.

I frowned my displeasure at Esther. I'd deal with her later. "Thank you, Esther." I moved away from the door. "Won't you come in, Miss Turner?"

"You know," Esther said, "I used to do a little acting out in Hollywood myself."

I rolled my eyes. Esther Pilaster had been retired for as long as I could remember. She hadn't worked since the local five and dime closed fifteen years ago.

I asked Ava if she would care for something to drink and invited her to sit. I crossed to the open window and looked down at Ruby's Diner. There were several cars in the lot, but the Harley was long gone.

I pulled the curtains shut and took a seat in the chair across from the actress.

"You heard what happened today, I suppose?" she began.

"About the shooting at your house? Yes. Have the police come up with anything?"

She said they hadn't. "Rumor has it that *Annie Get Your Gun* may continue, after all."

I explained how I'd been trying to get Lou Ferris and August Mantooth to agree to continue with the production. "It's for the good of the theater and the entire town."

"Still," she said, "I wonder if that's wise?"

"Believe me," I said, "I know how difficult it must be for you, the thought of returning to the theater." I ran my tongue over my upper lip. "Your dressing room."

She nodded somberly.

"Do you have any idea what Miss Klein was doing in your dressing room?"

The actress shrugged. "The woman was always flitting about, in and out. It was her job."

That made sense. "Did you notice anything . . ." I struggled for words. ". . . different in your dressing room?" I cleared my throat. "I mean, after the murder?"

Her brow creased ever so slightly. "How do you mean?"

"Was there anything missing, for instance?"

"Not a thing," Ava replied, twirling a diamond ring

on her left hand. "All perfectly ordinary. Except . . ." She hesitated.

"Yes?"

"Now that you mention it, I noticed the wardrobe trunk had been moved." She laughed lightly. "But it was nothing. Anyone might have moved it."

"Did you mention that to the police?"

"No," she said, solemnly. "It can't possibly have been important. Nothing in that trunk but costumes."

I closed my eyes and pictured her dressing room at the theater. The leather-sided wardrobe trunk was a large, rectangular portable clothes closet on locking wheels with a stiff wooden rod to hold the clothing. It stood about six feet tall and was maybe two and a half feet wide.

"Besides, it couldn't have been moved more than a foot or two." She smiled. "I'm probably the only person to notice or care. I'm considered somewhat of a diva."

I assured her that was not the case.

The actress rose and went to the window, running her fingers along the edge of the curtain. "I am quite concerned."

"For your safety?"

"For all of our safety," Miss Turner confessed, tugging at the material. I heard the sound of a car's backfire in the distance.

I felt my skin prickle. Something in her tone made me believe her. "Is that why you're here?" It was after ten, not exactly the witching hour, but still. I barely knew the woman and suddenly she was showing up unannounced in my apartment. What did she want?

"This may have been a mistake." Ava turned suddenly and headed for the door.

I rose. "Where are you going?"

She had already reached the door and was opening it. "Good night, Miss Simms."

"But—"

"I'll show myself out."

"Would you like me to drive you home?" I knew the actress didn't drive. That's why Cousin Riley chauffeured her to and from the theater for rehearsals.

"That won't be necessary. Gail is downstairs."

Nonetheless, I followed her down the steps to the door. Paul and Craig were coming in, their shirts untucked and their eyes glassy. "What are you two doing coming in the front?" I admonished them. "The front door is for customers. You're supposed to use the back door." A previous owner of the house had installed an exterior stairs leading from the ground to the second floor—thereby keeping renters from coming through the downstairs. Unfortunately, those stairs had been in a dangerous state of decay and proven too expensive to repair, so I'd asked my contractor to remove them, which had cost me a fraction of the money. Now I had no choice but to let renters use the interior stairs. I drew the line at using the front door, however. I seemed to be the only one aware of that line.

"Sorry." Craig giggled. I smelled beer on his breath.

"Say," Paul said, watching as Ava Turner slid into the back of a dark sedan at the curb, "what was Miss Turner doing here?"

"None of your business," I said. Not that I would

have admitted what she was doing here even if I'd known.

"The movie actress?" asked Craig.

Sure, he probably wanted to hit on her.

"You're both drunk," I said, pushing both men toward the stairs.

"Research," Paul explained with an impish grin.

"Yeah," said Craig. "Menu planning."

I followed them to their apartment, then banged on Esther's door. I heard a muffled meow, some scratching and murmuring. A moment later, Ester opened the door a crack. "It's late," she complained. "What do you want? I was trying to sleep."

A blast of lemony fresh air hit me in the face. That unnatural lemony smell that comes in a spray can. I narrowed my eyes at her. I looked at the space between her feet. "I heard a cat."

"*Animal Planet.*"

"You said you were asleep."

"I said I was trying to sleep. Watching the TV helps. Now, if you don't mind?" She slammed the door in my face.

"Don't let strangers in the store after dark!" I hollered at the door.

"Trying to sleep!" was her reply.

I trounced back to the third floor and locked up. I heard the sound of a motorcycle and pulled the curtain aside. I was about to let it drop back when something odd caught my eye.

"What the—" I ran my finger over the glass and gasped. There was a funnel-shaped hole in the glass. Was that a bullet hole?!

I inspected the curtain itself. A small hole had also punctured the fabric.

I drew away from the window quickly, bracing my back against the wall. I listened to my heart beating against my chest and debated what I should do. That hole had not been there earlier.

27

"Ichecked it out, like you said, Chief." Officer Reynolds came bouncing down the stairs. He tossed me my apartment keys. "Looks like the hole was made by a twenty-two of some sort. Maybe only an air rifle or pellet gun or something."

Jerry snorted and shot me a withering look. "Like I told you, Simms. It was nothing. Probably just some kids out having fun." He popped open the bin of shelled peanuts and thrust his hand inside.

I opened my mouth to complain, but I'd done it so frequently, and to no avail, that I decided it wasn't worth the breath. It was a good thing I had waited until morning to call the police. If I had dragged Jerry and his men down here at night to look at my window he'd have been even less interested in pursuing the matter.

"Maybe a bird hit your window," Reynolds suggested.

"Birds don't make bullet holes. Unless they're carrying rifles." Did these guys have any law enforcement training at all?

Reynolds reached in next and popped a handful of peanuts in his mouth. "No sign of the projectile."

Riley burst in. "Good morning, Amy!" He said hello to the chief and Officer Reynolds. "Need a ride to the theater?"

I told him no. "I'll take my van. I've got some errands to run." A meeting had been called for the cast and crew of *Annie Get Your Gun* over at TOTS. We'd be deciding whether or not to continue the show. A lot was at stake. I looked out to the street. Cousin Riley's pickup truck was empty. "Where's Rhonda?"

Riley frowned. "She says she's quitting. Not going back. This whole murder thing's got her mighty upset." He gave Chief Kennedy an accusatory look that bounced harmlessly off him.

"I can't say that I blame her." I thought about Ava Turner. Had that been her reason for stopping by last night? Had she wanted to tell me that she was quitting the show? If I were the actress, I'd probably be in a first-class seat on a plane to St. Tropez by now, soaking up the sun someplace safe until whatever was going around here was firmly resolved.

I guessed we'd all find out soon enough.

Riley left.

"I figure we're done here, too," said Jerry, hitching up his trousers.

"Done?" I exclaimed. "Aren't you going to investigate any further?"

"What's to investigate?"

"Jerry," I said, taking a deep breath, "Ava Turner

was in my apartment last night. Somebody shot at her yesterday morning. They shot at her again last night." I pointed angrily upstairs. "In *my* apartment!"

"Did they, Simms?" Chief Kennedy said with irritation. "Or did they try to shoot *you*?"

I opened my mouth to speak, then clamped it shut. *What the—?*

Jerry chuckled and winked at Officer Reynolds, which riled me all the more.

Was Jerry right? Had someone been shooting at me? It was horrible enough to think of somebody trying to shoot Ava Turner. But to think that same person was trying to shoot me . . .

"By the way, Simms," said the chief, with a voice of triumph. "I checked on T-Bone Crawford yesterday. He *was* at the diner to get his supper."

I snorted. "Sure, what else was he going to say? That he was staking out Birds and Bees?" I folded my arms across my chest. "Before trying to shoot me? Or Miss Turner."

"The man got off work and went to the diner for dinner. Hundreds of folks around here do exactly that same thing each day. Are they all trying to kill you too?"

"Come on, Reynolds." Chief Kennedy waved for the officer to follow him to the door. "Leave this investigation to me, Simms. We'll all be better off. I'll figure out who killed Kleinerman all in good time.

"And when I do," he said, turning in the open door as a customer came through, "I'll know who's behind all this mischief being perpetrated on Miss Turner!"

He stomped down the brick path to his squad car, Officer Reynolds following in his wake.

Mischief? Shootings, stabbings, and attempted murder were mischief?

Then I froze.

"What is it?" asked Mom, an expression of worry on her face. "Are you okay?"

I ran outside and banged on the car window. The chief was behind the wheel. He frowned and ordered Reynolds to roll down the window. "What is it, Amy?"

"You said Kleinerman? Who's Kleinerman?"

The chief shook his head and looked down the street a moment before answering. "We now know that Patsy's real name was Kleinerman, not Klein."

"Really? I wonder—"

Jerry interrupted. "And, get this, she was related to some guy that Ava Turner killed in self-defense twenty years ago." The chief twisted the key in the ignition and gunned the engine. Reynolds raised the window. I was being dismissed.

I stepped quickly away from the vehicle before Jerry ran over my toes.

I stood at the side of the road thinking. Could it be? Could Ava have murdered Patsy? Maybe because she thought Patsy was going to blackmail her or kill her in an act of revenge?

I went back inside as a large moving van pulled up next door and began dumping crates on the sidewalk. Work on the brew pub appeared to be going quickly. I hoped work on Anderson's house was doing the same.

"Mind watching the store, Mom?" I knew it was

hard for her to be on her feet all day, but I had the
meeting at TOTS and some errands to take care of as
well. Kim was due in around three to take over.

Mom said it would be fine. "Don't worry. I'll call
Betty. She can help, too."

"Thanks." Aunt Betty was always happy to oblige,
though it was hard to get her to focus on any one
thing for long. Still, she'd be good for at least a couple of hours. "I left a message for Aaron. He might
be coming by with some new birdhouses. Can you
give him a check, please? The book is under the till."

Mom agreed. She also promised to call the contractor to see about getting the upstairs window replaced.

I grabbed my keys and left, knowing that Birds &
Bees and my mother would be well taken care of.
Still, I felt a bit guilty over how much time I was
spending away from my store. When this show was all
over, one way or the other, I vowed to buckle down
and take care of business.

My first stop was the bookstore on the square. "Do
you have books on Ava Turner?" I inquired of the
young woman behind the register.

She swept a lock of long, blond hair behind her
ear. "The actress? Sure. Follow me."

I followed the young lady to a section of books of
local interest. As she walked, my eyes fell on the silver
and turquoise dream-catcher earrings that adorned
her ears.

She waved to an entire row dedicated to the actress. "We may have a few more in the biography section, but because she's local, we keep her stuff up
front."

"Thanks, this is a big help." I studied the titles. Some were bios; others were big coffee-table-style books full of photographs.

"Of course, the Ava Turner Museum also contains a selection of books. If you don't find what you like here, you might try there."

There was a modest Ava Turner Museum dedicated to the silver-screen legend next to Ginger Curry, the Chinese restaurant, around the corner from town square. It had opened in my absence and I'd never been inside.

The clerk slid a book off the shelf. "You won't find this one, though." She handed me the thick hardcover book.

"Ava Turner: The Unauthorized Biography?"

The woman smiled. "It's a popular title. But not," she said, "with Ava Turner. There are some stories told in it that Miss Turner is not very happy about." Her eyes twinkled. "And would just as soon forget, I'll bet."

"You've read it?"

"Yes." She laughed. "The woman led an exciting life once she left Ruby Lake. Far more exciting than mine, I'll tell you that! Did you know she once dated Frank Sinatra?"

I flipped through the book. There were a number of photos as well. "Do you remember if there was anything in here about a murder she was involved in some years ago?"

"Oh, yeah," the young lady drawled. "That was quite a scandal."

I handed her the book. "I'll take it." She rang up my purchase. "I don't need a bag," I said as she pulled one from under the counter. I glanced at my watch. I had an hour before the meeting at the theater. I took my new purchase and walked over to The Coffee and Tea House.

"Everything all right, Amy?" My friend Sherry refilled my coffee mug and pulled up a chair next to mine. "You look like your head is about to explode."

I squeezed my temples. "I feel like it, too." I slammed the book shut.

Sherry studied the cover. "Reading up on our most famous resident?"

"Something like that. Thanks for the coffee." I took a big swallow. "I have to get to TOTS." I could see the front of the theater from the window.

"What's happening with the show?" asked Sherry. "Will you open?"

I stood and placed some money atop the check. "I have no idea," I admitted. "I don't know about anything anymore. You remember the night of the murder?"

"Of course."

"You said Miss Turner was here that evening."

"That's right. Why?"

I shook my head. I had no idea why and said so.

Could Ava Turner have stabbed Patsy Klein— Kleinerman—to death and then walked to The Coffee and Tea House for an alibi?

How had she gotten out of the dressing room? The door had been locked and chained from the inside. Besides, at that point, an unknown assailant had already tried to kill the actress using that board with the nail in it. Could that have been Patsy?

Had the two women become engaged in some sort of deadly cat-and-mouse game? Trying to see who could murder the other first?

I walked slowly to the theater, deep in thought. The front door was unlocked. I found everyone sitting scattered about the seats. Even Chief Kennedy was there. "What are you doing here?" I asked him.

"Lou asked me to say a word."

I took a seat next to Ben Harlan and Dick Feller. They were eyeing Lou Ferris and August Mantooth, who were in the corner of the stage, locked in animated conversation.

"If Mantooth's arms fly any faster, he's going to take flight and hit the rafters," I muttered.

Ben chuckled. "How are you holding up, Amy?"

"Think the show will continue?" Dick sounded nervous.

I craned my neck. I spotted Eli Wallace sitting close to Amy Harlan. On seeing me, she shot me a look so cold it sent an icy dagger clear through my heart. She was dressed to kill in skintight designer jeans and a hot red scoop-neck shirt that looked so tight I feared her breasts would burst free any second. Maybe that was what Eli was hoping for, too.

Nathan Longfellow sat removed from the rest of us, two rows back. Robert LaChance, Mac MacDonald, and T-Bone Crawford, Robert's wrench man and henchman, swaggered down the aisle and took up seats in the front, nearest to the stage.

The black jeans, black leather vest over black T-shirt, and the skull-and-crossbones bandana covering his head gave the mechanic more the look of a rough-and-tumble biker dude than some guy I wanted to trust with my next brake job.

"Glad you could make it," I called to Robert and the mayor. "How was the *hunting* trip?"

"Just fine," said the mayor, looking from Robert to me.

"Tell me, Robert, how do you manage to go shooting with a broken arm? Or did Mac do all the shooting?"

Robert fumed. "Not that it's any of your business, but I couldn't shoot. I only went because our hunting trip had been planned months ago."

Funny that they would have scheduled a camping trip in the middle of show rehearsals. "Where did you go?" I noticed everybody was looking at us now, but I didn't care.

"We rented a cabin in the Smokies."

"Any witnesses?"

"What do I need witnesses for?"

I turned to Jerry. "Did you check their alibis?" Instead of traipsing around in the Smoky Mountains, they might have been skulking around the hills near Ava Turner's estate.

The chief's face turned bright red. "I do not need to check the mayor's alibi," he hissed, sinking down in his seat.

"Come on, Robert." The mayor grabbed his buddy, and they moved to some seats across the aisle. T-Bone nodded to the chief as he passed us and joined his boss.

"Where's Miss Turner?" I asked Ben and Dick.

"I have no idea," answered Ben. The attorney had gone casual today, brown trousers and a white polo shirt. He was trim for his age and elegantly handsome in a quiet way. I could see how my mother might be attracted to him.

A moment later, the great lady herself appeared from behind the stage curtains. Making her grand entrance. Riley led the way. Maybe she could hire him as her bodyguard-slash-chauffeur.

Aaron Maddley was also in the house, seated next to another crew member. I waved, and he actually waved back. Maybe there would be a thaw in our relationship. Such as it was. Paul Anderson plopped down in the empty seat next to him. That wouldn't be good. Who knew what Craig's friend might say about me? None of it good, that was for certain.

Lou paced a moment at the edge of the stage, then clapped his hands. "Thank you for coming, everyone. I know you are all wondering what will happen with *Annie Get Your Gun*."

He paused with a smile. "I'm wondering the same thing myself. Of course, we would all love for the show to continue."

He stopped at the end of the stage, his toes jutting out. "If Chief Kennedy can assure us of our safety." He turned to August. "And our esteemed director agrees to guide us."

Lou unfolded his arm toward Ava Turner. "And if our beloved and beautiful star, Miss Ava Turner, concurs"—he smiled warmly—"perhaps we can continue." He waved to Chief Kennedy.

Kennedy pushed himself up from his seat and began pacing back and forth in front of the stage. He assured us that the killer would be caught and that he was doing everything in his power to protect our star. "Each and every one of you," he added, slapping his holster. "Annie can get her gun," he quipped. "Me, I'm going to get me a murderer."

The room broke out in applause. I even clapped once or twice myself. It was a good act. Too bad I wasn't buying it.

"Does that mean you're close to catching the killer?" Aaron asked.

Several voices chimed in with the same question. Jerry raised his hand to quiet them. "You all know I can't comment on that directly." I saw his eyes land on a man in the audience. It was Lance Jennings from the *Ruby Lake Weekender*. Lance had his pad and pencil in hand and was writing furiously. Obviously, Jerry didn't want to be quoted as saying anything that could make him look bad down the road.

"Come on," cajoled Lance. "Can't you give our readers something?"

"Now, now," interrupted Lou, saving the chief from further inquiry and/or putting his foot in his mouth. "Thank you, Chief." He shook the chief's hand. "What do you all say?" Lou rubbed his hands together in anticipation. "Are we putting on a show?"

In the end, a vote was held and the majority agreed to continue with the production. Personally, as much as I would have been happy to give up show business, I knew it was in the theater's and the town's best interests and had cast my vote, reluctantly, in the affirmative.

I only hoped there would be no more murders. I had no idea what I could do to prevent it, but knew I had to try. If I got hurt in the process, I could only hope somebody found me and succored me the way those two children had that poor, injured towhee.

28

I separated from the group and wandered back-stage. I wanted a fresh look at Ava Turner's dressing room. The hall was well lit. As I approached, I heard noises coming from around the corner. A man was inside the electrical closet. His back was to me. I tiptoed past. I didn't need witnesses.

The door to the star's dressing room was shut. But there was nothing to indicate that the room was off-limits. I wasn't sure I would have let it stop me if there had been. Nonetheless, I rapped lightly on the door. There was no reply. I put my ear to the door and strained to hear.

Deadly silence.

I opened the door and flipped on the light switch. A mop and bucket sat in the middle of the floor. Cleaning supplies, various props, and unmarked cardboard boxes filled the room.

The chair Patsy had been found in had been pushed back up against the makeup dresser. The large wardrobe that Ava had mentioned—the one she suggested may have been moved—sat open. Several of the actress's costume changes hung on the hook. The small, lone window near the ceiling was firmly shut.

Everything looked perfectly ordinary. Perfectly harmless.

Yet a woman had been stabbed to death in this locked room.

"Everything okay?"

I screamed and turned, my hands balled into fists. I lowered them when I saw Cassius "Cash" Calderon, the local contractor, standing in the open doorway. "Oh, it's you, Mr. Calderon."

"Everything okay, Miss Simms?" the big man asked again. "I was working next door and noticed the light on in here." He peered around the room. "Isn't this where . . . you know?"

I nodded.

"I didn't think anybody was allowed in here." Cash was barrel chested, with dark blue eyes and a bristly crew cut. A small brown mole below his left earlobe, the size of a pencil eraser, gave him character. Though I knew he was somewhere between fifty and sixty years old, he was as fit as any forty-year-old. Definitely more fit than I.

Kim had suggested Zumba, but I was thinking more along the lines of organized bird-watching hikes. Why not combine my love of bird-watching with a little heart-healthy exercise? In my book, it beat flailing around in a room full of strangers while trying to cardio-dance to complicated Latin rhythms.

"I was just looking around. What's all this stuff doing in here? This is supposed to be Ava Turner's dressing room."

Cash's black T-shirt bore the name of his construction company, CC CONSTRUCTION. "Not anymore. Lou said she refused to come in here." He pulled a face. "I can't say that I blame her."

"Neither can I," I agreed. There was something macabre about the space.

"That's why Lou's using it as a storage room." He pointed at the wall. "I'm fixing up the electric panel and repairing the walls from the fire. That's why I moved some of the stuff from there over to here for now."

"That's good. Now that the theater is staying open, Lou says the repairs have to be made before he can officially open for business. That reminds me," I said, "I have a window in my apartment that needs replacing. Did Mom call you?"

Cash dug his cell phone from the pocket of his jeans. "No, not yet, anyway." He thumbed through his phone, checking his calendar. "I can stop by in a couple of days, if that works for you?"

I said it did. I wiped a line of sweat from my brow. "I hope you'll get the AC issues around here straightened out."

Cash pulled a face. "We'll see. Mr. Ferris still says he can't afford the repairs. But I keep telling him, he can't afford *not* to make the repairs."

The contractor stamped his right foot against the floor. "The basement is crisscrossed with ancient duct work. Not to mention the plumbing and electrical." He shook his head. "I've been a contractor for over thirty years and it scares *me* to go down there. It's a wonder this whole place doesn't collapse on itself."

"That bad, huh?" I expressed my hopes that the contractor could work his miracles and keep TOTS up and running. "At least see us through the summer season," I said, encouragingly. "Lou will be grateful for anything you can do."

"I'll do my best," the contractor promised. "Well, gotta get back to work," he announced. "I warn you, the electricity will be going out in here in a minute. I have to disconnect the power to the panel while I do a reinstall."

"No problem. I need to get back to the store." I left, but not to go back to the store. I was hoping to catch August Mantooth, aka August Manfred, before he left the theater. I had a couple of questions for the man, and I hoped he would be more forthcoming this time than he had been the last.

As an added inducement, I had the news article I'd discovered in Patsy's motel room in my purse.

The director was in his cubby-sized office, behind an ancient desk, staring at a laptop screen. "Miss Simms," he said, looking up guiltily from his computer. "What do you want?" He closed the lid of his laptop.

I sat on the folding director's chair across from the desk. "I wanted to talk to you about Patsy Klein." I eyed him carefully. "Or should I say Patsy Kleinerman?"

"I have no idea what you are talking about." He pushed back his chair and stood. "Nor do I wish to. So, if you don't mind." He motioned to the door.

I ignored the not-so-subtle hint. "I also wanted to talk to you about this." I unclasped my purse and took out my wallet. I removed the newspaper clipping and smoothed it open on the corner of the desk.

August looked down at the newspaper. His lips moved in silence. He looked at me, then slumped back down in his seat. "Where did you get that?"

"At the Ruby Lake Motor Inn. In Patsy Klein's room."

"But that's not possible," he blustered. "I—" The director stopped himself. He pulled his scarf tighter around his neck. The room was frigid. The contractor was right, the HVAC system needed a complete overhaul.

"You were going to say you searched her room and came up empty-handed?"

August flushed and reached for the newspaper. I was quicker. "Sorry," I said. "I might need this. Something tells me Chief Kennedy might want to read it, too." I had a feeling he was unaware of August Mantooth's somewhat dubious past.

Mantooth folded his arms across his chest as he glared across the desk at me. "Go ahead. I have nothing to hide."

"Not even the fact that you were burgling Miss Klein's room?"

"The door was ajar," he said, unconvincingly. "I was merely making sure all was in order. What were *you* doing there?"

"Let's stop playing games, shall we?" I said, leaning closer. I'd folded the news article and returned it to the safety of my wallet. Though I was now beginning to fear for my own safety. I may not be confronting merely a man accused of financial misconduct; I could be confronting a cold-blooded killer. "I know all about your past and I know all about Patsy Klein, aka Kleinerman. What I don't know is why you murdered her."

August jumped up.

"And why you are trying to murder Ava Turner." I turned and looked at the door, judging the distance and August's poor physical condition. There was every chance I could outrun him.

Of course, if he had a gun, I couldn't outrun a bullet.

Realizing I may have put myself in a difficult and dangerous situation, I rose. It was time to exit stage right.

"Patsy was blackmailing me, if you must know," August confessed suddenly. He tugged at his orange scarf and glanced at the door as if contemplating making a run for it. In the end, he sank into his chair like a deflated balloon.

"She wanted money?"

His big, sad eyes looked at me. "No, she only wanted a job here and there." He turned his attention to his hands. "She was actually good at what she did. So I obliged by getting her backstage work on my shows, everything from costume prep to scenery design. She liked to call herself a Jill-of-all-trades. In any case, it was far cheaper than paying her off or suffering the consequences. This is a small world. If word got out about even a hint of impropriety, my career could have been ruined."

August shook his finger at me. "And if you're thinking of telling Lou Ferris, you can save your breath. I told him myself after the murder."

"So why kill Ava Turner now? How does she fit into this?"

"I didn't kill Patsy and I'm not trying to kill Miss Turner!" cried Mantooth. "You saw me. I was outside with you and the others when Patsy was murdered. Besides," he added, "why would I kill her?"

"Maybe Patsy Klein was tired of small jobs and wanted one big payoff."

August shook his head no. "It wasn't like that. Besides, like you said, Ms. Simms, the killer was really after Ava Turner. Patsy was murdered by mistake. I don't know who is trying to kill Miss Turner. Believe me, I want to keep our star alive almost as much as Lou does."

I couldn't help smiling. "He does care a lot about the theater."

The director gave me a wry look. "And a lot about Miss Turner."

"Meaning?"

"Meaning I do believe the dear man adores her."

I said I wasn't surprised. "My cousin feels the same way." A sudden thought came to mind. "You don't suppose Lou could have murdered Patsy?"

He smiled in amusement. "Just how would he have managed that, Miss Simms? Lou was farthest from the scene than any of us."

I sighed and rubbed my face. Lou had been on the opposite side of the theater in his office. He'd come running after I'd arrived. How, indeed?

"I suggest you leave finding the killer to your chief of police," said August, grabbing a stack of papers beside him. "Focus on learning your lines. We've got a show to do."

"There still may not be a show unless we can catch whoever it is that is trying to murder your star."

"It seems to me," said August, clearly losing patience, "that more people want Ava Turner alive than dead. So who is our mysterious killer?"

I told him that I wasn't so sure of any of that anymore. I wasn't so sure of anything. I tried coming at the truth from another angle. "So it was Patsy Klein's idea to come here to Ruby Lake and work on *Annie Get Your Gun?*"

August nodded. "She was quite insistent."

I thought for a moment. "Did you know she was really Patsy Kleinerman, the stepdaughter of the man that Ava Turner shot in self-defense?"

August shook his head glumly, pulling his fingers through his thick and curly beard. "Not at all. At least, not until your Chief Kennedy mentioned as much. He told me Patsy was Rex's stepdaughter from a previous marriage."

"Do you think Patsy might have wanted to kill Ava Turner?"

A sick smile crossed the director's face. "I wouldn't be surprised, given the history between the two women. Ava Turner shot and killed Patsy's stepdad, Rex Richardson, in defense of her daughter." His gray eyes hinted at me. "Some say that the real story is quite different than the one that was released to the papers."

I felt a chill run up my arms. "What do you mean?"

He shrugged. "Some say it was Ava's daughter, Lavinia, who shot Rex. That he hadn't been assaulting her at all and was simply trying to take the gun away from her for her own safety." August tapped his temple. "The rumor was that the girl wasn't quite . . . stable."

There was a cold silence in the room, and it wasn't merely the out-of-whack HVAC system.

"Do you think Ava Turner might have murdered Miss Klein? Maybe she discovered the truth about the woman. Or maybe Patsy confronted her and Ava decided that the best way to deal with the woman was to silence her forever?"

August's mouth twisted down. "I don't know," he said, finally, his fingers pressed against the desktop. "But if she did"—he pulled up his brow—"it wouldn't be the first time she'd killed, would it?"

29

I left August Mantooth to his own devices and went in search of Lou. What the director had said about Ava had rocked me to the core. I wanted to see what, if anything, Lou could corroborate about what August had said. If there was one thing I knew about people in general, and men in particular, it was that they were not above lying when it suited them.

The sign thumbtacked to Lou's office door said NO ADMITTANCE, but up ahead I saw T-Bone Crawford open the door and duck inside. What did he want to see the theater manager about? He'd be more likely to want a word with the show's director.

I tiptoed to the door and pressed my ear against it. I didn't hear a thing. Not even a murmur. Very funny. I tried the door. It wasn't locked, so I went in.

"Lou?"

T-Bone Walker stood behind Lou's desk. There was a glistening knife in his hand that he was using to attempt to pry open the side desk drawer.

"Hey, what are you—"

T-Bone snarled and lunged across the desk for me.

I would have screamed, but I never got the chance. I dodged to the right and rolled a wobbly office chair at him. He bellowed and chased me behind the desk.

T-Bone lunged for me once more. This time, I did yell. At the top of my lungs. "Help! Help!"

I didn't know what good it would do. Lou Ferris's office was clear over on the other side of the theater, away from the dressing rooms. Away from where big, strong Cash Calderon was working on the electrical panel.

I grabbed anything and everything in reach and started throwing the whole lot at him. Books, pens, lamps, the telephone book, a portable radio, and stuff I barely comprehended before it left my hands. But it all either missed horribly or bounced off the over-muscled monster harmlessly.

"Stop moving!" snarled the ex-con. "You're only making it tougher on yourself."

"That's funny," I said, near breathless, as I swung around the desk to evade the point of his knife once again. "I thought I was keeping myself alive."

T-Bone hissed and dodged to the left. Unfortunately, I'd dodged to my right, which put me directly in his path. "Ha!" His eyes filled with fire and mirth.

I drove the heel of my shoe into his foot and he howled. I retreated behind the desk again and watched with terror—and a little bit of joy—as the big man hopped awkwardly on one foot, bellowing with rage.

Sadly, he hadn't dropped the knife.

"Is that what you told Patsy Klein, or should I say

Kleinerman?" I was shouting now. Partly because my adrenaline was running uncontrollably. Partly because I hoped somebody, anybody, would hear the commotion and come running, like the cavalry to the rescue. "That if she didn't put up a struggle it wouldn't hurt as much when you stabbed her to death?!"

"Shut the hell up!" he screamed at the top of his lungs.

I caught a movement out of the corner of my eye. Lou came in, put a finger to his lips. I tried desperately not to give any indication that the other man was in the room. If T-Bone caught sight of Lou, we'd both be dead. As it was, I couldn't imagine what the doughy theater manager could do for either of us. My eyes pleaded with him to run and call the police.

But Lou was crouching now, like a sandpiper preparing to descend on a small crab. Soundlessly, his hands wrapped around the black motorcycle helmet on the floor next to the door.

"You'll never get away with this!" I shouted in a desperate attempt to keep T-Bone's eyes on me. What the devil did Lou hope to accomplish? My arms were shaking as I clutched Lou's desk chair before me as a shield.

If he was planning on stealing the man's helmet, he'd only make him all the madder!

"I am going to cut you, b—"

T-Bone Crawford never got to finish his sentence. Lou drove the motorcycle helmet down on the biker's head. He went down like a proverbial dead duck.

I felt the floor shake as his dead weight hit the ground. "Lou, Lou!" I shouted, running out from behind the desk. "Thank you!"

Lou let the helmet fall to the ground. It hit T-Bone's back and rolled across the rug.

"I don't know what I—"

And then the lights went out.

30

"What the hell?" gasped Lou. I heard him trip over T-Bone's inert body.

"Don't worry," I said, using my hands to feel around in the dark, windowless office. "It's probably Mr. Calderon. He told me he was going to have to turn off the power while he works on the electric panel."

I could hear Lou fumbling around in his desk drawers. "Why didn't he tell me? I'm the one paying the bills after all. Besides, I told him not to worry about it today." A drawer slammed. Another fell to the floor.

"What are you doing?"

"Looking for a flashlight," explained Lou. "I know there's one here someplace."

"Shouldn't we be calling the police?"

Lou must have stopped because the commotion ceased. "Of course," he said, finally. "I don't have my phone. Can I borrow yours?"

I nodded, though I don't know why. If I couldn't

see him, he couldn't see me. I dug out my phone and placed it in Lou's hands. Fortunately, not a peep was coming from the fallen ex-con. Soon to be new-con. I'd known there was something fishy about that guy. While I was all for helping reformed criminals, my intuition had told me that T-Bone wasn't interested in going down the straight and narrow path.

Lou's face lit up in the glow of my phone. His fingers hesitated over the screen.

"Just dial 9-1-1," I said. I was concerned that fear had taken over and that the poor guy was falling into shock. "Want me to do it?"

"No, I've got—"

"Shush. Listen." I strained to hear. "What is that?"

"I don't hear anything," wheezed Lou. His face was ashen with ugly red blotches.

"That sounds like somebody shouting. . . ." I slowly turned around. There was a faint glow coming from behind a door behind the desk. I worked my way over to it. "Hey, I think there's a light on down here." I jiggled the handle. The door stuck. "What's in here?"

"Nothing," replied Lou. "It's a closet."

I jiggled the door once more, then pulled with both hands. The door flew toward me.

I found myself looking at a steep wooden stairway leading down. "Hey, I thought you said this was a closet? This looks like it leads to the basement."

"I thought you meant the other one." Lou fiddled with the phone. "I can hardly see a thing."

"Help! Help!" The muffled cry came from below.

"Somebody's down there!" I cried, chills running up my spine. "I'm going down."

"No!" returned Lou. "It may not be safe. Mr. Calderon said we shouldn't go in the basement."

I ignored Lou and started down the stairs. The warm glow cast by a couple of candles on the bare concrete floor provided just enough light to see.

"Help!" Pause. "Is somebody there?" It was a woman's voice.

I reached the bottom of the stairs and stopped to collect my bearings. Cash Calderon was right. The basement was a mishmash of rusted metal ductwork, drooping electrical wiring, and seeping plumbing. "Hello?" My voice was absorbed by the black ominous space.

It was a good thing I did not believe in monsters. Nonetheless, I was keeping my eyes open. If Dracula was lurking down here, I didn't want him sucking a pint of blood from my neck.

In several spaces, the basement had been roughed out with two-by-fours and Sheetrock to create smaller rooms. Cobwebs decorated the dark, damp space like some cheesy Hollywood movie set.

"Hello?" I whispered. "Is anybody here?" I found myself rubbing my itchy neck, checking for fang marks.

After a moment, I heard a rattle emanate from a thick wooden plank door. A single white candle on a saucer flickered weakly beside it. "Who's there?" The woman's voice sounded both hopeful and fearful.

"It's me, Amy Simms." I skipped to the door. "Hold on!"

There was a simple steel pin placed through a metal latch. I pulled it free with a twist, and the woman came tumbling out. "Miss Turner!"

The actress looked dazed and weak but otherwise unharmed. Her white dress was covered in dirty smudges.

At the sound of hippopotami stampeding down the narrow stairs, we both looked up. "I told you not to come down here!" Lou shouted with an anger I hadn't known he was capable of. He was carrying a small gauge rifle, a twenty-two as far as I could tell.

Lou raised the rifle at us. "Now look what you've made me do!"

I did the only thing I could think of. I kicked the candle and shoved the actress back inside her makeshift cell. The gun exploded and the bullet pinged as it shattered the cement block a foot from me. I dropped to the floor as Lou spun in fury. Two more shots ricocheted around the basement like angry hummingbirds.

On hands and knees, I scurried madly, my shoulder brushing the wall, in a desperate attempt to reach the second candle. Another bullet exploded above me, and bits of debris hit me in the face.

I launched myself forward and blew out a breath like I was blowing out the biggest birthday candle the world had ever seen.

If this didn't work and I couldn't find a way out of this mess, it would be the last candle I ever blew out!

Moving as quietly as possible, I turned myself around. I couldn't see a thing. Then again, neither could Lou. Not a peep came from Ava Turner. I hoped she kept quiet. It was probably the only thing keeping her alive.

"Miss Turner," Lou said, plaintively, "please don't be alarmed. I would never do anything to hurt you. I love you. You must know I love you!"

What on earth? Lou had lost his mind!

I scurried across the hard surface, my hands searching blindly, desperately for something I could use as a weapon. "Is that how you show somebody you love them?" I yelled at the top of my lungs. "By locking them in a basement closet?" Please, please let there be somebody up above who heard us.

"Quiet!" screamed Lou. He fired blindly. "It was for her own protection. It was for your own protection, Ava!"

"Who's going to protect her from you, Lou?" I shouted.

"Not you!" He fired again.

"Careful," I taunted. "You might hit your love, Ava!" Was I as crazy as Lou? I'd gotten him so worked up he was shooting blindly. Ava and I were both at risk of being shot and killed.

"No!" Lou bellowed with rage. "Miss Turner, are you all right? Please, talk to me. Tell me that you love me and I can make everything right for you." His breath came out in ragged snatches. "I will take care of you!"

I had worked myself up close now. I could sense Lou's legs right in front of me and, from the sound of his voice, I knew he had his back to me.

I swallowed purposefully and extended my arms. If I could get him to lose his balance, maybe he'd drop the rifle and Ava and I could run for help.

I threw myself at Lou's knees, grabbed his calves and yanked.

Lou screamed in surprise. But things didn't turn out the way I'd planned. Lou fell on top of me. I heard the rifle clatter to the ground.

I reached for it in the dark. I felt Lou's hand instead, gripping the barrel. I climbed over his belly and grabbed the barrel too.

Lou pulled and I pulled back. I didn't know how long I could keep up this lopsided wrestling match. The theater manager was bigger and stronger than me.

The lights came on suddenly. We both winced as the bulbs overhead illuminated our battle. Lou started to sit up and I slammed my free elbow into his flabby chin. He dropped his hold on the rifle and wrapped both hands around my exposed neck.

My heart froze in fear as his fingers pressed into my soft flesh. Everything was looking blurry and dark.

I heard steps running. Hands snatched the rifle from my fingers as if it were a toy.

"Let her go."

Lou's grip fell from my neck. As my vision cleared, I saw Cash Calderon standing to one side of Lou. The barrel of the rifle was pressed against his skull.

31

"Thanks for bringing the kids, Derek." I snapped the lid back on the potato salad and returned it to the picnic basket. I halfheartedly shooed a fly away from my tuna sandwich and took a bite.

"My pleasure." Derek was stretched out on the red and orange checked picnic blanket, propped up on his elbows. He looked decidedly un-lawyer-like but no less handsome in a navy-blue T-shirt, khaki shorts, and sneakers.

"Hey, what are you putting that potato salad away for?" growled Karl. "I could use seconds."

"Of course," I said. I plopped a generous scoop of Mom's potato salad onto Karl's paper plate, though I knew full well the ex-chief of police had passed seconds several servings ago.

"Me, too," said Floyd. "*Please*," he added. He was looking at his friend when he said it. Floyd held out his plate as I filled it.

"More lemonade?" Both men nodded.

"Any for you?" I said, turning my attention to Derek.

"Nope." He patted his flat belly. "All full up."

Derek's daughter, Maeve, and her friend Will sat with their legs crossed on the grass. The small cage containing the now-recuperated towhee rested between them.

I noticed Ms. Bryant with a T looking at us from behind a holly bush. I waved for her to come join us, and she took off in the other direction.

"Well, I suppose it's about time, kids."

"Can I do it?" asked Maeve, blue eyes wide with hope and anticipation.

"It's okay with me if it's okay with Will," I replied.

"I'll hold the cage," Will said.

Smiling wide, Derek's daughter spoke softly to the towhee. "Okay, Sammy. You are all better. So you go fly free. Find your family or find a new one to adopt you." The little towhee hopped toward the open door. She waved her finger at him. "And please try not to get hurt again."

The towhee cocked his eye at her. Sammy hesitated at the door, his claws grasping the lip. Suddenly, he fluttered his wings and flew upward.

Maeve and Will were jumping up and down, shouting words of encouragement. We watched as Sammy circled the lawn several times then landed on the bird feeder, the one that I'd brought from Floyd's old house. He snatched a sunflower and carried it over to a nearby pine, where he worked the nut free.

I noticed tears pooling up in Floyd's eyes, but I wasn't going to say anything. Karl saw them too and even he kept his mouth shut. Quite a feat for the garrulous old man.

I sighed wistfully.

"Everything okay?" asked Derek, sitting up beside me, his shoulder brushing mine.

"Huh?" I blushed. "Oh, sure." What was I going to say? That I suddenly wondered when I would be a wife and mother? Watching children of my own play on the lawn? Going on picnics? I forced a smile. "Hey, how about some blueberry crumb pie? You've got to have room for some of my Aunt Betty's blueberry pie."

"That definitely sounds too good to pass up." He rubbed his hands in anticipation.

"Me, too!" said Karl, scooting closer, even as he wolfed down the rest of his potato salad.

I chuckled and cut slices for all of us. I gave Will and Maeve generous slices.

"Thanks again for everything, Amy," Floyd said between mouthfuls, his lips and tongue a pleasant purple. "The residents love the feeders."

"Yeah," said Karl, who had already wiped his plate clean, "even the administration has decided it's a good thing."

"They've added a bird identification book to the center's library." Floyd's eyes were on the feeder as he ran his fingers through his beard.

I patted his other hand lovingly. "I'm happy for you."

"What about you?" asked Floyd. "What's going to happen to Birds and Bees?"

I sighed heavily. "I'm not sure." I'd done what I could. Hopefully, the townspeople would rally around the idea of keeping the old house at the corner and not allowing the redevelopment that a handful of others so desperately were pushing for.

"I'd hate to see you lose the place," added Derek. "But I'm not sure what more we can do." He explained how he'd searched through all the town rules and regulations and even dug through the building records going back a hundred years.

"If it's any consolation," he said, "if they do demolish your house, your ex-boyfriend and his partner will lose a portion of their outdoor patio."

My back stiffened. "They will?" I noticed my hand was clutched around his forearm. Since he wasn't complaining, I didn't remove it. "How come?"

"Their business sits a couple of feet over on your property. The previous owners of both your property and the brew pub signed an agreement years ago granting the business use of your land. That outdoor space had been undeveloped land before the garden center began operating business there. That agreement ended when Gertrude Hammer sold the property to you."

I squeezed his arm tighter. "Are you sure?"

Derek shrugged. "As sure as can be. Why? It's not exactly good news."

I smiled and kissed him on the cheek. "I wonder . . ."

Floyd rose and dusted off the crumbs off his trousers.

"Where are you going?" demanded Karl.

"The feeders are getting low."

"Sit back down. I want to hear what happened when you nabbed those killers, Amy. You and your boyfriend can play kissy-face later."

My face heated up and I released Derek's hand.

Derek chuckled. "I wouldn't mind hearing myself. I've only heard bits and snatches. And even those bits came from Dad, who got his information from Chief Kennedy."

"Well," I began, warming to my subject, replaying the events in my mind like I was reliving a Broadway show, "at first I was certain that Patsy Klein had been murdered by mistake."

"In the wrong place at the wrong time," interjected Floyd. "I remember you saying that."

I nodded. "But I couldn't figure out why. Then, the more I talked to people, the more I learned, the more confused I got. I couldn't come up with any reason that anyone would want to murder Ava Turner.

"Then, when I learned that Patsy had been blackmailing August Mantooth, I started wondering if I had been wrong about my original theory."

"You started thinking that Patsy had been killed on purpose," said Karl, "by this August Mantooth fellow."

"Or somebody else," suggested Derek. "From what you and Dad have told me, plenty of people Miss Klein worked with disliked her immensely. Including your cousin Rhonda."

"She'd made a fool out of Eli Wallace and tangled with Nathan Longfellow just to name two," Karl said. "Right, Amy?"

"That's right. She seemed to be a real trouble-maker. Chief Kennedy told me they'd found several of the missing items from the theater in her room afterward."

"I'll bet she was responsible for all those accidents

around the theater," said Karl. "I've seen my share of loonies, I'll have you know."

"Be quiet and let Amy tell it," complained Floyd.

"You're right, Karl," I said in response to his earlier remarks. "I did suspect August. When I confronted him, he said he had been on the phone with his agent the entire time. He couldn't have murdered Patsy."

"Was he telling the truth?" asked Derek.

"According to Chief Kennedy, yes. August Mantooth had been on the phone with his agent in New York the entire time. The agent swears to it. Besides, we know now that Lou Ferris had murdered Patsy after all."

"I still don't get why," Floyd said, scratching his head. "She didn't mean anything to him."

"No," I agreed. "But Ava Turner did. Lou was completely smitten with her." I explained that police had found his home overflowing with memorabilia related to the actress and her career.

"Dad said Lou Ferris was on the board of trustees of the Ava Turner Museum."

I nodded. "Not only that, he was the driving force behind getting the museum set up in the first place."

"All for the love of a woman," sighed Floyd.

"Sick obsession, more like it." I looked at Floyd out of the corner of my eye. Was the dear man missing his wife?

"She is a real beauty," Karl said with a wink.

"I don't know if Lou figured out who Patsy Klein really was—the stepdaughter of the actor Miss Turner shot and killed twenty years ago.

"But he confessed to Ava, when he had her under

lock and key, that he'd discovered that it was Patsy who was causing all the trouble at TOTS. First it was little things, like disrupting the show and some petty thievery. Then it escalated to sabotage and attempted murder."

"Like the rigged curtain rod that fell on LaChance and that Sampson woman," Karl interrupted once more.

"That's right. Lou told Ava that he'd seen Patsy descending from the catwalk above the stage moments after the incident. That's when he said he knew he had to get rid of her for good. And remember, witnesses say it fell only a foot from where Miss Turner was standing."

"So obviously it was intended for her." Derek waved to his daughter, who was doing cartwheels on the grass. "A blow on the head from that height could have been lethal."

I concurred. "Lou couldn't let it go on. He decided that the only way to save the show and, more importantly, Ava Turner, was to murder Patsy before she succeeded in doing away with Ava."

"Why didn't Lou tell the police what was going on?" asked Karl, the ex-cop.

"Who knows?" I answered. "Maybe he was afraid that without any evidence, the police wouldn't take him seriously. Ava might have been killed before Chief Kennedy took any real action."

"I still don't understand how he did it, Amy," Floyd said. "You said it was a locked dressing room."

"It was," I explained. "But there was a trapdoor under the wardrobe that led down to the basement. Having been at TOTS forever, Lou knew every inch of the place. And, as I discovered, there's an entrance to the basement from Lou's office." That explained why Lou had refused to let Cash go down in the basement to work on the HVAC system.

Floyd expressed surprise. "Trapdoor?"

I nodded. "With one of those folding stairs attached."

"I know what you mean," said Floyd. "We had one of those going up to our attic."

"Before it was a dressing room," I explained, "the room had been part of a larger storeroom with access to the basement for convenience. We didn't see the trapdoor earlier because of the Persian rug and wardrobe on top of it." Lou had maneuvered the big, wheeled wardrobe over the trapdoor some days after the murder in an effort to keep its existence secret. "The way the rug was positioned, it simply flopped back into place once he'd stabbed Patsy and used the trapdoor to make his escape."

"No one would think to look for a murderer under a rug," quipped Karl.

"And all Lou had to do was go from his office, through the basement—" began Derek.

"And up into Ava Turner's locked dressing room!" finished Karl.

Floyd pulled a face. "What about the gun?"

I shrugged. "Lou admitted that he'd fired the gun. He wanted everyone to go to the dressing room. And he wanted to provide himself with an alibi. He was seen coming from his office."

"Clever," admitted Floyd. "Lou stabbed Patsy Klein to death to keep her from harming Miss Turner. . . ."

Floyd plucked at a blade of grass and stuck it between his lips.

"He had taken Ava's phone himself," I said.

Karl asked, "So Lou was the one who sent that text
from Ava's phone saying how she was going to kill
herself?"

"Yep," I replied. "You have to hand it to Lou. He
was pretty adept at creating confusion. He could
have killed Patsy anytime, anywhere. But he chose to
create an intriguing scene."

"All those years in show business must have
rubbed off on him," suggested Karl. "Man thought
he was staging a show."

I nodded. "Instead, he was staging a murder."

"And, don't forget," said Derek after we were all
silent for a moment, "he planted the murder weapon
in the dressing room locker days after."

"And he went around taking potshots at Miss
Turner!" Floyd said quickly, beating Karl to the punch.

I nodded. "Again, clever. When he saw that folks
thought that Ava Turner was the intended victim, he
milked it for all it was worth. Instead of looking for
motives for Patsy Klein's murder, we were looking for
someone trying, still trying, to murder Ava."

"That's why he took shots at her out in her garden
and she didn't get hurt."

"Yep. He was even following her the night she
came by my apartment. He shot my window after
she'd left." Lou, despite his harmless-looking appearance, had once been in the Navy and was an expert
shot. That explained the tattoo swallow I'd first noticed on his wrist. He'd had it done in the Navy. The

swallow is supposed to be good luck for sailors. Lou was going to need all the luck he could get now. "In the end, Lou decided the only way to really protect Ava was to lock her up. He locked her in the basement at TOTS and was planning to take her back to his house that night. He left her there with nothing but a couple of candles burning so nobody would notice the lights, a bottle of water, and a box of crackers."

"Talk about crackers," quipped Karl. "Lou Ferris is as cracked as it gets."

"Maybe that will be his defense," suggested Derek.

"What about when Miss Turner got smacked in the head with that board with the nail in it?" asked Karl. "Patsy did that?"

I shook my head. "Actually, Ava admitted that she'd done that herself."

"She did?" There was disbelief in Derek's voice. "Why?"

I arched my brow. "According to her, she did it to *create drama.*" I formed air quotes with my fingers.

"Actresses." Floyd chuckled. "That explains why she didn't really get hurt. Only the very tiniest of knots on her skull."

"If you ask me, a man's got to be unhinged to do all the things Lou Ferris did for a woman." Karl wiggled his cane.

"I don't know about that," replied Derek. "Not that I'm suggesting anything so extreme as murder, but for the right woman, there are a lot of things a man might consider."

I blushed and turned aside. Was he talking about me?

"Kennedy tells me they've transferred Lou to the county jail," Karl said.

"Good. He and T-Bone Crawford can share a cell."

Derek ruffled my hair. "That was crazy, what you did. Confronting T-Bone like that."

I laughed. "I didn't know I would be confronting him. Believe me! If I had known I was going to stumble across him breaking into Lou's desk, I would have run the other way!"

"Good to know," replied Derek. "He could have killed you."

"Him and Lou both." Floyd broke a bit of crust loose from the pie tin. "It was a good thing Mr. Calderon showed up."

I nodded. I owed the man my life.

"What was T-Bone doing in Lou's office in the first place?" asked Karl.

"It seems he overheard Lou saying to someone how he kept the receipts for sales, both cash and checks, in a drawer in his desk. I guess T-Bone thought a little extra cash was too good a thing to pass up."

"What about the show, Amy?" wondered Floyd. "Are we going to get to see you in *Annie Get Your Gun*?"

"Yeah," teased Derek. "Are we?"

"I'm afraid so," I groaned. I explained how August was staying on to direct the show. Aaron Maddley had agreed to run the theater operations until the town could find someone to take on the job on a regular basis.

The good news for The Theater On The Square's fans was that Ruby Lake officials had decided not only to keep the theater open, but to give it a complete renovation. It seemed they had finally become convinced of the benefits of keeping the historic old theater around.

"I can't wait to see you act," Floyd said.

"I can't wait to hear you sing!" snorted Karl.

I glared at Derek. "And you?"

"I can't wait to watch you . . . dance?"

I swiveled my finger at the three of them. "All I can say is, I better hear all three of you clapping," I said sternly. "Loudly."

32

After we'd cleaned up the remains of our picnic and dropped our gear in the trunk of Derek's car, he gave me a ride back to Birds & Bees.

"Come inside for a cup of coffee?" I offered, picnic basket dangling from my elbow as I stood on the curb.

Derek's eyes bounced off the *biergarten*, where workers were busy setting up tables. The place must be getting close to opening. Thank goodness. "No, I'd better get back to the office."

My spirits fell. "Are you sure?"

He looked toward Birds & Bees. "I'm sure."

I turned to go. Derek's hand on my arm stopped me, pulled me back. "What—" He didn't give me a chance to finish my sentence, but I didn't mind. His lips met mine. My eyes closed and my body heated up. After a moment, he released me.

"Call you later?" he asked.

I nodded numbly and watched as Derek drove off.

A little voice inside my head told me that he hadn't wanted to come in because he didn't want to run into Craig. Another little voice told me that if he kissed me like that again and didn't do anything about it, I was going to need a cold shower.

Another little voice told me that Craig had to go. And soon.

I set the picnic basket, blanket, and cooler behind the front counter. Mom was ringing up a sack of bird food. "Hi, Mom."

"Hello, dear. How was the picnic?"

"Heavenly," I replied.

"What?"

I laughed to cover my embarrassment. "I mean, good." I could still feel the warmth of Derek's lips on mine and the aftereffects of what the kiss had done to me. It had been a long time since I'd had a man in my life. "How are you doing, Mom?" I gave her a gentle pat on the back. "Holding up?"

Mom ran a finger through her limp hair. "A little tired, actually. It's been crazy around here."

"Sorry about that." I looked around the store. "Where's Kim? Where's Aunt Betty?" Both were supposed to be helping out. Neither was in sight.

Mom said good-bye to her customer. "Kim had to run out. Randy called. Some sort of emergency over at that house they're rehabbing."

"Emergency?"

"Burst plumbing or something."

"And he expects Kim to help?" We both laughed. "What about Aunt Betty?"

"Betty had to leave. She and Sterling had plans."

I felt terrible. Poor Mom, all alone in the shop.

And in her condition, with the muscular dystrophy, it was important that she not overdo things.

"You need to take it easy, Mom." I reached behind and untied her store apron. "Why don't you go upstairs and rest. I've got it from here. You must be exhausted."

"It hasn't been all that bad," countered my mother. She slid her behind onto the stool beside the counter. "Oh, Amy." She grabbed my hands. "I almost forgot! You'll never guess what. It's the most wonderful news!" She laughed with glee. "Don't you think?"

"I might if I knew what that news was," I answered with a grin.

"Of course. Well, the mayor was in here and—"

"Mac? He was in here?"

Mom nodded. "Paul Anderson, too."

"What did they want?"

Mom tapped my arm. "That's what I'm trying to tell you. He said the town has decided to drop the whole eminent domain proceeding on your house."

My eyes grew. "They have?" Mom bobbed her head up and down. "Why?"

She shrugged. "Well, in the first place, they've decided to put a lot of the town's available funds into keeping TOTS open so they don't appear to have the funds required to proceed. In the second place, it seems that they've had a lot of calls, letters, and folks going down to town hall and complaining, urging that the town maintain its historic charm."

A man's voice added, "And not allow a national franchise to set up shop."

I spun around. Paul Anderson stood before us, hands in the pockets of his jeans.

"Hi, Paul. I was just explaining to Amy what you told me."

I cocked my head at the man. "This was your doing?"

"Not exactly. I mean, I can't take credit for it. But I did explain to the town fathers and my fellow planning commission members that it might be in everyone's best interest to keep things as they are. There's nothing wrong with the status quo, is there?"

"Everyone's interest," I said, wrapping Mom's apron around my waist, "including yours?"

Paul shrugged. "Maybe."

"And maybe you know that your *biergarten* is sitting on *my* property."

Paul frowned. "You know about that?"

I nodded silently.

"I'm sure we can come to some sort of arrangement," began Paul.

I smiled. "I'm sure we can. Number one will be keeping your partner as far away from me as possible."

Paul laughed. "Already done. His girlfriend blew into town unexpectedly and he headed back to Raleigh with her. After they spend a few days up in Asheville, that is."

So the jerk had a girlfriend even as he was making renewed moves on me. "Good riddance."

"So we're good here?" Paul asked. He made for the door.

"For the moment," I said, watching him leave. "For the moment." I caught a movement out of the corner of my eye. Esther, in a flowery peach dress and low black heels, was moving up and down the aisles. She had a feather duster in her hand—which just seemed so, so wrong in a shop selling birdseed and gifts for bird lovers—and had a green store apron tied around her front.

"What," I asked my mother, my face scrunching up in disbelief, "is that all about?"

"Huh?"

I pointed to Esther, who was now dusting down the hummingbird feeders. "That," I whispered.

Mom beamed. "Somebody's got to work a few shifts around here." Mom headed for the stairs to our apartment. "After all, Amy dear, you're never around."

"But—"

"You're always off solving mysteries and things."

"But—"

Mom wiggled her fingers in good-bye from the bottom step. "Kim's busy with her business with Randy. And Aunt Betty, well, I don't have to tell you how unreliable she is."

"I know, Mother, but—"

Mom looked at me sideways. "You don't expect me to be on my feet working here day and night, do you?"

I hung my head. "No, Mom."

"Besides you always running around town, you've been saying the shop could use some extra help." Mom slowly disappeared up the steps.

"But Esther?"

"Who better?" Mom called down pleasantly. "She lives here."

I turned to my renter. "But you? I mean, no offense, Esther, but what do you know about birds?"

Esther pulled herself up to her full height. Which

wasn't much. "What's to know? Customers come in and I sell them stuff. I'm no dummy," she said confidently.

"They come in looking for one thing, I try to sell them two!" She held up two fingers of her left hand as proof of concept or something. Maybe she didn't think I could count to two.

Esther walked over to within inches of where I stood and looked up at me. Her breath smelled like cigarettes and chewing gum. "Your mom, Barbara, told me you'd pay me fifteen dollars an hour."

Fifteen dollars an hour? I was pretty sure *I* didn't make fifteen bucks an hour!

"And I don't work Sundays and I don't clean up after no birds."

"There are no birds to clean up after, Esther. This isn't a pet store."

"I'll say," quipped Esther. "You offer benefits?"

"Benefits?"

"I always wanted one of them 401(k)s."

"I don't even have one myself, Esther." And I doubted she even knew what one was.

Esther frowned.

"You know"—Esther raised her voice to match the volume of construction noise that had kicked up next door and was driving a wedge of pain into my skull—"you're lucky I was available to help you."

I smiled weakly. Luck didn't begin to describe it. It wasn't enough that Esther the Pester lived in my house; now she had to work in my store?

Esther stuck out her jaw. "In fact, you never even thanked me."

"Thanked you for what exactly?"

"I got that heap of a camper ticketed, didn't I? What an eyesore!"

I gawped at her. "That was you?"

Cousin Riley suddenly appeared from nowhere.

"Where did you come from?"

Riley jerked his thumb over his shoulder. "I finished putting up those shelves that Aunt Barbara asked me to install in the storeroom."

"Shelves?" I was feeling a bit light-headed.

"Yeah." Riley filled in the details about how my mother didn't think all the stock should be spread inconveniently on the floor, where it was always getting tripped over and one had to stoop down all the time to get to it, so she'd asked him to install some shelving. "Then I'm going to start on refinishing the floors."

I frowned. "Refinishing the floors?"

"Yeah, Aunt Barbara gave me a part-time job. Didn't she tell you?"

I shook my head no. I was feeling a little sick all of a sudden, and I didn't think it was the tuna salad.

"You okay?" asked Riley.

"She looks awful," Esther said. "I had an aunt once who looked like that," she elaborated, waving a crooked gnarly knuckled finger at me, "right before she dropped dead."

"Maybe you should go lie down." Riley felt my forehead.

I walked over to the glass display case and removed a pair of brand-new binoculars. I unknotted the strap and draped the binocs over my neck.

"What are you doing?" asked Riley.

"Where are you going?" demanded Esther, her

hands planted on her hips. She'd stuffed the feather duster down the front of her dress.

I swung the door open and groaned with pleasure as the warm sunshine splashed over me. "Bird-watching," I said with a smile.

I ripped off the apron I suddenly realized I was still wearing and tossed it at Esther with a flourish. "You're in charge!"

Please turn the page for an exciting sneak peek of
J.R. Ripley's next Bird Lover's Mystery
THE WOODPECKER ALWAYS PECKS TWICE
Now on sale!

1

Rat-a-tat-tat-brrr.

I peeked at the clock on the bedside table: 6:30 a.m. As usual. "Good morning to you, too," I said with a groan. I sat up. My feet bounced around on the pine floor in search of my pink slippers.

Rat-a-tat-tat-brrr. The sound was loud and dissonant—hardly the stuff of "Peachum's Morning Hymn" from *The Threepenny Opera.*

I came to my feet and rubbed my fists into my eyes. "You're killing me, bird." It had been a late night. I'd had a real, honest-to-goodness date with Derek Harlan. Dinner and a movie, the whole nine yards. Now if I could have only followed it up with nine hours of sleep. Heck, I'd have settled for six, but it hadn't been in the cards.

Rat-a-tat-tat-brrr. The bird could've used a music lesson from Kurt Weill.

Nonetheless, I crossed to the dresser and picked up my binoculars, determined to get a better look at him. I removed the tethered lens covers, pulled the

curtains, and brought the binocs to eye level. There
he was, a beautiful red-bellied woodpecker, clinging
to the gray bark of the big bitternut hickory outside
my bedroom window, tapping away at the twisted hol-
low branch hanging closest to the house.

Waking me up, like he did every morning lately—
the relentless pounding reverberating across my
skull as if he were perched on my head and not in
the tree. The woodpecker wasn't tapping to drive me
crazy. He—and I recognized the bird as a male by the
intense red coloration on the back of his neck and
top of his head; a female only has the red coloration
adorning its neck—was tapping to drive out carpen-
ter ants and other insects. In other words, breakfast.

I moved the binoculars out over the street toward
Ruby Lake. There was a doozy of a storm brewing.
The sky was the color of lead with streaks of black
running like watercolor down a page. Jagged bolts of
lightning streaked across the distant sky.

The woodpecker went about its business, oblivious
to the storm. When a bird's got to eat, a bird's got to
eat. Don't ask me why it was named a red-bellied
woodpecker when it was the bird's head that was the
most clearly and visibly colored red. A small patch of
red is distinguishable on a red-bellied woodpecker's
lower belly but that's all. Perhaps it was because the
scientists had already proclaimed another woodpecker to be the red-headed woodpecker. First come,
first served. I was no ornithologist. I had been an
English major in college and now run a small-town
store selling birdwatching and feeding supplies.

I scanned the distant treetops, wondering if I might

spot any other interesting or unusual bird species this morning. There was no avian activity to be seen along the shoreline. Generally, I would spot duck, kingbirds, swamp sparrows, and the occasional swallow flying low across Ruby Lake.

A small motor-powered fishing boat sat alone in the lake, bobbing side to side in the windblown water. I searched the woods for signs of bird life. With the heavy clouds blocking the sun, there was little to see besides shadows. Lately, a pair of red-shouldered hawks had spent early mornings settled on the broad limbs of a tall oak whose branches loomed over the water. But not this morning. They seemed to have taken the day off. I suddenly wished I could do the same.

I was about to retreat in search of my own breakfast—I smelled fresh-ground coffee brewing—when my eyes fell on the old McKutcheon house. The McKutcheons had been one of the Town of Ruby Lake's first families, having settled in our small North Carolina town back in the early 1800s. The house was nearly that old—even older than the late nineteenth century home that now housed both me and my business, Birds & Bees. Though much of the original McKutcheon house had burned to the ground in the 1890s, family members had rebuilt the house and barn and added various other outbuildings around the turn of the century.

Then, fortunes failing, the McKutcheon house had sat empty for decades when the last members of the family moved to Boston, or so I seemed to remember hearing. But there was a light on in one of the upstairs windows now. Wisps of smoke fought to rise from the central chimney against the onslaught of rain abruptly falling in heavy sheets.

I heard a flutter and turned. My woodpecker friend shook himself to rid his feathers of raindrops, then returned to digging into the hickory bark.

I trained my eyes once more on the McKutcheon house. The light coming from the upstairs window danced like flame, but I knew this to be a trick of the rain, which blurred and bent the light until it looked almost alive. I was about to turn away, when a man stepped into view. At least, I thought it was a man. It was really too dark to be certain at first. I was too far away. The rain was falling too hard.

A second, smaller shape stepped into view. He, if it was a he, moved quickly, arms flailing. A slouchy, gray beanie capped the top of his head. The larger man threw up his arms as if to ward off an impending blow.

It wasn't a blow that came next. It was a full steam attack. The smaller man launched himself at the larger one as if to tackle him. Both fell in a heap. I gasped. What were the two fighting about?

They disappeared from sight, the window ledge blocking my view. A moment later, one of the men's heads came into view. He crossed the floor on his knees, stood and opened the window.

What on earth was he up to?

My hands were shaking as I tried to see what would happen next. The glasses were bouncing so much, the room jumped in and out of my sight. I squeezed my elbows against my ribs to steady the binoculars and narrowed in on the room once more.

The smaller man threw open the window and hoisted something up over the sill. I fiddled with the binocs' focus, trying to get a sharper look. I now realized what I was seeing. A pair of legs dangled over the window ledge, nothing more distinguishable than a pair of charcoal trousers with two bare feet protruding.

Rat-a-tat-tat-brrr! My heart skipped a beat.

The smaller man stooped and lifted the other man, pushing him up. The larger man put up no struggle. Was he unconscious? Was he dead?

A moment later, the smaller man heaved. His victim fell silently, tumbling like a sack filled with wet straw, from the upstairs window to the ground below. If he wasn't dead before, he most certainly was now.

I gasped. The startled red-bellied woodpecker took flight. I ran to the phone.

2

"What on earth?" my mother exclaimed as I came running into the kitchen.

"Phone!" I cried. "Where's the phone?"

Mom set the coffee carafe back on the warming plate. "Right here." She lifted the portable phone from the base on the corner of the counter and handed it to me.

The landline doubled as the Birds & Bees business line. I punched in 911 and reported what I'd seen. Mom looked at me gape-jawed.

I dropped the phone on the counter and pressed my face against the cool window. The rain was letting up. If I turned my head just right, I could make out the McKutcheon house from this vantage.

Mom poured two cups of coffee and handed one to me. She cinched her robe around her waist, sat and motioned for me to do the same. "You saw some man throw another man out a window?" There was shock, surprise, and maybe a smidgen of disbelief in her voice.

My hand trembled as I lifted the cup to my lips and sipped. "Yes. I mean, at first I wasn't sure what I was seeing. But it was definitely a couple of people fighting." I took a steadying drink. The coffee was black and unsweetened but I didn't mind for a change.

Mom broke off a piece of her breakfast cookie. "At the McKutcheon house? Across the lake?"

I nodded and glanced out the window. How long would it take the police to reach the house?

"I thought the old place was empty," Mom said. "What were you doing looking at the McKutcheon house?"

I turned back to my mother. I felt terrible to be causing her any concern or alarm. Mom's got muscular dystrophy and, though it is still very manageable, I was concerned for her health and didn't want to say or do anything that might cause her undue stress.

Unfortunately, in practice, I seemed to be doing the opposite despite my good intentions. "I'm sure it's nothing." I patted Mom's hand. "Jerry will get it all sorted out." Jerry Kennedy was Ruby Lake's chief of police. I didn't exactly have the highest opinion of him, but then, his opinion of me wasn't exactly the stuff upon which friendships are formed.

I explained to Mom how I had picked up the binoculars to watch our resident alarm clock, then happened to be perusing Ruby Lake for further bird sightings. I kept a chalkboard behind the counter in the store where I and anyone else could post local bird sightings on a weekly basis.

"Ah, Drummy." Mom smiled. Drummy was the name we'd given to what we had come to think of as *our* woodpecker. After all, if he was going to come around every morning, noon, and night giving us a solo drum performance, he might as well have a name.

Curses are much more personal if you can attach a name to them.

Mom slid the package of breakfast cookies my way. She'd begun eating one of the prepackaged oatmeal raisin cookies each morning with her coffee since discovering them in the cereal aisle in the market a month ago.

I declined. "I don't think I could eat a thing." My stomach was churning. I thrummed my fingers against the kitchen table as I glanced at the clock on the wall. "How long do you think before we hear something?"

"You need to be patient, Amy." Mom is a retired high school teacher and still knows how to talk to me, when necessary, like I'm a troubled teenaged student in need of a calming, steadying, grown-up in-fluence, instead of the mature thirty-four-year-old woman my driver's license claims I am. Dad passed away a while back and Mom and I shared the third-floor apartment above Birds & Bees. "I'm sure Jerry will call us the minute he has the situation under control."

I stood and began pacing. "I don't think I can stand to wait."

Mom grinned. "I can call Anita if you like." Anita Brown is one of my mother's best friends, pinochle partner and, more importantly in this case, part-time dispatcher for the Ruby Lake Police Department. If anybody else knew what was happening, Anita would.

The doorbell interrupted my answer. I opened the door. "Esther?" Esther Pilaster, or "Esther the Pester" and "Esther Pester" as I sometimes interchangeably referred to her, was a tenant of mine. She came with the house when I bought it and, until her lease was up, I was stuck with her. Her apartment was on the second floor of Birds & Bees.

"You've got company," snapped Esther. Esther is a long-in-the-tooth spinster in her seventies. Narrow shoulders only barely supported the flowery dress she wore. She's a small woman with a hawkish nose, sagging eyelids, and silver ponytail. Wispy white eyebrows topped off a pair of rheumy gray-blue eyes that looked at me funny. "Hey! What's that? Kittens?"

"What?"

She pointed a crooked finger at my pajama top. "Your jammies are covered in kittens." She squinted at me. "I thought you said you didn't like cats?"

I tugged at my pjs and blushed. "I'm allergic to cats, Esther. I never said I didn't like them."

Footsteps pounded up the steps. "What the devil is going on up here?" Chief Kennedy's head appeared at the top of the stairs. His cap was damp and dripping.

"Jerry—Chief Kennedy." I pulled my collar closed.

He took off his cap and thumped it against the side of his thigh. "If you're not coming down, I'm coming up." The chief pushed past me and Esther and into my apartment. "You got coffee?"

"Please"—I cleared my throat—"come on in," I said, hoping the sarcasm wasn't too heavily laced. I wanted to learn what he'd discovered at the McKutcheon house, so this wasn't the time to start sparring with the man.

"Thank you, Esther," I said, turning to my renter. "Shouldn't you be prepping the store for opening? Thank you." I shut the door on her before she could object.

Not only was I stuck with Esther the Pester as a tenant, I was now stuck with her as an employee of Birds & Bees. That was Mom's fault. Mom figured I needed more help around the store, as if she and my best friend, Kim Christy, weren't enough assistance.

To tell the truth, Mom was right. Somehow, I seemed to be spending as much time out of Birds & Bees as I did within. Mom had made the executive decision to hire Esther part-time. As much as it irritated me, it made sense. And, so far, Esther had been a pretty decent employee. Sales were up. I was pretty sure that was because customers were afraid of her. But, hey, a sale's a sale.

"Dammit, Mrs. Simms," I heard Jerry say as I crossed the living room to the kitchen, "I mean, no disrespect, but that daughter of yours is daft as a brush and half as useful!"

"What's that supposed to mean?" I shot back, feeling my pulse quicken. Jerry has a way of making my blood boil faster than most—dropping me in a cauldron of boiling oil wouldn't heat me up any faster than Jerry did. "Name calling? That's the thanks I get for reporting a crime?"

Jerry snorted. "Crime?" His two-tone brown uniform was sodden, especially around the shoulders and cuffs. He'd left a trail of wet footprints across the floor. That meant there'd be mopping in my future today. Oh, joy.

Mom handed Jerry a steaming coffee mug. "Drink this. You'll feel better." Mom had been one of Jerry's teachers in high school. Neither of us would have suspected he'd grow up to be Ruby Lake's chief of police one day. Personally, I wasn't so sure Jerry would ever grow up mentally.

"The only crime is that you wasted a perfectly good morning sending me out on a wild goose chase, Amy Simms!"

I threw out my chest. "Wild goose chase? That's what you call reporting a murder, Jerry?"

Jerry twisted one of the kitchen chairs around and threw himself down in it backwards. He thumped his mug against the table. "There is no crime, Simms."

Mom slid the plate of cellophane-wrapped breakfast cookies the chief's way. She's become a real proponent of them. Jerry wasted no time peeling one out of its wrapper and wolfing it down.

He slapped at his trousers. "My squad car's filthy. I'm filthy. It's storming out, in case you didn't realize. And it's a dirt road out around the lake to the McKutcheon homestead."

Mom took a seat and said calmly, "Tell us what you found, Jerry."

Jerry huffed. "The place is a hostel of some sort."

"Hostile?" I jumped in. "You see? I told you there was something nefarious going on over there."

"I didn't say they were *hostile*." The chief growled. "I said they're running a hostel. H-O-S-T-E-L. All sorts of foreigners and such running around over there."

"You mean like a bed and breakfast?" Mom inquired.

Jerry shrugged. "Young fellow at the door called it a hostel, so hostel it is. Guster McKutcheon is running it. He wasn't home."

"Guster McKutcheon," Mom said thoughtfully. "I'm not sure I remember him. Who were his folks?"

"I've no idea," answered Chief Kennedy. "Apparently he works out at the diner. Nobody at the house knew anything about a murder. And there was no body!"

"But—"

Jerry's hand chopped through the air between us. "Not on the ground, not in the house, not in the air circling the property like a freaking pigeon! Do you have any idea how big a fool you made me look, Amy?"

I was pretty sure Jerry didn't need my help in that department but knew better than to say so. Mom shot me a warning look just in case. "I know what I saw, Jerry."

"Maybe you were hallucinating." He stuck his nose in my face. "Your eyes are red. Are you hung over?"

"Of course, not!" I backed away. I may have had the teeniest bit too much to drink last night and I may have had a teeny bit too little sleep but still, I knew what saw.

Jerry leaned across the table toward me. "Explain to me how you happened to see anything at all?" He shook his arm at the window. "The McKutcheon place must be a mile away from here."

I looked at my mother for support. "We were bird watching," Mom said.

"Bird watching!" Jerry chuckled. "Lord, I had no idea what this town was getting into when you came back and opened that silly store of yours." I refrained from protesting because no good could come of it.

He thumped his fist and the table jumped an inch. "Sorry, Mrs. Simms," the chief said, grabbing a paper napkin from the vintage brass holder on the table and wiping up the few drops of coffee that had spilled from his cup. He squinted at my mother. "Do you mean you saw this so-called murder, too?"

Oh, sure, if my mother, his former history teacher, says she saw a murder, he'd be all over that.

"Actually, no," admitted Mom. "You see, Amy was holding the binoculars." Oh, well. She'd tried.

Jerry nodded as if everything was now clear as day, though not this rainy morning.

"Then what was that I saw being tossed down if not a man?"

"Junk," replied Jerry Kennedy. "Plain and simple. Nothing but junk. At the time of your so-called fight, a couple of the youngsters were cleaning out that upstairs room the fastest way possible—tossing garbage out the window. The roof's got a leak and water was getting in. Same thing in the barn. Several others were out there in the barn covering some boxes of supplies with plastic.

"There was a whole pile of trash on the ground outside the window when I arrived. Bits of furniture, piles of newspapers, clothes and," he screwed up his eyes at me, "even an old dressmaker dummy."

"But, I saw—"

Jerry interrupted. "The kid at the house explained that the room had been used to store all kinds of stuff. They're turning the room back into a bedroom."

He turned to my mother as if she was the only one even worth trying to explain anything to. "You should see the place, Mrs. Simms. There are a bunch of young foreigners staying there. Some of them barely spoke English."

Mom rose and started a fresh pot of coffee. "I had no idea one of the McKutcheons had come back to town. It will be nice to see the house come alive again."

"Come alive?" I couldn't help quipping. "Mom, somebody only this morning got defenestrated there."

Jerry looked nonplussed.

"It means thrown out a window, Jerry," I filled in.

Jerry's only reply was an eye roll.

"Look, I don't know what you saw." Jerry stood and shoved a couple packs of breakfast cookies in his trousers. I waited eagerly for Mom to berate him, but she didn't. She's way too nice to the man.

"Maybe you saw a big old bird," Jerry said. "Maybe you saw the wind shaking the branches." He wiggled his arms for effect. "It was storming out pretty good. Hell, maybe you saw the widow in the lake!"

Everyone in town knew the story of the widow in the lake. The story goes that she'd drowned herself after her husband was murdered by marauders around the time of the Civil War. She'd laid a curse on the men and they had died one by one, each death more hideous than the previous.

After the last man died, she walked into the lake and disappeared. Some say she still rises from the center of the lake once a year, on the anniversary of her husband's death. Today was not that day. I pursed my lips. At least, I didn't think today was the day.

"All I do know is that you did not see one man throw another man out that window." Chief Kennedy was pointing across Ruby Lake at the McKutcheon house. He headed for the apartment door and threw it open. "Nice jammies, by the way!"

My cheeks burned as I slammed the door and turned the lock in case Jerry decided to come back. Mom offered me a third cup of coffee and I didn't refuse it. I carried my steaming mug to the kitchen window and looked out. The sky was brightening now. In a couple of hours, we might actually get some sunshine.

"Maybe Jerry's right," Mom said, coming up behind me. "Maybe your eyes were playing tricks on you. It was early. You were tired. The storm."

I exhaled deeply, turned, and smiled. "You know, I hate it when you're right."

"I know."

"And I doubly hate to even think that Jerry Kennedy could be right."

Mom chuckled. "You don't have to tell me that, Amy. How was your date last night?"

"Great." I couldn't resist smiling at the memory. "How was yours?" I knew she'd had a date of her own with Ben Harlan last night. It was a little funny and maybe a little weird that she happened to be dating Ben and I happened to be dating his son.

Mom deftly evaded the question and fingered my lapel. "Shouldn't you be getting dressed and down to the store? I hate to think of Esther being stuck down there opening up all alone."

I handed Mom my mug. Thoughts of Esther running around the store unsupervised took precedence over nearly everything else, including dating gossip. "Me too." Who knew what trouble the Pester might get into?

I took a quick shower, then brushed my teeth and hair—puzzling at the frazzled brown-haired, blue-eyed woman in the mirror as I did so. Were Jerry and Mom right? Had my imagination run away with me? I threw on a comfortable pair of slacks and a red Birds & Bees logoed polo shirt.

Before leaving the bedroom, I picked up the binoculars from the bed where I'd dropped them in my hurry to telephone the police. I retrained them on the house across the lake. There was nothing out of the ordinary going on. A couple of lights were on upstairs and down. The rain had diminished to nothing more than a fine drizzle that created a gloomy pall over the lake.

Somewhere deep in those waters, the bones of the widow in the lake were said to be stirring restlessly. I could picture her white skeleton rolling along the

THE WOODPECKER ALWAYS PECKS TWICE   315

lake floor in search of a peace that would never come.

The storm had quieted, the wind had died. As I laid the binocs back atop the dresser, I couldn't help wondering if someone else had died this morning too.

3

"Amy, dear, before you go, I was hoping we could have a little talk." Mom sat in the big chair next to the sofa, a copy of the *Ruby Lake Weekender*, our town's small local paper, in her lap. She was still in her robe. Mom had been letting her unnaturally blonde hair grow out. Soon it would be a similar shade of chestnut to my own hair. I could see a lot of myself in her as she reverted to her natural color.

"Can it wait, Mom?" I said. "Esther's probably opened by now. Plus, there's a delivery truck due."

Mom opened her mouth, tapped the thin newspaper against her leg. There's not a lot of news in Ruby Lake—not that that's a bad thing. "Of course, dear. I'll be down a little later myself."

"Tell me, do you believe in this whole widow in the lake thing that Jerry was blathering about?"

Mom shook her head. "A town like Ruby Lake has a lot of local stories. I'm not that familiar with this one though the story has cropped up now and again." She pointed a finger at me. "I'm a historian, remember, so I believe in facts, not fairy tales. If I'm remembering correctly, anecdotal evidence does suggest that a crime was committed, a woman's husband brutally murdered.

"Perhaps she even committed suicide afterward. I doubt we'll ever know the entire story. There was no one around to tweet then or post the news on Facebook or some blog." Mom leaned forward. "Why? You didn't see the widow in the lake too, did you?"

"No!" Thank heavens.

"Then I'd worry about the lady running around downstairs in Birds and Bees and not the widow in the lake," Mom said with a big grin.

Esther. "Thanks." I planted a kiss on her warm cheek and headed downstairs.

There's a small kitchenette and seating area where customers can have a drink or a snack and peruse some of the bird literature, books, and magazines I keep available on a built-in wooden bookshelf between a pair of rocking chairs. I found Esther hovering over the kitchen sink. She'd added a green Birds & Bees logoed apron to her ensemble.

"Trouble with the cops again?" Esther asked, her eyes flashing with delight. She had a pot of coffee going and was filling a jar for iced tea with tap water.

I smothered a yawn. My stomach grumbled. I should have taken Mom up on the breakfast cookies. The only food on hand downstairs this morning was a plate of Danish butter cookies, the remains of a tin I'd bought a couple of days before at the Lakeside Market up the street. Hardly the breakfast of champions. Or shopkeepers. "Not exactly." I helped myself to a small stack of cookies, then glanced at the front door. "Have you opened up?"

"Five minutes ago." She stared at me like a dog waiting for a juicy treat. "So what did Chief Kennedy want, busting in here all wet and covered in mud first thing in the morning?"

I sighed. Esther was obviously not going to let go of this figurative bone. "Look, Esther," I began, "you've lived here a long time—"

"My whole life."

"Yes," I said, "your whole life. What do you know about the McKutcheons? Do you remember them?"

Her wispy white eyebrows formed a V above her nose. "Them from the farm on the other side of the lake?"

"Yes," I said, nibbling at my final cookie. After this, I'd look for some real nutrition. Maybe a candy bar.

"What do you want to know about them for?"

The corners of my mouth turned down. Why did she seem to answer every question with a question? "If you must know, I—" I hesitated. Did I really want to tell Esther the Pester what I'd seen? Or thought I saw. Finally, I began again. "If you must know," I said quickly, before I could come to my senses and change my mind, "I saw a man throw another man out the window this morning." I folded my arms across my chest and stared her down.

"At the McKutcheon house?!" Esther hooted.

"Yes," I said sharply. "At the McKutcheon house."

Esther had finished filling the tea jar. She added a half-dozen tea bags, sugar, and lemon and set it in the window to warm in the sun. Not that I was certain we'd see any sun today. No matter. We could always warm the water in the microwave if it came to that.

"What were you doing at the McKutcheon house?" demanded Esther.

"I wasn't *at* the McKutcheon house."

"Then how did you see what you say you saw?"

I explained how I had been birdwatching and happened to glance across the lake.

"And you just happened to see a murder?" Esther pulled the plate of cookies out of my reach as I extended my hand for a second helping. "These are for the customers."

As if waiting for their cue, a pair of women walked through the front door and Esther followed me as I went to greet them. I inquired if they were looking for something specific but they said they wanted to take a look around. I retreated to the cash register and checked to make sure I had sufficient change to get through the day. If not, I'd need a trip to the bank.

"Nobody has lived in the McKutcheon house for some years," Esther said from the other side of the sales counter. "Last McKutcheon moved out before you were born."

"Well, according to Jerry Kennedy, there's one living there now."

Esther was clearly surprised. She scratched at her ear. "You don't say?"

"Apparently a Guster McKutcheon has come back to Ruby Lake. He's opened the house up as a hostel."

"You mean like a hotel?"

"Something like that." I gazed across the street to Ruby's Diner. "Apparently Mr. McKutcheon also has a job over at the diner."

"I never thought we'd ever see a McKutcheon living in that old place again," Esther said.

"Why not?" I pushed the cash register closed. Esther was interrupted by the approach of our two customers. One carried a birdhouse constructed of recycled material.

The blonde held the birdhouse aloft. "Will I get robins to nest with a birdhouse like this?"

I took the birdhouse from her hands. "This house would be perfect for chickadees and wrens," I explained. "See this opening?" I ran my fingers around the edges of the hole. "It's an inch and a quarter. It's designed for cavity nesters, like wrens and black-capped chickadees, but too small for others like house sparrows and bluebirds."

The woman looked disappointed. "So, no robins?"

I smiled to lessen the blow. "Sorry. Robins build their nests on shelves and ledges. You can build them a nesting platform yourself." The two women looked at each other dubiously.

"We do sell a selection of nesting platforms. I can show you, if you like."

The women agreed and followed me over to a wall where I had different types of birdhouses and nesting boxes arranged by the species of bird they were best suited for. I helped them select a simple cedar nesting platform. The platforms look like a typical birdhouse with the front removed, except for a low border along the front to keep the nesting material from spilling out.

"I'll take it," the customer said.

"And I'll take the other birdhouse, Claire," added her friend. "The one for wrens and such."

"Perfect, Eden." The woman named Claire explained that the two were next-door neighbors. "We can share."

I gave them instructions on how to mount the birdhouses—they'd both opted for pole mounts, rather than affixing them to trees—and rang up the sale.

I caught up to Esther, who was ordering around the deliveryman as he rolled boxes of supplies in through the back door using his red hand truck. I pulled her aside. "About what you were saying before, Esther," I said out of the side of my mouth.

"About what?" Esther cocked her head. "Do you want the seed back here or out front?"

"Out front, like always," I said, struggling to maintain my calm. We always keep the twenty-five pound bags of unshelled black oil sunflower seeds up front in the corner beside the bins. There was no point lugging them from back to front one at a time when there was such a nice, compliant worker who'd move them all at once for us.

I chased after Esther as she directed Ralph, our young deliveryman, out to the sales side of Birds & Bees. Of course, he'd been delivering here for six weeks or more already, so he knew perfectly well where everything went.

He was too nice to point that out to Esther. "Thank you, Ms. Pilaster," he said with a nod of his cap. "Anything else I can do for you, ma'am?"

"Well," Esther said, tapping her foot against the hardwood, "there is that pile of pallets in the storeroom doing nothing but collecting dust and cobwebs. An old lady like me can't just pluck the lot of 'em up and toss 'em in the dumpster alone, can she?"

Ralph grinned. "Yes, ma'am. I'll get right on it." Ralph has short red hair, green eyes, and an arc of light freckles running across his face. He looked all of eighteen, but I knew for a fact he was twenty-four. I'd asked to see his driver's license.

"Ralph," I said, "you'll do no such thing. Kim and I can handle that." I turned to my employee—though sometimes I felt it was the other way around and I was working for Esther. "I'm sure Ralph has a lot of other important deliveries to make today." Ralph has a route running from Charlotte to the south to Asheville to the north and all points in between.

"Harrumph," snorted Esther.

Ralph grinned. "It's no problem at all, Miss Simms." He rubbed his hands together. "I'll get those pallets and be on my way."

I thanked Ralph and held Esther in place by clamping my arms on her shoulders. The woman was harder to keep still than a nervous chicken. "Okay, Esther." I resisted shaking the woman—just barely. "Tell me why you said what you said."

She squinted in puzzlement.

"About the McKutcheon place." I nudged her some more when an answer wasn't forthcoming.

"You said you didn't think you would ever see a McKutcheon living there again. What did you mean by that?"

The door chimed and Esther swiveled—a shark catching the scent of fresh blood in the water.

"Oh, no you don't," I whispered. Over Esther's shoulder, I called to the gentleman as he marched toward the book section. "Be with you in a minute!" I turned my attention back to Esther. "So?"

Esther removed my hands from her shoulders. "The McKutcheons never had much luck on that homestead. The ground's no good for growing. It's evil. Haunted. Old Indian burial grounds, too."

I chuckled. "Please, next you'll be telling me Ruby Lake has its own Loch Ness Monster."

Esther smirked. "We sort of do, don't we? We've got the widow in the lake."

I waved a disparaging hand. "An old wives' tale." I was trying hard to believe the story was as phony as a three-dollar bill.

"Mary McKutcheon was no old wives' tale," Esther shot back. "She was a real life, flesh and blood, saliva spitting pioneer woman."

"The widow in the lake was a McKutcheon?" Why had I never heard that before?

"Of course." Esther folded her arms across her chest. "After she passed, the life just sort of went out of the place. Family tried to keep the farm going for years and years. But trouble always followed. My grandpappy, rest his soul, said that nobody was safe living there, not a McKutcheon or anybody else."

She twisted her head towards our customer who

was working his way back toward the door and his escape. "Can I go now?"

A few more steps and the man would have made his escape. "Fine, go."

Esther called out to the sitting duck cum customer, then turned back to me. "I'd stay away from the McKutcheon house if you know what's good for you!"

Sadly, I rarely did.

ABOUT THE AUTHOR

J.R. Ripley is the pen name of Glenn Meganck, the critically acclaimed author of the Tony Kozol mystery series, the Maggie Miller Mysteries, and the Kitty Karlyle Pet Chef Mysteries (written as Marie Celine), among other novels. For more information about him, visit www.glennmeganck.com.

Books by Bestselling Author
Fern Michaels

___**The Jury**	0-8217-7878-1	$6.99US/$9.99CAN
___**Sweet Revenge**	0-8217-7879-X	$6.99US/$9.99CAN
___**Lethal Justice**	0-8217-7880-3	$6.99US/$9.99CAN
___**Free Fall**	0-8217-7881-1	$6.99US/$9.99CAN
___**Fool Me Once**	0-8217-8071-9	$7.99US/$10.99CAN
___**Vegas Rich**	0-8217-8112-X	$7.99US/$10.99CAN
___**Hide and Seek**	1-4201-0184-6	$6.99US/$9.99CAN
___**Hokus Pokus**	1-4201-0185-4	$6.99US/$9.99CAN
___**Fast Track**	1-4201-0186-2	$6.99US/$9.99CAN
___**Collateral Damage**	1-4201-0187-0	$6.99US/$9.99CAN
___**Final Justice**	1-4201-0188-9	$6.99US/$9.99CAN
___**Up Close and Personal**	0-8217-7956-7	$7.99US/$9.99CAN
___**Under the Radar**	1-4201-0683-X	$6.99US/$9.99CAN
___**Razor Sharp**	1-4201-0684-8	$7.99US/$10.99CAN
___**Yesterday**	1-4201-1494-8	$5.99US/$6.99CAN
___**Vanishing Act**	1-4201-0685-6	$7.99US/$10.99CAN
___**Sara's Song**	1-4201-1493-X	$5.99US/$6.99CAN
___**Deadly Deals**	1-4201-0686-4	$7.99US/$10.99CAN
___**Game Over**	1-4201-0687-2	$7.99US/$10.99CAN
___**Sins of Omission**	1-4201-1153-1	$7.99US/$10.99CAN
___**Sins of the Flesh**	1-4201-1154-X	$7.99US/$10.99CAN
___**Cross Roads**	1-4201-1192-2	$7.99US/$10.99CAN

Available Wherever Books Are Sold!
Check out our website at **www.kensingtonbooks.com**

Romantic Suspense from
Lisa Jackson

Available Wherever Books Are Sold!
Visit our website at **www.kensingtonbooks.com**

Books by Bestselling Author
Victoria Alexander

His Mistress by Christmas	1-4201-1708-4	$7.99US/$9.99CAN
The Importance of Being Wicked	1-4201-1707-6	$7.99US/$9.99CAN
My Wicked Little Lies	1-4201-1706-8	$7.99US/$8.99CAN
The Perfect Mistress	1-4201-1705-X	$7.99US/$9.99CAN
The Scandalous Adventures of the Sister of the Bride	1-4201-3224-5	$7.99US/$9.99CAN
The Shocking Secret of a Guest at the Wedding	1-4201-3226-1	$7.99US/$9.99CAN
What Happens at Christmas	1-4201-1709-2	$7.99US/$9.99CAN

Available Wherever Books Are Sold!

Visit our website at **www.kensingtonbooks.com**

Thrilling Fiction from

GEORGINA GENTRY

My Heroes Have Always Been Cowboys	978-0-8217-7959-0	$6.99US/$8.99CAN
Rio: The Texans	978-1-4201-0851-4	$6.99US/$8.99CAN
Diablo: The Texans	978-1-4201-0850-7	$6.99US/$8.99CAN
To Seduce a Texan	978-0-8217-7992-7	$6.99US/$8.49CAN
To Wed a Texan	978-0-8217-7991-0	$6.99US/$8.49CAN

Available Wherever Books Are Sold!

Visit our website at www.kensingtonbooks.com